CANDLELAND

When Newcastle based journalist Stephen Larkin is called down to London to help find a missing girl, he is unprepared for the violence of life in the capital's under-belly. Caught up in a world of transsexual prostitutes, gun-toting Yardies and psychotic hitmen, Larkin must learn to fight dirty if he is to survive the experience...

Please note: *This book contains material which may not be suitable to all our readers.*

CANDLELAND

CANDLELAND

by

Martyn Waites

Magna Large Print Books
Long Preston, North Yorkshire,
BD23 4ND, England.

British Library Cataloguing in Publication Data.

Waites, Martyn
    Candleland.

    A catalogue record of this book is
    available from the British Library

    ISBN   0-7505-2139-2

First published in Great Britain in 2000, 2001 by
Allison & Busby Ltd.

Published in Large Print 2004 by arrangement with
Allison & Busby Ltd.

Magna Large Print is an imprint of Library Magna Books Ltd.

Printed and bound in Great Britain by
T.J. (International) Ltd., Cornwall, PL28 8RW

For Nina and Betty

A lot of people helped, either wittingly or unwittingly, with this book and it's only fair they should get a mention. So, in no particular order, big thanks to: Graham Falco, Stephen Falco, Heather Grottick, Caroline Montgomery, David Shelley, Shend, Ray Trickett, Cathi Unsworth and Styal White. The mistakes are, needless to say, theirs, and the good bits are all mine.

Detective Inspector Christy Kennedy appears by arrangement with his creator, Paul Charles, and can be found in his own excellent series of novels which I thoroughly recommend.

If there is a pub called The Volunteer in Hackney then it isn't the one in this book. This one's only pretend.

Lastly, a really huge above-and-beyond-type thank you to my wife Linda.

Part One

A Better Place

She opened her eyes, saw bleached-bone white sky. A pale, deathly heaven. She sighed, sending a blade of pain through her ribs. Unable to move, she lay still, allowing consciousness to dribble back slowly.

She could feel wet wooden planks beneath her back, the dampness soaking her clothes, a slow, incessant drizzle of rain on her face. White noise filled her head. Her hearing was damaged, she knew, but she managed to make out rushing water underneath the planking. A river's quick current. It stank of decay and pollutants: things had died in that water.

That sudden, chill thought jolted her. That would be her fate if she didn't escape. The realisation came like a stone, thrown and wedged in her heart. Frantically she tried to move her arms, lever herself up, but all she succeeded in doing was unleashing a cacophony of pain through her body. The bones in her arms and fingers, like those in her legs and torso, had been systematically shattered. She would be going nowhere.

The torture had been thorough; the men almost clinical in their application of agony. They had broken her fingers one by one, burnt her, hit her. She had passed out, but they had just brought her round and started again. They had tried to extract her teeth with pliers, twist her hair out with an iron bar and worse. But she wouldn't talk. As their sadism increased, so did their sexual energy. They had raped her in turn, using her battered body as a receptacle for their lust and hatred.

The pain had been enormous but, perversely, it strengthened her resolve. She still wouldn't talk, no matter what. Too much rested on silence.

They destroyed her body, but not her soul. That she kept for her lover – the person she was trying to protect. Her lover had given her strength, hope and a reason for living. A pure, unconditional love, totally unlike any she had ever known in her life. If positions had been reversed her lover would have gladly done the same for her; of that she was absolutely certain.

Suddenly she heard footsteps. Her tormentors were returning. Her stomach lurched in fearful anticipation as they approached. They stopped at either side of her, looked down. One of them, the big one, knelt, pushing his face into hers. His dead eyes flicked over her body, taking in the damage he had inflicted. He grunted, content with the results of his labours.

He moved away from her slightly and, without a change of expression, pulled his arm back. She just had time to see his fist speeding towards her eyes before her head exploded into hot fireworks, subsiding to a smothering, comforting purple darkness.

The cold water hit her, enveloping her in ice, rushing her back to consciousness. She was in the river, sinking. She tried to move her broken limbs, swim to the surface, but it was no good. She was constrained by ropes, weighed down by breezeblocks, the sodden knots tightening as she struggled. She didn't want to die, she was scared, this was all wrong. She was losing her life when she had just started to find it. She held her breath, shattered lungs bursting, clinging on to that last precious piece of trapped air. Down she went, writhing, the blocks dragging her quickly, pressure bursting her eardrums. It soon became too dark to see anything as the toxic depths of black, brown and green began to claim her.

Realising no one would come to help her, she stopped fighting. She wasn't going to be saved. She was no longer a person, just a sack of bones, rope and stone. It was too much, she was tired from the effort of living. Her head was stinging from holding the air inside her body and, resigned, she let it go.

As it escaped and the rank, toxic water flooded in, she saw her lover's face smiling at her. She smiled back, grabbing the image, desperately hoping her love would be enough to carry her to a better place.

The white noise in her head dissipated and she imagined she heard the angels singing, beckoning

13

her. A sound so heavenly-sweet she could listen to it forever. The desire to follow the song was so strong she could do nothing but let her mind drift towards it.

Her heart stopped, her body lay unmoving; caught in the tangled waste at the river's bottom. Dead. Missed by her lover, perhaps, but no one else. To the rest of the world just another statistic, another biodegradable mass in an unmarked grave. Another lost child.

Amen Corner

Seven am, Sunday. Larkin walked down Mosely Street pulling his leather close around him to keep out the sharp February chill. The Victorian buildings loomed, malformed and unfinished in the sodium-etched dawn, the sky struggling to turn night into day, the dark not giving up without a fight. He walked on, purposefully but not quickly. At such an unsociable hour, he doubted the person he was going to meet would want to share good news with him.

He had walked from Jesmond through the city centre and found it practically deserted. It was the dead hours between Saturday night and Sunday morning – a transitional time – and the city had either fallen into a restless sleep, or an alcoholic stupor. On the roads were the odd taxi, a crack-of-dawn bus, and a few vans: market traders humping their wares down to be hawked on the quayside. The occasional shop doorways were filled by huddled homeless bundles, their bodies embalmed by meths and alcohol, entombed by blankets and cardboard. Perfectly still, imitating death so the cold wouldn't claim them. On the pavement straggled a Saturday night clubber, bombed out and dazed, wondering where the party went and how he got left behind; directionless as a dog that has lost its scent in the rain.

Larkin rounded a corner to an open, paved square with wooden benches and civically administered concrete flower tubs. Where once had been bulbs now bloomed old burger boxes, kebab wrappers and beer cans. Pools of vomit, broken glass and dried blood on the paving stones told their squalid Saturday night stories. Larkin ignored them. He'd heard them before.

Beyond the square stood St Nicholas' Cathedral, gothic and imposing; so dark it seemed to suck all the available surrounding light into itself like an ecclesiastical black hole. The Cathedral held memories for Larkin, not least of which was a murdered lover and a prayer said for a sad, dead woman he had never known. The dead

15

woman had, in a way, turned out to be his lover all along. The memory sprang up quickly and sharply, like a knife-wielding jack-in-the-box, and he tried to shut it out but it was impossible. It was just one more unpleasant reminder of his past in a city full of them.

He walked past the front of the Cathedral, the huge wooden doors not yet admitting the believers, and rounded the corner to a closed-in area of slabbed ground upon which sat a couple of dilapidated benches and which led off to a narrow lane sided by mugger-camo bushes. Once an area where the faithful would gather in fellowship, now a desolate place beloved of winos, junkies or just those who either through deliberation or circumstance chose to make a career of losing themselves. The faithless were drawn to this spot, congregated on it, some of them considering it home. Its name was spelt out on a plaque on the cold stone wall above the benches. Amen Corner. There were no winos or junkies there this morning, though. None would have dared. Because there, slap in the middle of one of the benches, sat Detective Inspector Henry Moir.

'About fuckin' time,' he said by way of a greeting.

'A pleasure to see you too, Henry,' Larkin replied, his breath curling into steam as he spoke.

Silence. Moir seemed not to have heard him.

'So,' said Larkin, feeling uncomfortable but trying to keep the conversation light, 'you said on the phone something about breakfast? Where we going?'

Moir grunted and gestured to a paper bag and polystyrene cup on the bench next to him. 'There. Haven't been waitin' too long for you. Should still be this side of luke-warm.'

Larkin sat down, picked up the bag. Its contents could only be termed a bacon sandwich in the most literal sense: a thick, gristle-fat slab of pink meat, heavily soaked in ketchup and grease, stuck between two lumps of white bread that seemed to have been cut by someone wearing boxing gloves. 'Thanks, Henry.' He put it back where he found it.

'You not gonna eat it?' Moir asked as if personally insulted.

'It's a bit early. But it's the thought that counts.' He picked up the polystyrene cup, took a mouthful of tea. It was the liquid equivalent of the sandwich but he drank it. He knew it was a big gesture on Moir's part and he didn't want to appear ungrateful.

'So,' said Larkin, setting the cup down. He wasn't looking forward to the next bit. 'You said on the phone you wanted to ask me a favour...'

'Aye...' Moir nodded, distracted. He opened his mouth to speak but no sound came out. Shit, thought Larkin, this wasn't going to be easy for either of them.

He took a good look at Moir. Although he was still a big man, he had lost a lot of weight since they'd last met. There was a gap between his collar and neck wide enough to slip a finger or two. His clothing was more unkempt than usual – mis-matching overcoat, jacket and trousers, worn and grubby, thrown over a washed-out red polo shirt, now home to a varied array of stains. Moir looked like he'd come last in a dressing-in-the-dark competition. His unwashed smell was unsuccessfully masked by stale booze and tobacco.

To delay speaking, Moir rummaged through his pockets for something. He found it. A half empty half-bottle of whisky. With trembling but eager hands he poured a large shot into the tea and took a sip. As an afterthought he bobbed the bottle in the direction of Larkin, who lifted a refusing hand. He then fumbled out a packet of Marlboros and lit one. Ritual completed he settled back, allowing the various hits to enter his body.

The Bell's and fags diet, thought Larkin. Poor sod.

'You were saying?' he said quietly.

'Aye...' Moir glanced quickly at Larkin,

eyes refusing to make contact. 'You know I've been away recently...' He spoke to the ground. Larkin didn't interrupt. 'An' you know where I've been. Lookin' for Karen. My youngest. Daughter.' His breathing quickened. Moir took a drag to steady himself. 'She's a ... a junkie–' The word was painfully spat out. 'Heroin. An' she's got the, got the Aids, y'know.'

Larkin nodded.

'So I went lookin' for her. To try an'...' His voice tailed off. He sighed. 'You know me an' her didn't ... didn't get on. So I thought I'd best try an' sort things out before...' He gave a useless gesture with his hand and fell silent. He swallowed down half the cup of tea, replenishing the whisky afterwards.

'And,' Larkin began cautiously, 'did you ... find her?'

Moir gave an exhalation that was both sigh and grunt of pain. 'No. I went all round Edinburgh, her old haunts, the crowd she used to hang with...' He tensed. 'Her mother... Nothin'.' Moir fell silent again and stared ahead. Larkin glanced across to where he was looking but Moir's eyes were focused on a deeper and distant place, further away than Larkin could see.

'I'm sorry,' said Larkin.

Moir turned to him, startled, as if he was seeing Larkin for the first time. 'I said she's not in Edinburgh, I didn't say she was–' He stopped himself and took a quick drag. 'She's in London. One of her mates told me.'

'What about your lot? The Missing Persons Bureau isn't it? Can't they help?'

'No. I can't...' His fingers contorted into rigid claws. 'I don't want... No. She just doesn't want to be found. No,' He took a deep drag, held it. 'I've had an agency lookin' for her. No joy so far.' He sighed again, expelling smoke. 'They're a waste of fuckin' money, you know that?' The sudden volume in Moir's voice startled Larkin. 'I should be lookin' for her myself. I'm a detective!' he suddenly shouted. His voice, like his hands, was shaking. 'I should be lookin' for her! I should be out there!' He threw the cigarette to the stone and ground it out. 'I shouldn't be sittin' here, I should be ... I ...' He trailed off, head dropping into his chest, eyes screwed tight with the effort of keeping it all in. His hands balled themselves into fists and began uselessly smacking against each other. Larkin could do nothing but sit and watch helplessly.

Not without effort, Moir brought himself under control again. He reached into his pocket and, with shaking hands, lit up another Marlboro. He kept his eyes fixed on the flagstones as if ashamed of his outburst. When a dignified period of time had elapsed, Larkin spoke.

'So what are you going to do?'

'I'm goin' to London. I'm goin' to find her.'

'D'you know where she is?'

'Aye,' said Moir, anger and irritation clouding his voice, 'London.'

'It's a big place—'

'I know it's a fuckin' big place, you patronisin' bastard, I've been there before!'

'I know you've been there before. But you can't look for her on your own, you won't know where to look. You need someone who knows the area.'

'I'm not a fuckin' tourist!'

'I didn't say you were!' Larkin just looked at him in exasperation.

Moir caught his eye, dropped his head again and sighed. 'Sorry.' He drank from his cup, hands still shaking. Larkin nodded absently.

Moir looked at him again. His eyes were red-rimmed and bloodshot – like miniature scarlet galaxies exploding. At their corners were the beginnings of long-dammed tears. The man was unravelling before Larkin.

'That's why you wanted to meet me,' Larkin stated flatly. 'You want me to come with you, show you round, right?'

Moir said nothing. He just chewed his bottom lip and slowly nodded. 'Aye, but it's all right. Stupid idea. It might take days, weeks, I don't know. You've got your own life here. You can't just walk away from that.'

Larkin didn't reply.

'Anyway,' said Moir, his voice lightening falsely, 'I hear you've got a new woman, that right?'

'Yeah.'

'What's her name?'

Larkin knew Moir was trying to make him feel as if he could cope on his own, erecting barriers, too proud to ask outright for help. Larkin played along. 'Jo. She works at The Bridge.'

'Barmaid, eh? Free drinks. You don't want tae give that up, eh?' Moir gave a small, unconvincing laugh. 'You've got your job, too. Still with Bolland?'

'For the time being.'

Moir took another swig. 'Aye. Stupid idea, see. You've got your own life. Shouldn't have asked you to meet me. You don't need to get involved in my problems.' He looked into his polystyrene cup, trying to convince himself.

'I haven't lived there for a long time, Henry. London. The lay of the land's probably changed.'

'There you are, see?' said Moir with desperate joviality. 'You won't know your way around either.'

'I didn't say that, Henry. I said my knowledge might be a bit rusty. You'll have to be prepared for that.'

'What d'you mean?'

'I'm coming with you.'

The first sign of hope appeared across Moir's features. 'But–'

'No arguments. Count me in. Just let me sort some things out and I'll be with you.' He stood up to go, looking at the lightening sky. 'Going to be cloudy today.'

Moir gave a snort. 'It's cloudy every fuckin' day. You've got to make the most of the sunny spells because you know they won't last.'

Larkin began to move away. He didn't want to hear Moir's gratitude. It was difficult enough for the big man to ask.

'Listen, er...'

Larkin turned. Too late. Moir was standing now, his eyes imploring, his mouth twitching inarticulately. 'Yeah?'

Moir seemed on the verge of saying something important, but he couldn't quite take those last few steps. Instead he sat back down on the bench. 'I'll see you later,' he mumbled.

Larkin nodded and began to walk. Reaching the road he paused and looked back. Moir was still in the same position on the bench, drinking. But now he'd dispensed with the cup and the tea and was drinking straight from the bottle.

He should wait until the Cathedral opens, thought Larkin. Then he could go inside and say a prayer to St Jude. An obscure but relevant saint. The patron saint of hopeless causes.

In Transit

Three days after Larkin's early morning meeting with Moir, he found himself in the passenger seat of his Saab 90 with the policeman at full stretch on the back seat and Andy Brennan in the driving seat, travelling down the A1. The Saab was new or new to Larkin at any rate – an early Nineties black soft-top in the classic Saab shape: a Giger-designed bathtub. Larkin loved the car and had happily traded in his Golf for it.

The three men had started the journey with only the most cursory of small talk – Moir making it quite clear that Andy was there only on the greatest of sufferance, because he had promised them wonderful accommodation at a house he knew in Clapham – and had soon lapsed into silence. None of them was looking forward to the trip.

Larkin glanced over his shoulder. Moir was asleep, his mouth wide open.

'He gone?' asked Andy.

'Spark out,' Larkin replied.

'Not surprised, poor bastard,' said Andy. He rummaged about in the glove box, his eyes darting between that and the road, until he found a tape he could listen to.

'Stick it on but don't wake him,' said Larkin.

'More than my life's worth to get on the wrong side of him, innit? The way he thinks of me,' Andy replied with a smile. He looked through the tapes he found, tossing one after another back into the glove box. 'All this shit you listen to, it's a struggle to find anythin' decent. Look at this,' he said rummaging, 'The Smiths ... The Pixies ... Husker Du – Husker Du? Who the fuck were they?'

Larkin began to answer.

'Never mind, I don't wanna know. An' I certainly don't wanna hear them. Look at this lot. It's all either Eighties indie shite, country and western, or professional miserable bastards! Mind you, that's all the same thing really.'

'From someone whose idea of music revolves around overweight black men boasting about their genitalia, I'll take that as a compliment.' Larkin hated to have his musical taste called into question. 'If you don't like it, there's the door.'

'Touchy. Oh...' Andy smiled in surprise and took out a tape. 'Don't know how this one crept in but we'd better make the most of it.' He slipped it in the player.

The tape led in and Angel by Massive Attack started up. Andy tapped the steering wheel in time to the repetitive bass riff. The drums thumped in, then the rest. Dark, foreboding, hypnotic. Larkin checked on Moir. He stirred slightly but kept on sleeping. Larkin doubted he'd wake up before they arrived if he'd consumed as much alcohol as the smell coming off him seemed to suggest.

Larkin settled back, the music casting its spell on him. He checked out, mentally replaying the last few days...

'Look at the state of that. Fucking disgrace...'

The Baltic Flour Mills stood on the south bank of the Tyne, Gateshead side. To Larkin, it was one of the last remaining symbols of Newcastle as a bustling port, of locally built ships on the Tyne, of work and industry, of pride and optimism in the region. That era was gone, disappeared, a fading, eroding memory. The building was being converted into an arts and leisure centre to house orchestras, art galleries, the lot. Larkin had argued, strongly and loudly, that since the North East was now officially the poorest area in England, and the only growth industry was call centres, the local council should be doing something more than this gesture, which he took to be a symbolically cynical one.

'Elitist shite,' said Larkin.

'Yeah,' said Andy from the sofa, 'I think I read something about that. Now, who was it...?' He pretended to think. 'Very well argued. Very angry. Had the City Council quaking in their boots. And good lord!' Andy suddenly mock exclaimed. 'If that isn't the very author in my front room!' His voice dropped. 'And if he doesn't change his fuckin' tune he'll be out that window.'

'Yeah, well,' said Larkin, turning his back on the view. He'd given up expecting reasoned debate from Andy.

'An' don't go givin' me that "We used to build ships, now we answer the phone" bollocks. That dignity of labour crap. Save it for your readers.' Andy sat down. 'Anyway, think about it. What would you rather do? Risk your life weldin' steel plate thirty feet up or sit in a comfy chair and yak on all day?'

Larkin didn't reply. 'That's better, Sunday's a day of rest, remember? You can take time off from the fight,' Andy said through a mouthful of toast. 'Now, to what do I owe the pleasure?'

Larkin had called in to see Andy a couple of hours after leaving Moir sitting on his bench, drinking himself into amnesia. In the

27

meantime he had been walking, trying to straighten the thoughts in his head. He had guessed the reason for Moir's summons, or at least narrowed it down to a set of possibilities on the same theme. As soon as Moir had broached the subject, Larkin knew what his answer was going to be. Moir was a friend and Larkin couldn't let him down. But the speed with which Larkin had agreed had both surprised and confused himself.

Andy's flat was in an old warehouse that had been gentrified into expensive living accommodation. An open-plan space with bare brick walls and modernist furniture, his camera equipment and a huge TV and video setup dominated one corner while a minimalist CD system backed by stacked and indexed discs sat in the opposite corner next to a state-of-the-art PC setup. Walls were adorned by occasional framed photographs – all Andy's own work. Good quality rugs were strategically placed on the polished wood floors and a select library of art and photography books were shelved to one side of the window. It wasn't to Larkin's taste but, he had to admit, it had more style than he would have given Andy credit for. Larkin had expected Andy's taste to run more towards purple shagpile, waterbeds and Barry White, but he'd yet to see inside the bedroom. Maybe he should reserve final judgement until he'd seen the inner sanctum.

Andy Brennan was Larkin's partner, a South London gobshite and top photographer who snapped the pictures to Larkin's words. A textbook case of opposites attracting, their personal friction sparked a great working relationship. They also had a friendship that had been tested to the full and still held strong.

'Came round for a couple of things,' Larkin started. He stared at his coffee cup. 'First, I won't be looking at that,' he jerked his thumb towards the window, 'for a while.'

'What?' asked Andy incredulously. 'You goin' on 'oliday, then?'

Larkin gave a grim laugh. 'Not exactly. But I'll be out of Newcastle.'

'How long for?'

Larkin swirled the remains of the coffee round his mug, watched the patterns. 'Don't know. Depends. Could be indefinitely.'

'Indefinitely? Fuckin' 'ell!' Andy shouted. 'I've only just bought this place! I'm only 'ere 'cos you did a number on me about this town. Now you wanna piss off an' leave me?'

'Just listen a minute–' Larkin began.

'What about that new bird of yours?' Andy was in full flow now. 'What's her name? Jo? She's gonna be well over the moon. You told 'er yet?'

'Not yet, but–'

'For fuck's sake, what d'you wanna jack it in now for? Look at the work you're doin'. Look at the money you're makin' from it. What's the matter with you?'

It was true. Larkin was doing well. It had happened quite suddenly, taking him by surprise. He was writing the pieces he wanted to write – political exposés, name-and-shame stories, damning indictments of social issues – stuff that had led him to be described by one bitter rival as 'the journalistic Jiminy Cricket of the North East'. He didn't care, though, he took it as a compliment. There was a growing audience for his writing, and, amazingly, he was making good money from it.

The business with Swanson had had a profound effect on him. There was no way it could have been otherwise. He had seen stuff – fucking awful stuff – that made him want to tell people the truth – to rage about it – and transfer that anger to others. He'd wilfully yanked his old investigative instinct out of hibernation, where he was startled to discover that it was still functioning with razor-sharp capability. That, together with his guiding lights and guardian angels of rage and truth, was the engine that drove him. He concentrated only on the things he wanted to write about – injustice, inequality, giving voice to the voiceless – but in a way that avoided the usual patronising preachiness and worthiness that went with such stories. The resultant pieces sounded like they were written by an outsider kicking in the doors of power, a One Of Us. People started to take notice.

There was, of course, a 'but' to all this, because things weren't that simple with Larkin. Although his work was taking off, giving him a sense of handsomely rewarded vindication, there was something else inside him, gnawing away. Fear.

'Just listen a minute, will you?' Larkin was getting agitated. This wasn't turning out the way he'd planned it in his head. 'Listen. I'm going down to London. That's what I came to tell you. But not to live. I don't think. I've been given a job to do down there and I don't know how long it'll take.'

'A job? Bolland never said anythin' to me about a job.'

'It's not from Bolland.'

Andy began to quieten down. This was starting to sound interesting. 'Who, then?'

'Moir.'

'Eh?' Andy resumed his seat.

Larkin explained about the meeting. Andy listened in silence.

'So,' said Andy eventually. 'You're gonna go to London with Henry, find his daughter – or try at least – and then what?'

Larkin thought of his writing. His work. And the doubts. 'I don't know, Andy. I honestly don't know.'

The two lapsed into silence, the coffee growing colder between them.

'How is 'e?' Andy asked eventually.

'Henry? Awful.' Larkin swirled the murky liquid in his mug. 'Looked like he'd been up for the last week trying to get in the Guinness Book of Records for single-handedly keeping the Scottish whisky industry going.'

'Shit.'

'Yeah, it's really got to him. I've seen this building up for a while. He's been carrying it around inside for too long. It's tearing him apart.'

Andy slowly shook his head, sighed. 'You got anywhere to stay?'

'Not yet.'

'Any contacts down there?'

Larkin shook his head. 'Not any more.'

Andy laughed. 'You're lucky you've got me to look after you, you know that? You wouldn't last five fuckin' minutes on your own.' He put his mug on the floor. 'I'm comin' with you.'

Larkin did a double take. 'I don't think Moir–'

'I don't care.' Andy looked straight at Larkin. 'You need someone who knows the ins an' outs,' he said, his south London accent thickening up. 'Someone with a place to stay. An' one that you'll really love, I might add. In short, you need me.'

'Aren't you busy at the moment?'

'Nothing that can't wait. When're we goin?'

Despite the seriousness of the situation, Larkin smiled. 'I'll talk to Moir first.'

'Good,' said Andy smiling, 'but I'm comin'. We're a team, you an' me. They can't break up a winnin' act like us.'

'That's what they said about the Spice Girls.' Larkin looked at his mug. 'Any chance of a refill? This is cold.'

'No chance.'

'Why not?'

'Because it's Sunday lunchtime, the hangover's gone and the pubs are open. An' whether you think you belong here or not, that's where we're goin'.'

They didn't get far from Andy's quayside flat, round the corner to the Crown Pasada. They had made their way through the anoraked hordes thronging the quayside, searching vainly through stalls chocca with cheap imports, looking for the Holy Grail of bargains, knowing it didn't exist, but enjoying the process because it filled in the day's hours.

The Crown was a poky little pub, unwilling and unlikely to attract the Sunday strollers. Dark wooden booths gave it the feel of a Catholic confessional. Tobacco-stained walls and a high ceiling lent it an almost grave formality.

'Well,' said Andy, as they installed themselves and their pints in a booth, 'this is all a
bit sudden, ain't it?'

Larkin nodded absently in reply.

Andy frowned. 'So what made you drop
everythin' and up sticks just 'cos Henry
asked you to?'

'He's a mate,' Larkin replied quickly. 'He
needs help.'

'So you, who haven't lived in London for
years, or spoken to anyone from there in
years, go runnin'? Yeah right.' Andy leaned
forward. 'What's the real deal?'

Larkin started to speak, but hesitated.
Andy's perception could still surprise him.
He sighed. 'I don't know, Andy. I've been
having ... doubts.'

Andy took a mouthful of beer and sat
back, listening, settled in for a long haul.
'Yeah?' he offered.

'Yeah,' said Larkin, a difficult look on his
face. 'Not the actual work itself, that's fine.
No, just what comes with it.' He took a swig
of beer. 'I'm unhappy about that.'

Andy laughed. 'What you on about? That's
nothin' new, you're always fuckin' miserable.
You can make Radiohead sound like Ken
Dodd, you can mate.'

Larkin managed a smile. 'Piss off, Andy.'
His face became serious. 'No, I think I know
what it is. And I think maybe that's why I

34

said yes to Moir so quickly.' He took another mouthful and said nothing.

Andy looked at him. 'You gonna tell me then, or you gonna be a man of mystery still?'

Larkin smiled, slightly. 'I'm scared, Andy. That's all it is. Scared of success.'

Andy sat back, nodded. He knew where this was leading.

'Last time my work made waves I lost Sophie and Joe. I'm just worried history will repeat itself.'

'Yeah, I can see that,' replied Andy, 'but it's different this time. You're goin' in with your eyes open. Older an' wiser, mate.'

Larkin gave a weak smile. 'I know, but once you start thinking these things, it's a bugger to stop.'

'So how d'you think goin' to London is gonna help?'

'I don't know, Andy. I mean, I want to help Moir, but I think I've still got some ghosts down there. Maybe I can finally lay them to rest and get on with things up here.' He straightened his back, looked around. 'Anyway,' he said, aiming for levity, 'It's nothing to worry about. Something for me to sort out myself. But not now.' He picked up his pint, drank deep. 'Let's talk about something else. You've got better things to do than sit here all day listening to a miserable twat like me moaning on.'

'You're right,' said Andy. 'I do.'

They both smiled, and started to talk: work, music, football, films – subjects that can seem inconsequential and superficial, but in reality are shared experiences, affirmations of connection. Larkin was glad of the conversation. Eventually, though, they then lapsed into silence, just drinking. Eventually Andy spoke.

'You reckon we'll find 'er?' he asked, his voice solemn.

'Truth?' Larkin replied. 'I doubt it. Not in a city the size of London. Not if she doesn't want to be found. That's if she's still–' He didn't finish his sentence.

'Yeah,' said Andy sadly, mentally finishing it for him. 'Poor Henry.'

'Aye,' said Larkin, 'I can't see a happy ending to this one.'

Tying up and casting off. That's what the next two days had involved for Larkin. He informed Jo that he was going to London indefinitely. She took the news stoically. They'd met when she had taken Larkin home one night after he'd found himself on an accidental solo bender in the pub where she worked. It wasn't a deep relationship, and they both knew it never would be. It was based on mutual physical need. Sex and virtually nothing more. She was almost as emotionally scarred as he was and told him she didn't want commitment either. He had chosen to believe her.

Telling her had been easy. He imagined she'd heard similar before. She even offered him one last fuck – for friendship, for old times' sake. He refused. As he walked away he'd felt guilty at the way he'd just used her to fill the gaps in his life, but comforted himself with the thought that she said she'd been doing the same thing. But he also felt a twist of self-disgust, because he knew he'd really wanted to take her up on her offer.

After that it had been Bolland's turn for a visit. The boss of the news agency Larkin freelanced for sat impassively while Larkin explained where he and Andy were going. When he asked how long Larkin was planning on being away, the only answer he received was a shrug. Bolland got the picture. He told Larkin that if he didn't hurry back, there might not be a job for him at all. Larkin nodded and left.

He was ready to leave Newcastle.

Teardrops, the third track, was just coming to an end. Larkin shifted in his seat and looked out of the window. There was a power station somewhere at the bottom of Yorkshire, and since his first trip to London by road Larkin had regarded that as the border between North and South.

Its huge towers belched noxious smoke that enveloped you in a toxic cloud. He had taken that to be symbolic: the North gripping you in its clutches, throwing up a forcefield from which you had to break free if you wanted to progress with your journey.

Larkin had always thought that but now, as he stared out at bare fields, barren hedges and denuded trees, all rendered bleak by the unrelenting stranglehold of late winter, flowing past the car like some looped cinematic back projection, he realised he didn't know whether they'd passed it or not. He didn't know if he was North, South or wherever. He hadn't a clue where he was.

Arrival

By the time they'd reached south London the city had hit Larkin with the force of a baseball bat. The years fell away quickly and he began to pick up the vibe of the place once again, his body tingling as he re-attuned himself to the sounds, the rhythms. Elegant, angular cadences; the gritty poetry of the streets. It was a city like no other and he had to admit he was, just at that moment, excited to be back.

He knew the euphoria would soon wear

off, though, and he would begin to see the city as it really was. Just a huge, pounding heart. Neither good nor bad, just raw, alive, throbbing. Unfortunately its arteries were currently blocked. The roads were gridlocked – cars moving only occasionally and sluggishly like mud down a bankside in the rain. The pavements were equally gridlocked – pedestrians internalising their rage, struggling to hold on to their own space. Larkin remembered that people didn't walk in London, they engaged in a perambulatory turf war measured in millimetres. Newcastle, although a busy, bustling city in its own right, still had the feel of a market town compared to this. Welcome back, Larkin. Whatever you wanted to make of it.

Andy, who came down to London more regularly than Larkin, was unfazed by being back. He drove like a native son, throwing the car down sidestreets and rat-runs as if he was still intent on proving his local knowledge to the other two, showing off driving skills he seemed to have learned from Seventies cop shows. The perfect London driver.

'Careful,' said Larkin as Andy had just narrowly won a game of chicken with an oncoming Mondeo down a double-parked street in Kennington. 'This is my new car, remember.'

'Don't worry mate,' said Andy, his road

concentration up to video game standard, 'All the time I've been driving in London I've never had an accident.'

'No,' replied Larkin, 'but I bet you've seen plenty.'

Andy opened his mouth to give a retort, but the sudden appearance of a skateboarding teenager forced him into some fancy manoeuvring. The car's pitch and roll elicited a groan and a grumble from the back seat.

'Now look what you've done,' said Larkin. 'The Kraken wakes.'

'Nearly there, mate,' Andy cabbied over his shoulder to the slowly rousing Moir. 'No worries.'

The policeman ignored him and looked out the window only half awake, numbly taking in the sights as if he'd been drugged, kidnapped and woken up in a foreign continent.

Twenty minutes later the car was pulling up at its destination; one in a street of large houses. Victorian or Edwardian, blonde brick, three storeys high with original sash windows and stained, leaded door inserts. It was situated opposite a block of Sixties flats in what Larkin took to be quite an affluent area behind Clapham North tube station.

'Nice place,' said Larkin, meaning it.

'Thanks,' Andy replied, an air of pride in his voice.

Getting out of the car, Larkin was still slightly mystified. Andy hadn't told them who they'd be staying with or who owned the house. Larkin had asked him but he wouldn't give a straight answer. He tried again.

'You'll see,' was the only answer he received.

Moir came round enough to swing himself out of the car and make his way to the house while Larkin took the bags from the boot. Larkin saw the front door being opened by a female figure who hugged Andy and kissed him on the cheek, then beckoned the others in.

The woman, Larkin noticed as he got nearer, was in her mid to late forties, possibly, since the only indicator of age was the slight collection of lines at the corners of her eyes and mouth. Her long, hennaed hair was pulled from her face, falling down her back. The velvet scoop-necked top and long, flowing batik skirt showed off her firm, full figure. She looked like the kind who had been pretty as a girl and had matured into a deeply attractive woman. Even Moir, who a moment ago had been comatose, was taking interest.

'Hi,' she smiled, extending her hand, 'I'm Faye.'

'Stephen Larkin.'

'I thought so. I've heard a lot about you.'

'Really?' Larkin was taken aback. 'Andy's never mentioned you before.'

Her smile became wry. 'I doubt he would. Come in.'

Larkin entered. The hall was large and tall, with a wide staircase going up to the first floor. What appeared to be a study was on the right and old panelled doors led off to the main downstairs rooms on the left. Under the stairs was another door, presumably leading to the cellar, Larkin surmised, and beyond that, the kitchen. As far as Larkin could tell, the house had all its original features with anything additional in keeping. This hadn't been done in an obvious, heritage way, just a comfortable functional, homely way.

'Come through,' said Faye over her shoulder as she entered the kitchen. 'Leave the bags, we'll sort them in a while.' Moir shut the front door and they all followed Faye.

The kitchen, with its centrally placed, old, scarred pine table, cooker and dressers, seemed, on first glance, the obvious heart of the house. On the stove were steaming pots.

'I thought you boys would be hungry after such a long trip. Sit yourselves down.'

'Thanks,' said Larkin. 'You've gone to a lot of trouble.'

'No trouble,' replied Faye. She gave a quick, bright smile. Maybe too quick. 'Nice

42

to have people in the house. Someone to cook for. Sort that out, Andy.' She handed him a corkscrew and he trotted over to the wine rack, selected a couple of reds, found glasses, opened and poured.

'Cheers,' said Faye. Larkin and Moir mumbled in response, Andy replied loudly 'Cheers, yourself.'

'I hope you all find what you're looking for.' She drank, they followed.

Larkin and Moir sat down, Larkin looking at him. All the life seemed to have been drained out of the man. Moir stared at the table, not so much avoiding eye contact as oblivious to it.

Poor bastard, thought Larkin. Now that you're here you don't know if you want answers or not. Or even if you'll find them. Then an unbidden thought came into Larkin's head: Neither do I. He took another slug of wine, shook his head. One thing at a time, he thought, one thing at a time.

Faye then went on to tell them to treat her house as their own, and that they were welcome to stay as long as they liked. 'As long as it takes,' she said. 'As I said, it's nice to have the company.' They thanked her, solemnly.

The meal was served – pasta, meatballs, salad – and they all ate and drank heartily, like hungry, condemned men. Conversation was light, superficial and strained, Moir casting a massive, inhibiting shadow.

'So,' Larkin asked of Faye, 'how d'you know Andy?'

A look passed between Andy and Faye, bookended by conspiratorial smiles.

'Oh, we go way back. Don't we, Andy?'

'We do.'

'You see,' said Faye, leaning forward, the candlelight from the table defining her cleavage in a most flattering and, to Larkin, highly desirable way. 'I'm Andy's mother.'

Larkin almost dropped his fork. Even Moir phased into the present long enough to allow his jaw to slacken. Faye and Andy smiled, enjoying the confusion.

'Well, Andy mate,' said Larkin, mentally retracting his earlier thoughts about Faye's breasts, 'I didn't think you were capable of surprising me any more, but I've been proved wrong.'

Andy raised his glass in salute, a broad grin on his face. Ice well and truly broken, the meal, and the conversation, began to pick up.

'So what's the story, if you don't mind me asking?' said Larkin.

'Doesn't Andy tell you anything?' asked Faye.

'Not as much as I thought he did.'

Faye smiled again. 'Well, if he doesn't

mind–' Andy shrugged '–and you two don't
mind listening–' Larkin nodded, Moir
raised his eyebrows. 'OK then.' Draining her
glass then refilling it, she began to fill in the
missing bits of Andy's life story.

She fell pregnant with Andy when she was
very young. 'Too young, really. Andy's
father and I were just a couple of sheltered
kids out in the back of beyond. We didn't
have much of a clue what we were doing.
Still, Andy's father was very sweet about it.
It was a small village and he wanted to
protect me, so he thought the gentlemanly
thing to do was marry me. So he did. And it
was hell. There we were, playing at being
grown-ups, trying to bring up a kid when
we'd only just left school.' She took a drink
of wine. 'Anyway, to cut a tedious story
short, Andy's father's family weren't short
of a bob or two so they paid me off and
brought Andy up themselves.' She smiled. 'I
think they were relieved, really. Gentry, you
see. Gentleman farmers. They despise
commoners like me,' she said with a laugh.

'Right bunch of humourless tossers,'
chimed in Andy.

'Don't be bitter, Andy, they can't help it.'
Andy gave a deferential shrug. Faye
continued. She told how it had hurt to leave
her baby, but she knew he'd be well looked
after. 'And I went travelling. Europe, India,
that's what we did at the time. Anyway,

potted history. I eventually ended up in London, enrolled in art school, fell in love with one of my tutors, married him, moved in here.'

Faye's eyes fell on a painting on the wall. Larkin followed her gaze. An abstract in rich crimson and blue hues, the muted light of the candles gave it intensity and depth. Larkin glanced around. It wasn't the only painting there. The walls were full of them and, Larkin noticed for the first time, they were all original.

'He was an artist and a sculptor,' Faye continued, reluctantly tearing her eyes away from the memories she could see painted into the canvas. 'The paintings were all his. The sculpture and ceramics are both of ours. His are the good ones,' she said with a self-deprecating laugh.

Larkin smiled and looked around the table. He had to admit he was having a good time. He was starting to relax in his temporary new home. They all were, by the looks of things. Andy was enjoying himself, but he very rarely didn't. Then Faye. For all her good looks and stimulating nature, she carried an air of loneliness about her. She seemed genuinely pleased to have company. He looked at Moir. Even he appeared less preoccupied, his mouth giving an occasional twitch at the corners. It was such a simple thing: food, drink, company, conversation.

Simple, but it looked like something none of them had had too much of recently. Good, thought Larkin. They needed this tonight. Because tomorrow was going to be a different matter.

'So,' Faye continued, 'once I got settled here Andy started to come and visit. School holidays and such.' She laughed. 'I tried to do the motherly bit, make up for lost time, teach him things about art and culture, but he wasn't interested. All he wanted to do was talk in that ridiculous assumed accent and pretend he was streetwise.'

Andy reddened.

'Still does,' said Larkin. The harder they laughed, the redder Andy became.

'So where's your husband tonight, then?' asked Larkin. Andy shot him a look that was picked up by the others, causing the laughter to thin.

Faye made eye contact only with her wine glass. 'Jeavon, my husband, died suddenly. Car crash.' Silence. She looked up, eyes glinting from the candlelight. 'I got a job teaching art and ceramics at South London Uni. I was going to sell this place at first, get rid of all the stuff, but then I decided not to. I liked being surrounded by Jeavon's things, it made me feel ... close to him somehow.' She looked into her wine, playing with the stem of the glass.

Faye looked up, smiled. 'But let's not

47

dwell on that. This is a house that should have people in it, that's what I decided. I usually rent to students, but I'm inbetween lodgers at the moment so you're welcome to stay as long as you like. Treat this place as your home. I mean that.'

Larkin and Moir thanked her.

'So,' said Faye, 'what are your plans?'

Moir spoke in a shaky voice. 'We're goin' lookin' tomorrow…'

Larkin glanced at him, saw that was all they would be getting. He took over. 'Yeah,' he said, 'we'll start with the agency Henry employed to trace his daughter and take it from there. After that, who knows? Go round the charities, hostels, drop-in centres, that sort of thing. Ask around, show some photos. Keep our eyes peeled, perhaps even flypost some pictures of her…' Larkin shrugged. 'I doubt anyone will want to talk to us. We'll have to do what we can to win people's trust. Anything to find her.'

'Good luck. I hope you do. It's a big place.'

'We'll give it our best,' said Andy.

'Er…'

All heads turned. Moir was about to speak. 'I, er think I'll turn in. Tired. Busy day.' He stood up, gripping the table with trembling hands, and looked to Faye. 'Could you…?'

She smiled and led him through the door, going upstairs to show him to his room.

'Bit of a fuckin' state, isn't he?' said Andy when Moir was safely out of earshot.

'Yeah,' agreed Larkin, 'I think we'd better leave him here tomorrow. He's more of a liability than anything else.'

Andy nodded.

'Hey,' said Larkin smiling, 'you kept quiet about your mother.'

Andy shrugged. 'What was I supposed to say? Yeah, she gave birth to me, an' that, but I don't think of her as me mother. More like an aunt, or somethin', a sister. She's just Faye.'

'She's lovely.' Larkin smiled.

'Yeah,' Andy said, his face stern. 'I know. An' don't you go gettin' ideas.'

Larkin smiled, knowing it would annoy Andy. 'But you don't think of her as your mother. More as your sister.'

'Yeah, an' I wouldn't want me sister gettin' involved with you neither,' he said grumpily.

Faye chose that moment to reappear. 'I put him in one of the attic rooms, poor man,' she said, resuming her place at the table. 'Early for him to be going to bed.'

'I think he's got something in his bag to help him sleep,' said Larkin.

'Ah,' replied Faye, understanding dawning on her. 'So,' she said, pouring herself some more wine, 'what are you two planning for the night?'

'Dunno,' replied Andy. He looked between

Larkin and Faye. 'Fancy a pint Stevie?'

'Yeah,' said Larkin. 'I used to know this area quite well. There's a pub round the corner ... the Coach and Horses, is it? Nice place. Comfortable, I seem to remember. Let's go there.' He looked at Andy. 'What's that smirk for?'

'You'll see. Come on.'

'What about you, Faye?' Larkin looked at her. The candlelight radiance made her look ten years younger. At least. He was undeniably attracted to her. 'You coming?'

She smiled. 'I've got a bit of reading to do. Have fun and I'll see you both later.'

More than three hours passed before Larkin let himself back into the house with Andy's key. He had soon found out why Andy had been smiling. The Coach and Horses with its carpeting, warming fire and polished brass had gone. In its place was a bar known by a single vowel sound with bare walls, a huge MTV screen and furniture out of Architectural Salvage R Us. It was aiming for cool but bordering on hypothermia. Larkin took one look at the skinny young girl behind the bar, her studied disinterest bordering on vapidity, and refused to drink there. Andy, laughing and calling him an old fart, followed him out and down the road.

The other places they tried were, if anything, even worse. The Falcon now had yellow canopies stuck to it and was known by an Egyptian symbol. The Railway Tavern, which used to be a retreat for old men to play dominoes, had been redecorated in primary colours by either a retarded toddler or a sixth form art student.

It was a long time since Larkin had been to London, in particular south London, and he had expected change, but not this much. Clapham High Street was somewhere he'd once known very well. He'd lived around there. Now he found that familiarity alien, disorientating, like something from a dream he couldn't quite remember correctly. It was all there, but not in the right places. It made him realise that whole swathes of his past had gone, disappeared. Of course there were parts that clung to him, stuff he doubted he'd ever shake, but equally there were things that were lost forever. The thought reminded him of Moir's daughter, Karen. People, like memories, can just slip out of sight, vanish through the cracks, never come back.

They passed a new chrome and steel construct that on first glance appeared to be a landing pad for alien spaceships but on closer inspection turned out to be a new Sainsbury's, and headed into the old town, specifically the Prince Of Wales. It was comforting to see that this place hadn't changed much. With the same collection of

51

artefacts, antiques and junk stuck to every available piece of wall or ceiling, it resembled Steptoe's yard with a bar in the middle.

They drank and talked there for a while until Andy struck up a conversation with a girl he claimed he used to know. Her friend was more interested in the barman than Larkin so, recognising an exit cue when he saw one, he drank up and left.

Walking back, he had thought of Sophie. There were places round here that had been special haunts for the both of them. He had found Newcastle to have its share of ghosts when he had moved back up there, and London was just the same. Of course, being melancholically half cut didn't help much.

As he entered the house he noticed light spilling under the door to the living room. Following it, he opened the door and saw Faye sitting in an armchair, book on her lap, wearing an oversized, white terrycloth bathrobe and damp hair. The only illumination in the room came from a reading lamp positioned to her right. When she heard the door go, she had swung her right hand over the side of the chair as if hiding something. There was no need because Larkin knew a spliff when he smelt one. She also had a large, empty glass resting on the floor by her foot.

'Hi,' she said, slurring. 'Good night?'

'OK,' he replied. 'He stayed in the doorway

and took in the scene. The room, and by extension the house, looked suddenly big, empty and cold. Faye's reading light wasn't throwing out any warmth, it just emphasised the shadows and the darkness unreached by effulgence. The distance between light and dark, warm and cold. In the centre sat Faye looking vulnerable, alone. And smashed.

'Where's Andy?' asked Faye, swivelling her head round.

Larkin explained what had happened.

'Same old Andy,' she said and laughed. 'Nothing changes, does it?'

Larkin didn't reply.

'Help yourself to a drink, if you like.' She held up her hand. 'Or d'you want some of this?' She gestured with the spliff.

'No thanks, I don't any more. But don't let me stop you.'

She smiled and gestured upstairs. 'I won't get done for this, will I?'

Larkin laughed. 'I doubt it.'

'Get a drink and I'll have a refill. G and T please.' She held out her glass and he made his way to the kitchen. He made the same for himself and on returning found that Faye had curled herself into a corner in one of the room's enormous sofas. Her legs were strong and shapely and Larkin could see the curve of her breasts through the gap in her robe. He sat down next to her.

'Cheers,' he said. They both drank.

'So,' she said, fixing him with a stoned yet penetratingly direct stare, 'Stephen Larkin. Andy's told me so much about you.'

'You said earlier.' Larkin laughed. 'Nothing good, I hope.'

She laughed too, a surprisingly strong, confident sound. 'Accurate, I think. A journalist. A bruised romantic wearing the mask of a cynic. A believer in truth.'

Larkin snorted. 'Andy said all that?'

'Not in as many words. I added the embellishment.' She looked into her drink. 'He also told me that you'd lost people close to you,' she said, looking right into his eyes.

'Yeah,' he mumbled.

'How long?' she asked quietly.

Larkin sighed. This was something he never talked about. But ... he didn't know. Maybe it was the drink, maybe it was just time to talk. Or perhaps it was Faye. He was certainly attracted to her, but she was a stranger to him. And sometimes it was easier to open up with total strangers. Especially ones who had suffered a similar loss, who might understand.

'Over ten years ago now,' he said. 'My wife and son have been dead that long. Killed by someone looking for me. Because he thought I'd destroyed his life. And then a couple of years ago, I lost someone else. Someone equally close.'

He fell silent. Faye moved along the sofa

towards him. He felt her arm snake towards his thigh, smelt her clean, fresh skin.

'When you lose someone suddenly you always blame yourself,' she said, her breath whispering close to Larkin's ear. 'I know I did. But you can't, you have to go on.'

'Yeah,' said Larkin. He moved his arm around her.

'When Jeavon died...' She sighed. 'God, I missed him. I still do. Because it was sudden like that, the car crash, it's like ... like you were talking to someone, telling them something important ... and now ... you'll never finish the sentence. Never speak to them again.' She sighed once more, moved in closer.

Despite, or maybe because of, the subject of conversation he found the closeness of Faye's body giving him an erection. He didn't know whether to hold her tighter or move away, so he stayed where he was.

'It's the intimacy I miss,' she said. 'Knowing everything about someone mentally, spiritually and physically ... you never find that again.'

Her head now rested on Larkin's shoulder. It suddenly dawned on him that her gin, like her spliff, was only the latest of many for the evening. He wondered if this was how she passed most evenings. He stayed where he was, listening while she talked.

'It gets so lonely...' she continued. 'Sometimes ... sometimes some student that lodges here ... I let him into my bedroom. And he holds me, and I hold him and he makes me feel wanted ... but they're only boys ... they don't last...' Both her arms were round Larkin now. Her lips were resting on his neck. 'You know what I mean...' she said in a dreamy voice, 'don't you?'

Larkin knew. He'd been to that place before, many times. Like Faye he was there now.

'Yes,' he said, his voice dry, 'I know.'

'Then come to bed with me.' Her voice was a desperate whisper, aching, imploring. 'Now.'

'OK,' said Larkin.

They both stood up. With a shy smile, Faye took his hand and led him from the room, up the stairs to her bedroom. Larkin paused on the landing. The only sound in the dark old house was Moir's booze-tranquillised snoring, the only light that which had seeped in from streetlights outside. He looked into the room where Faye was taking off her robe, her naked body silhouetted, backlit against the curtains. She looked beautiful. It was too dark to see the damage, the vulnerability, but he knew it was there. It just added to her appeal.

He went inside and closed the door behind him, like it was the most natural thing in the world.

Behind the Cross

The boy had big, round, eyes; trusting, cow-like. His hair was a straight blonde mop and he was wearing a T-shirt. He could have been any kid, anybody's kid. Above him were two other pictures, one of a woman: dark hair and glinting eyes, wide mouth. Built for fun, she looked like trouble. Next to her was a young man, blonde, with an unintelligent, bovine face but cunning eyes. Above the pictures, a message:

HAVE YOU SEEN THESE PEOPLE?
CASH REWARD FOR RETURN
OF MY SON.

Underneath were two phone numbers, a land line and a mobile. More imploring words but no extra details. Leaving it to the reader to fill in the story, sketch the heartbreak. The posters covered every bit of available space along Pentonville Road and Caledonian Road, stuck on abandoned shops, boarded-up windows and overslapped on the usual posters for bands, CDs and raves.

Larkin was the only one on the pavement looking at the poster, everyone else was

57

ignoring it, their own lives taking precedence. How easy it is, he thought, not for the first time, to slip wilfully through the cracks.

King's Cross was the same as it had always been, only more so. The odd, surprising pockets of gentrifying Islington trickle-over and attempts at hipness – E-ed up all-night danceathon clubs in barely converted ware-houses – were desperate and superficially cosmetic. It was still a place where lives dead-ended; the dispossessed's last port of call before they dropped off the screen altogether. The routes were clear and the facts now acknowledged – there were even sharps bins in the public toilets.

Larkin moved away from the poster and checked the piece of paper in his hand. The address he was looking for was down the Caledonian Road. As he walked he thought of the night before.

Sex with Faye had been, on a purely physical level, a wonderful experience. As he shut the bedroom door and turned to face her, she came over, put her arms around him, head on his shoulder.

'Damaged people make the best lovers,' she had whispered. 'They expect nothing and give everything. When two get together, it can be ... electric...'

And it had been. Inhibitions shredded by blow and booze, psychological needs transformed into physical wanting. So what if they thought of other people, said past partners' names with their minds' voices? It didn't matter. They were there for each other, in the here and now. That was the thing.

Afterwards they had lain in each other's arms, unmoving, unspeaking. Eyes not connecting. Touching not each other's bodies but those of the missing, the lost. No future together; the commonality that had brought them close would be the thing to stop them going further. Larkin had drifted off to sleep and when he had woken, he was alone.

He had gone downstairs to find Moir at the kitchen table, hands shaking their way through a breakfast fag. After exchanging tentative pleasantries, Larkin asked where Faye was.

'Out. Work.' Moir replied, his voice as trembling as his hands.

Larkin nodded. There was no sign of Andy. Larkin hadn't expected there to be. 'Just you and me then, Henry,' said Larkin.

'Look,' said Moir, 'd'you mind if I just stay here today? Just till I...'

Larkin looked at his friend, sitting there in an old T-shirt and shorts. All the fight seemed to have gone out of him. All the life. 'No,' said Larkin, 'that's OK. I'll go.'

Moir nodded, relieved. He said nothing

more, so Larkin finished up and left the house.

The first place Larkin would go was the agency Moir had employed to look for Karen. A private agency based on the Caledonian Road. Although he wasn't expecting any instant results, it seemed as good a place to start from as any.

Larkin walked down the filthy street, pulling his coat around him to keep out the cold and exhaust fumes, and stopped in front of a doorway set between an off-licence and a boarded-up store front. A piece of card tacked to a bell said Finders. He had the right place. He decided not to ring and set about climbing the bare, broken wooden staircase.

He reached the top. Two doors stood in front of him; one, battered and chipped, had a laminated cardboard sign pinned to it bearing the same name as the downstairs bell. Larkin knocked and waited.

'Come in,' called a fag-addled voice.

Larkin entered. The room was quite small and made smaller by the clutter. Shelves covered the walls, piled with box files, papers and text books. An old two-bar electric fire in the corner threw out heat to a six-inch radius. The skeletons of two chairs sat on a threadbare rug in front of a weathered mahogany desk. On the desk was another pile of papers, an Arsenal mug and a packet of Rothmans. Also on the desk was the room's only incongruity: a top-of-the-range PC and printer. The whole office spoke of cramped efficiency; too much work for too small a space. Behind the desk sat a middle-aged woman, grey-streaked, pudding basin haircut, glasses and a nondescript beige top. She held a pen in her right hand, a cigarette in her left. Karen Carpenter was abruptly silenced as she clicked off Melody FM on a portable.

'Morning,' said Larkin. 'I called earlier...'

'Oh, that's right,' she said, putting the pen down and sticking the fag in her mouth, 'Mr..' She consulted a desk diary, well-thumbed for only February. 'Larkin. Have a seat.'

Larkin took his chances on one of the chairs and looked at her. She reminded him of someone but he couldn't think who.

'Mo Mowlam,' she said, as if reading his mind.

'Sorry?'

'I saw the look you gave me. I remind you of someone but you don't know who. Mo Mowlam. Everyone says so.' She smiled. 'Shame it couldn't've been Sharon bloody Stone, but there you go.' She had the kind of music hall Cockney accent that seemed about to burst into song.

Larkin smiled. It sounded like a standard

line she trotted out to clients or potential clients, but it was a good technique, like a considerate dentist putting patients at ease. Any levity, any humanity, was welcome. Larkin found himself warming to her already.

'Anyway, my real name's Jackie Fairley and when I'm not sorting out Northern Ireland I run this place. What can I do for you?'

'Well, as I said on the phone,' began Larkin, 'I'm here on behalf of Henry Moir. He was a client of yours.'

She clicked a few keys on the keyboard and looked at the computer screen. 'That's right. He wanted us to find his daughter.'

'Yeah,' said Larkin. 'He sent me to pick up your findings and settle up with you.'

Jackie Fairley nodded. It was a professional nod, giving nothing away. She pressed a button and the printer whirred into life. She passed the A4 sheets to Larkin.

'There you are,' she said, 'Karen Moir.'

Larkin gave the pages a cursory once-over. 'Anything here that I should go to first?'

'You mean have we found her?' She gave a small, sad smile. 'No. Perhaps we would have done, given more time and money, but 'fraid not.'

Larkin put the pages on his lap. 'Thanks.' Looking round the office he found he was curious. 'How do you find a missing person?

Presumably they're missing because they don't want to be found.'

'Usually, yes.' She drew deep on the Rothmans. 'But not always. There's various routes. Most people looking for a misper – official slang, you can guess what it means – they start with the National Missing Persons Helpline. They're the ones who do the posters and have the appeals on TV. They also do detective work, counselling, checking records, the lot. They're bloody good, the best. We work with them from time to time, and vice versa. They know the routes to follow. There's also the Salvation Army, the National Missing Persons Bureau at Scotland Yard – although that mainly matches data on mispers with unidentified bodies the police have come across – those are the main ones. If they get no joy from any of them, people come to us. Or someone like us.'

'And then?'

'We talk to the people looking for the misper. Find out what they know. Try and find out what the misper is running away from. Sometimes they can't cope, sometimes they think they're unloved. Often they're running from some form of authority figure, parents, step-parents, children's home, whatever. If we find the runner and there's, say, a history of abuse, then we organise counselling and don't return them.' She gave a small laugh. 'We draft in extra strongarm operatives for the days when we have to give that news to people. If the people doing the looking are genuinely concerned, we do all we can to reunite them.' She took off her glasses, rubbed her eyes. 'Most of the kids on the street are just out of institutions and spiralling down.' She stubbed her fag out. 'We get the lucky ones. The ones with someone at home, waiting for them.'

Larkin nodded. 'Interesting you said authority figure.'

Jackie Fairley smiled grimly, looked at the screen. 'I see Mr Moir is a detective. Policemen are all the same. He might be in plain clothes but he still wears the uniform on the inside. A fair few runaways have police as parents. It's not unconnected.'

Larkin opened his mouth to speak.

'Now before you start,' she said, a teasing smile on her face, 'I was speaking generally. I had fifteen years in the force, so I should know.' She leaned back, lit up another fag. 'So Mr Larkin, why didn't Mr Moir go to his own to find his girl?'

'I don't think he wanted them involved. He didn't want them to see—' His pain, thought Larkin.

Jackie Fairley nodded. She seemed to finish the thought too. 'I see. I know what the force can be like. I had enough of it.'

'How d'you end up here, then?'

'This used to be my manor, the Cross. I used to work with runaway kids. All this here,' – she gestured round the office – 'is just an extension of that.'

Larkin looked again at the papers on his lap. 'I'll be having a go at looking for her myself.' She gave him an amused ironic look. 'Anything I should follow up first?'

'Just read the report. It's all in there.'

'Would you have told me if you'd found her?'

Jackie Fairley gave her grim smile again. 'Just remember what I said. Sometimes mispers don't want to be found, in which case we find out why and arrange for help. Sometimes they're already in a safe house or refuge, in which case we tell the parents we've found them but don't say where. We don't break confidentiality. And lastly,' she paused, took a drag. 'We don't find them. And that could be for any number of reasons.'

Larkin nodded, letting the unacknowledged word hang in the air between them. There was silence in the room, save for the traffic outside and the sound of Jackie Fairley sucking smoke down into her lungs, burning the paper wrapping on the cigarette as she did.

Larkin thanked her and took out his chequebook to settle up. That done, he stood up and made for the door.

'Oh, if you don't mind me asking,' Jackie Fairley said, after depositing the cheque in a locked safe, 'what's your job? How come you're involved in this?'

'I'm a friend of Henry's,' he replied. 'And a journalist.'

'Ooh,' she said, suddenly interested. 'D'you want to do a story about me, then?' She laughed.

Larkin smiled. 'I can think of worse ones. You do good work here.'

'Yeah,' she said, crossing to the window, looking down. 'We do what we can.' She turned back to him. 'Let me know how you get on. If you're successful at it, I might have a job for you.'

He smiled, shook her hand and left. As he walked down the stairs he heard the radio being switched back on; the comforting, soothing, escapist sounds of Andy Williams singing 'Can't Take My Eyes Off You' being totally at odds with their surroundings.

Outside on the street, he headed towards King's Cross. He walked, eyes front, ignoring the posters like the other pedestrians. He had to find a comfortable, stimulating environment in which to read the report. That meant a pub. But not one round here.

Larkin turned right on to Pentonville Road, the urban cocktail stink of human piss, bad garbage and carbon monoxide stinging his nostrils as he headed for the station. He didn't look back, didn't speculate on the whereabouts of the missing poster boy, told himself he had enough to think about, told himself he couldn't feel those wide, innocent, monochrome eyes bore into his back.

Spice of Life

The man, Arabic, Lebanese or something, was poorly dressed, overweight and dead-eyed. But he fed the machine in the corner of the café, hands moving over the buttons, eyes interpreting the lights and bleeps, with the solemn, dextrous skill and laser-locked attention of a Jedi master. Larkin, sitting at a nearby table, was supposed to be keeping watch through the window, but his gaze was involuntarily drawn to the man. Eventually, money consumed and none regurgitated, the man rolled out of the café and Larkin continued his vigil.

Nineteen years old, dark brown hair (now possibly dyed), last seen wearing black jeans, boots, an old grey sweatshirt and a blue denim jacket. A useless description. Also a photo, swiped by Moir from one of Karen's druggie buddies in Edinburgh: a teenager, sullen, with short hair, pouting mouth and dark-ringed eyes. A look, simultaneously brooding and haunted.

Larkin had gone to The Spice of Life, an old West End pub on the fringes of Soho, to read the report. All around him the lunchtime crowd were meeting, finding people, while he sat alone, searching, lost. The report was as Jackie Fairley said. The usual methods had been gone through – charities, institutions, hospitals, methadone treatment centres, social services, police, DSS – all blank.

The elder of two sisters, youngest still living with her mother. Parents divorced when Karen was twelve, pressure of father's work blamed. Father married to his job, policeman. Karen took the divorce hard. Father's favourite, now forced to live with her mother who refused the girls any contact with him, persuading them he was to blame for everything. Karen began to believe he had never loved her.

Her home life was unhappy – she and her mother had never got on. The mother remarried. Karen and the stepfather took a mutual dislike to each other. She began to run away, short jaunts at first, longer each time. Social Services brought her back, intervened, but were powerless to do anything. When she turned sixteen she left and didn't go back. Her mother washed her hands of her. With one daughter and a new husband, Karen was more trouble than she was worth.

Larkin had read Karen's biography uneasily, the details of her life rendered in a just-the-facts-ma'am Joe Friday kind of way, a form of journalism he had never been able to master. It was both personal and impersonal, like trespassing in a house, close yet distant from someone. He tried to be as objective as possible, but he couldn't help letting his imagination colour the heartache between the words.

Details now become sketchy. Her father moved to Newcastle. Despite efforts on his part, Karen refused to contact him, still blaming him for everything. She drifted into drugs, heroin in particular, and began to mix with people who dragged her down. It was during this time that she became HIV positive.

After a while she began to tell her peer group that she'd met someone and was going to London to make a new start. No one took much notice one way or the other. Junkies always talked like that. Then one day she was gone. At first her friends missed her, wondered where she was, but gradually began to forget she had ever been there as the need for the next fix took precedence.

Larkin put the report down and looked round. Suddenly the pub seemed grim, oppressive. He knew it wasn't really, that it was Karen's story affecting him. He ordered another pint and picked up the pages again, scouring through for something – anything

– that might give him a lead. His chest gave a sudden heart-gulp as his eyes fixed on a piece he'd somehow missed earlier. It wasn't much, but it was the nearest thing to a clue he'd seen.

Police had been called to a disturbance at 5 Cromwell House on the Atwell Estate in Shoreditch. A fight had been in progress, presumably a drug-related turf war, and everyone in the vicinity had been pulled in. Karen Moir was among the list of people questioned but never charged. She claimed she was just passing and had been drawn into it, and this couldn't be disproved. Reluctantly the police had let her go. That was well over six months ago and that was the last time her name had been recorded anywhere. Slim, admittedly, but all Larkin had to go on. He stuck the report in his pocket, drained his glass, got out his A to Z and, excited to be doing something positive, made his way to Shoreditch.

In conclusion, we failed to find Karen Moir. Whether she is still living under that name, or whether she is still out there at all, is a matter on which we can only speculate.

To get to Shoreditch, Larkin had to walk through Hoxton, the hippest, most happening part of London. A charmless stretch between Old Street and Shoreditch High Street, a no-man's-land where the City ends and inner city urbania starts, it had been overrun by artists, media folk and their attendant terminally hip hangers-on. This wasn't the gentrification of the Eighties City yuppie, however, this was a new kind of colonisation; the creatives carving out a new capital for themselves, literally in some cases, turning warehouses and old schools into lofts, studios. Everything had a neo-primitive look, as if the lack of amenities was something in itself to be proud of.

Larkin walked south from Old Street tube, down Rivington Street onto Curtain Road. Everyone he passed seemed to be wearing regulation fleeces and cargo pants with trainers on their feet. They all looked to be well into their twenties and thirties and dressed like seventeen-year-olds, except not that many seventeen-year-olds could afford the labels on the clothing and footwear they wore. Cropped hair and goatees were de rigueur for the men and the women all looked like they had shares in the Severe Black Glasses Company. The bars and cafes weren't just that, they were also galleries, film clubs and internet access centres. He caught snippets of conversation as he went, overheard customers loudly declaim themselves to each other. For people who make a living from communication, thought Larkin, they didn't seem to have anything to say beyond self-promotion. Larkin couldn't talk: if spouting bullshit in pubs was a crime, he'd have been locked up a long time ago. There was a real buzz about the place, though, a happening vibe that was worlds away from the smug City wine bars that lay half a mile to the west.

He crossed the road and walked over Hoxton Square itself. Leafless trees and threadbare grass, February-bleak. It looked like the kind of place where Sorenson and Sipowitz of *NYPD Blue* would find a dead body. Maybe the artists liked it that way, found it inspiring. He walked further and found the fashionable people thinning, and an unexceptional working-class area taking over. Shops, pubs, cafes. Nowhere near as hip as round the corner, but not that bad. It even had the Hackney Community College, a beige brick building done out in the architectural style of Modern Aspirational.

Larkin began to wonder why Jackie Fairley's people hadn't followed up the lead – this area didn't seem so threatening. Once he reached the Atwell Estate he had his answer. There would be no ultra-hip coffee shops here, no artists revelling in artfully arranged lo-fi surroundings. This wasn't just a sink estate, but seemed to have been designed by the same architect who did the old Soviet gulags. It probably served the same purpose too, as a sinkhole down which had been poured all the undesirables in the area: problem families, fucked-over adults, fucked-up kids, misfits, outcasts and those who through no fault of their own were just plainly poor. Council flats whose inhabitants had slipped as far down the food chain as it was possible to go.

Perhaps it hadn't started out as a slum, but that's how it had ended up. Police, local authority and social workers were afraid to enter, leaving the purest form of Darwinism to flourish. A warren of huge tenement blocks, bolted-together concrete slabs that managed to look both impermanent and as if they'd been there forever. As Larkin walked, he looked at the windows, wondered who was behind them, what wretched things had conspired to bring them here. The despair was almost palpable. Graffiti beginning to proliferate, wall-scrawled territorial, tribalist markings giving Dante-esque warnings to the unwary. Citizens stay out. Larkin entered.

He went down the deserted street, feeling unseen eyes chart his every step, a sharp-edged wind blowing dust and garbage around him. He had memorised the route, not wanting to bring out the A to Z for fear of looking like a tourist, and was tensed and ready for trouble. Were the streets really curling, taking him further and further towards the centre, spiralling deeper and deeper downwards, or was it just his imagination working on him? A slice of fear lodged itself in his subconscious. Was this Hell? He tried to dismiss the thought, and kept walking.

He turned the corner to Cromwell House and immediately knew which one was number five. The patch of earth at the front was decorated with strewn junk food cartons, discarded automotive parts and other forms of human waste. Shrivelled, stunted trees sprouted from patches of yellow grass, dying, starved of light and nutrients, wilting in the shadows of the concrete monoliths. The windows of the flat were boarded up and the door seemed to be made from reinforced battleship steel. Shit, he thought. Crack house.

Larkin checked the street. There was no way into the flat and he doubted the occupants would be in a hurry to answer his questions. That was why the report hadn't made such a fuss about the lead. With this kind of environment it was more of a dead end. Needing time and space to think of his next move, he had noticed a cafe opposite. It sat in a one-storey row of mostly boarded-up graffitied shops. The ones that were still open had grilled and barred fronts, the cafe no exception. It looked more like a testing ground for various strains of germ warfare, but Larkin had no alternative. He called at the newsagents, picked up a couple of tabloids for camouflage and entered.

He had seen them come and go; sidling up to the door, doing a coded knock, slipping folded money in, getting a poly-wrapped bundle in return. Some were even allowed inside. Occasionally a big flash car would pull up. Beamer or Merc, stereo bleeping and thumping fit to crack the tarmac, and a couple of young black guys dressed like wannabe gangsta rappers would get out, go inside then back in the car and away. Sometimes a young kid, who didn't look to be in double figures, would ride up on a pedal bike, shove something through the slit in the door and zoom off again. Once, a young mixed-race guy, well-built with muscle, wearing a leather bomber, trainers, oversized jeans, with dirty blonde cropped hair, emerged from the flat. Despite the February cold, he wore nothing underneath the bomber, which was unzipped as far as his flaunted six-pack. His posture said he knew how to handle himself. Standing four-square and squat at his side on a leash and harness was a Staffordshire bull terrier, muscle-packed back-up. He looked up and down the street, his attitude expecting either armed police or paparazzi to come running, and when none did, strode off, leading with his dick.

Larkin had read his way through the

papers twice, eaten a full English that was surprisingly good, and drunk three cups of coffee that, while not winning any awards, were comfortably the right side of poisonous. He wanted to keep watching, but out of the corner of his eye he could see the sole worker in the cafe, a small, aged West Indian, eyeing him suspiciously from his perch behind the counter. He seemed to be the only person working there, but Larkin kept catching glimpses of shadowy figures in the darkened kitchen area which was cordoned off from the front of the cafe by an old beaded curtain. Larkin didn't know what they were doing in there, but he doubted they were dishwashers. The last thing he wanted was to outstay his welcome in an area like this. The night was beginning to cut in, so Larkin decided to pay his bill and leave. He'd plan his next move later.

Larkin moved to the counter, took out some cash from his pocket. The West Indian was dressed in a dirty shirt covered by an apron so multi-coloured with unidentifiable stains it resembled a mid-period Jackson Pollock. He never took his eyes from Larkin all the time he rang up the money in the cash register. Leaning across to give Larkin his change, he spoke.

'Haven't seen you in here before,' he drawled in a rich Jamaican accent.

'No,' said Larkin.

'You're not from round here.' The man's left hand played under the counter. Larkin speculated what was there: a gun, baseball bat, machete, or even a panic button that would bring two dozen steroid-pumped friends running. He decided to choose his answers carefully.

'No, I'm not.'

'You givin' a lot of attention to that place opposite. You police? Mr John Law himself?' The man's posture stiffened. He was bracing himself.

At least Larkin could answer honestly. 'No, nothing like that. I'm just looking for somebody. Someone in there might know where she is.'

Some of the man's hostility dropped away. A look of intelligence, of calculation, entered his features. 'They won't tell you. Even if they know. They bad, bad boys.' Bitterness crept into the man's voice.

'I know, but that place is the only lead I've got.'

The man stared straight at Larkin, genuinely curious. 'Who are you, then? What you do?'

'My name's Stephen Larkin. I'm a journalist.'

The West Indian's eyes suddenly twinkled. A smile edged its way to the corners of his mouth. 'A journalist? A newspaper reporter? You lookin' for a story, man?' He puffed his chest out. 'Don't waste your time with those boys. Let me tell you the story of my life.'

Larkin smiled. Why does everyone I meet want me to write their life story today? he thought. 'I'm not working at the moment. I'm just doing a favour for a friend. Find his daughter for him.'

'An' take her home?'

Larkin nodded. 'Hopefully.'

The man's face became serious, as if he was considering something, weighing up a painful decision. Suddenly, decision apparently reached, he broke into a wide grin. His hand dropped from whatever it was behind the counter. 'Let me tell you my story. And who knows? If you listen good, and pay attention to an old man, and I take a liking to you, white boy, I might just be able to get you in there.' He gestured towards the crack house.

'Really?' Larkin couldn't hide his surprise.

'Really.' He looked round the cafe. 'Now, my customers seem to have deserted me today, so what say I shut up early and find us something a bit stronger than coffee to drink. That sound good to you?'

Larkin smiled. It certainly did.

The man, whose name was Raymond, 'but everyone be call me Rayman', closed the cafe, took off his apron, poured two huge shots of Jamaican rum and began to talk.

The shadowy figures still moved about in the kitchen, but since they posed no immediate threat, Larkin tried to ignore them and listen to the story.

Rayman came to Britain from the Caribbean in the Fifties. 'I was nine years old. Windrush. My parents thought there more jobs here, the land of opportunity.' He sighed. 'Ha. My father was trainin' to be a doctor. You not writin' this down?'

'I'm listening,' Larkin replied.

The answer seemed good enough. Rayman continued. 'Anyway, only work he could get here was shovlin' coal.' He laughed bitterly. 'Told him make no difference he wouldn't get dirty. His skin already too black. This wasn't the country we were promised, with fine buildings an' good manners an' all that. We were called wogs an' told to get back to the jungle. I saw all this, saw my parents stick in there, saw their dreams just disappear. I wouldn't go the same way. I's goin' make somethin' of my life.'

He told Larkin of his drift into petty crime, 'the only openin' for a black man in those days'. Stealing, shoplifting to start with, then it escalated. 'I was earnin' me good money, dressin' well, had fine-lookin' ladies on my arm. Good times. Then someone said he like to sleep with one of my ladies and pay well for it. So I got me a string of them, hired them out.' He paused

79

to take a mouthful of rum. 'But it was all fun, you know? Nothin' heavy, you know what I'm sayin'? We all got somethin' out of it. I wasn't hurtin' no one, the ladies got fine clothes, money in their pocket, I din't beat them up or nothin'...' His eyes misted over as he travelled back over the years. 'Yeah, we all enjoyed it.' Larkin doubted that, but didn't interrupt his cosy criminal history.

Rayman had started to deal cannabis, 'just weed, nothin' stronger,' and run a shebeen. 'Man, that was a success. High times for all. The black man loves to gamble, loves to drink, loves his women. An' I supplied all three. But then the big boys, the gangsters wanted to take over an' I knew it was time to get out.'

'So what did you do?'

'Bought this place an' a couple others round here. Good times a-comin' Maggie said. So I listened. Became a businessman. Started some Caribbean restaurants, owned some property round here.' He looked around. 'All I got left now is this.' He gestured towards the shadowy kitchen. 'An' my weed dealin'.' He shook his head. 'Should have known better'n trust that white bitch.'

Larkin agreed, and the conversation, fuelled by the rum, began to meander. Three glasses later, they had managed to sort out the majority of Britain's problems, and had an enjoyable time of it, but Larkin was still no further forward to gaining access to the crack house.

Rayman sat back, drained the last of his rum. 'So, you like my story?'

'Yeah,' said Larkin.

'But you're not goin' to write about me?'

'Not just yet.'

Rayman laughed. 'But you listened, an' we talked an' had us a fine time, an' that's good enough.' He leaned forward, suddenly conspiratorial. 'An' now you wanna know how to get in that crack house across the street?'

Larkin leaned in too. Partners in crime. 'Yeah.'

'Lemme think about it,' Rayman said, sitting back. 'Come here tomorrow for your breakfast an' we talk again.'

'You've got a great way of getting repeat business,' said Larkin.

Rayman laughed again, pointed. 'You're not bad for a white man.' He stood up. 'You better leave now.' He nodded towards the shadowy kitchen, his face suddenly serious. 'I got me some business to attend to.'

Larkin left, promising to return and made his way back through the estate. The darkness was full on now, and he attempted to stick to well-lighted areas, which wasn't easy. The further he got from the centre of the estate, the more relaxed he began to feel. He was even relieved to see the trendsetters of Hoxtonia sitting in their bars, oblivious to what lay around the corner. He wished he could have joined them.

He thought of Rayman and his promise. Could he trust him? Probably not. Should he be contemplating the course of action he was about to take? Probably not. Did he have a choice if he wanted to find Karen? Probably not.

With a sigh of relief at making his way out of the estate in one piece, but for little else, he made his way back to Clapham.

Shelter

By the time Larkin had reached Clapham, the skies had opened, letting squally rain join the cold and wind, perfect fag end of winter weather. Larkin wasn't soaked by the time he reached Faye's but he was certainly unpleasantly wet. That, along with being chilled and windswept, told him once again why most British suicides happen in February. Nothing to do with certain unfortunate people realising they couldn't keep their New Year's resolutions and they were condemned to live as failures, Larkin's surly thoughts went, just the weather.

Opening the front door, the first thing that struck him was the smell. Wonderful cooking aromas coming from the kitchen. It made the house feel warm, lived in, welcoming. He could get used to this, he thought. He squelched into the front room. Andy lay stretched out on the floor, hooked up to the TV in a tangle of wires and plastic, fighting Duke Nukem on his Playstation. Larkin smiled.

'Turned into an adolescent again now that you're back at your mam's?' he asked.

Andy stood up, inadvertently allowing himself to die onscreen. He looked sheepish. ''Allo, Stevie, mate. Look, about last night...'

Larkin began to walk away. 'You don't have to explain.'

'No,' said Andy, 'it's not what you think.' He paused and thought. 'Actually yeah, it is what you think, but there was a reason for that.'

'I'm sure.'

'I mean, what could I do? She's an old mate. And she's a bit of a dealer. Whenever I see her we get together, it's a done thing. I give her a bit of the old pork sword action and she gives me a discount on some blow and speed.'

Larkin smiled, milking his mock-superiority for all it was worth. 'Charming arrangement. I hope you took precautions.'

Andy looked morally offended. 'Course I did. What d'you take me for? Nice girl an' that, but she's been round the track more times than the greyhounds at Walthamstow, know what I mean?'

Larkin shook his head. He was in no position to judge. Not after what he'd done last night.

'I'll make it up to you, anyway,' said Andy. 'Whatever you want tomorrow, I'll do it.'

'Good,' said Larkin.

'How d'you get on, anyway?' Andy asked.

They sat down and Larkin told him.

'Fuckin' 'ell,' said Andy when he'd finished, 'You 'ad a busy day.'

'And it's going to get busier tomorrow,' said Larkin, and told him how he was going to gain entry into the crack house and what Andy's part was to be. Andy just listened quietly, his face turning paler and paler. Being brave with steroid-pumped cartoon characters was one thing, Larkin thought, real life was another.

'You're off your fuckin' 'ead, you know that?'

'You said you'd help, Andy.'

Andy grumbled and complained. 'Don't know why I let you talk me into these things,' he said, giving reluctant agreement.

'I just need you for backup,' said Larkin. 'I'll be taking the risks.'

Andy mumbled something less than complimentary, then went back to Duke Nukem.

Faye chose that moment to enter. She

stopped short when she saw Larkin.

'Oh. Hello, Stephen. I thought I heard voices. Is it raining out there?'

Larkin said hello then added, rather needlessly, that it was. They stared at each other, generating a sudden, difficult electricity. If Andy hadn't been so involved in his game he would have noticed.

'The kettle's just boiled ... if you'd like a drink.' She moved hesitantly towards the kitchen. Larkin followed.

Once there, she began making tea for them both, her back to him, eyes on the mugs. 'Good day?' she asked.

He repeated to her what he'd already said to Andy, playing down his attempted entry to the crack house. When he'd finished she said, 'Well, I hope you'll be careful.'

'Yes, Mum.'

They both smiled.

'How are you?' Larkin asked.

She looked at him, eyes meeting at last. 'Fine.' She handed him his mug and sat at the table, opposite him. 'Look,' she said, after darting a quick glance at the door to make sure they were alone, 'I'm sorry, I shouldn't have just left this morning. I should have said something.'

'That's OK,' Larkin replied quietly.

She smiled weakly. 'I don't ... make a habit of doing that,' she said to her mug, 'but I'd been drinking and smoking ... and thinking about … well, you know.'

'I know,' said Larkin. 'We were both there when we needed someone. You don't have to say any more.'

She looked up and smiled. She opened her mouth as if to say something important, something deeper, but instead announced, 'It's pasta carbonara tonight. But don't expect this every night. It'll be someone else's turn to cook tomorrow.' She stood up, began busying herself at the cooker.

'Where's Henry?'

'In his room.'

'I'll go and see him.' Larkin stood and crossed the kitchen. He stood behind her, looked at the curve of her neck under her piled-up hair, smooth and white. His hands began to move towards her shoulders.

Suddenly she turned, looked straight at him. Her eyes had none of the sexual directness of the previous night. Instead they held a kind of subdued claustrophobic fear. 'Tell him his dinner's ready, will you?' she said as brightly and evasively as possible.

Larkin knew that look. Fear of confinement, fear of involvement. Damage did that to people. He nodded and left the room. Faye went back to what she was doing.

He walked up the stairs all the way to the attic and knocked on the door of Moir's room.

'Yeah?' rumbled the familiar Scottish voice.

'It's Stephen.'

There was a heavy-footed scramble of indecent haste across the floor and the door was sharply pulled open. Cosmetically, Moir looked better than he had the previous night. His hair was clean, his face was shaved, his clothes didn't smell. But beyond that, he was just the same.

'Well?' Moir's eyes were half-crazed, half-imploring.

'I'll come in and tell you.'

Moir retreated into the room, sat on the bed.

Larkin entered and saw what Moir had in his hand. A revolver.

'What the fuck're you doing with that?' said Larkin.

'Just cleaning it. Why, d'you think I'm goin' tae top myself?' asked Moir with a sharp laugh.

'Well...' Larkin shrugged.

'Don't worry. Used to be my dad's. I brought it down in case there was goin' tae be any rough stuff. I was just givin' it a polish. You never know.'

'Just put it away, please, Henry. It's making me nervous.'

Moir bundled it up and slid it under the bed. Larkin breathed a sigh of relief and looked round the room. The slanting roof and drawn curtain together with the sparse furniture gave the room a sombre, cold feel.

Or perhaps that was just Moir's mood permeating the atmosphere. On the side of the bed was a bottle of Bell's, almost empty. One glass. Well, things can't be that bad, thought Larkin. At least he's not drinking straight from the bottle.

'D'you wanna drink?' asked Moir.

'There's only one glass.'

'For visitors.' He almost laughed. 'I'm takin' it straight from the bottle.'

Oh fuck, thought Larkin, things are that bad. Let's hope the gun's not loaded.

'So tell me.' Moir handed the glass to Larkin, who sat on the other end of the bed.

Larkin handed Moir the report Jackie Fairley had given him. Moir rifled through it, staring at the pages as if the words themselves might yield up secrets, answers. While he looked, Larkin ran through the story again. After finishing the report, Moir sat impassively, eyes focused on something Larkin couldn't see, something that wasn't in the room but that Moir carried with him. Larkin was going to tell him to expect the worst, but one look at Moir showed he had gone over every calamitous outcome in his mind. When Larkin had finished, Moir took a large slug from the bottle and turned to him.

'You're a good friend,' he said, tears welling in his eyes. 'Thanks.' It wasn't the response Larkin had been expecting.

He looked at Moir, waiting for something more, but nothing else was forthcoming. Moir just sat, looking like a man who'd reached the end of a long road, or was lost on one that he couldn't see the end of.

Larkin sipped his whisky and waited. Eventually, Moir spoke.

'When I was a boy,' he began, talking slowly as if he'd been practising in his head, 'I used to play a lot of chess.' He sighed. 'It was so simple. One black side, one white. One won, one lost. I always wanted to be white. And to win. So I joined the force. And looked at things in the same way. Black and white. Good and evil. Right and wrong.' He snorted, took a swig. 'Naive little bastard that I was. The job soon disabused me of that notion, because as we all know, there is no such thing as absolute right and wrong. And little by little my belief was traded off.' He flung his arms out, gesturing expansively. 'You know what I mean. Turn a blind eye to a small misdemeanour in order to stop a larger one ... convince yourself that a crime is not morally wrong if there's a kickback in it for you ... produce evidence to convict some unconvictable bastard that you know in your heart is guilty.' He sighed again, the sudden energy leaving him. 'Black and white began to merge into one huge fuckin' grey fog. Various shades, mind, but all grey. And I stopped bein' able to tell the good guys from

89

the villains, an' workin' out what was important an' what wasn't. An' I lost it. Lost sight of the board, the squares, the gameplan … lost my wife, my family…' He lowered his head. '…my self-respect. All my fault.' He sighed again, heavier this time. 'Lost the fuckin' lot… An' now whenever I see a chessboard, it reminds me what I lost, an' makes me wanna puke…'

They sat in silence. Larkin couldn't think of a single thing to say.

'Thanks for today,' said Moir eventually, his voice too small for his frame. 'I appreciate it.'

'No problem,' Larkin replied. He stood up. Placed his hand on Moir's shoulder. 'There's some food downstairs for you if you want it.'

'Aye, I'll be down in a wee while.'

Larkin nodded and left the room.

The dinner consisted of tasty, plentiful food and strained conviviality. Afterwards, while the men were complimenting Faye on her food, she picked up her glass of wine and announced, 'Don't expect me to cook, clean and look after you every day, you know. You're big enough to fend for yourselves.' With that she walked into the front room and sat down. Andy threw a tea towel to Moir, who regarded it with the same familiarity he would a piece of Mayan sculpture. The two men set about clearing up the kitchen.

Larkin, finding himself surplus to require-
ments, took his own glass of wine and joined
Faye in the front room. He found her on the
sofa and sat at the opposite end, leaving a
large distance between them.

'You OK?' Larkin asked.

'I am. But I won't be if you keep asking me
that.'

They both laughed, then fell silent.

'How's Henry been today?' asked Larkin.

'Still the same, I think,' she replied without
turning round. 'He went for a walk earlier
over the Common. I made him have a bath
and put his clothes in the wash. You wouldn't
have believed the state they were in.'

'I would.'

She laughed. 'Of course you would, you're
a man.' She took a drink. 'Look, I've got the
day off tomorrow. I'll see if he wants to go
out somewhere, do something. Might take
his mind off things.'

'Thanks. That would be good.'

They both fell silent again, drinking their
wine, trying to feel comfortable with the
space between them. Eventually conversation
started up, but nothing important. Micro-
scopic rather than small talk, but any
communication was better than none at all.

The evening slipped slowly away. Moir and
Andy came into the room and they all sat

drinking, watching TV. A biting wind lashed the rain against the window, and the four of them sat, bruised, damaged, but still hanging in there. The house kept them sheltered and safe from the suicidal February outside, while they wished for a similar kind of thing within themselves.

Over the Threshold

The next morning found Larkin again in the cafe, coat collar up, tabloids spread in front of him, mug of coffee at his side. Upon entering he had been surprised to discover not Rayman behind the counter but a surly young black guy.

'You waitin' for Rayman?' the man asked.

Larkin answered that he was.

'Sit there.' The man gestured to a table. 'He be here soon.'

Larkin had done as he was told, and sat there, waiting. He had thought of sitting at another table other than the one the man had specified, just to annoy him, but didn't think it was worth it. The man had just stared at him and stood in front of the doorway to the back of the kitchen, arms folded. He looked more like a sentry than a cafe worker, thought Larkin. His build showed he could handle himself, the faint scars on his face showed he had handled himself, and the bulge in his jacket pocket looked too heavy to be a mobile phone.

Larkin swallowed hard. The coffee seemed to be going down in lumps. He didn't quite know what he was getting into and he still had time to back out. He could just get up and walk away, and that would be that. Instead he stayed where he was and tried to read his paper. Waiting for Rayman to arrive.

About fifteen minutes later, the door opened and Rayman entered.

'Hey, my man Larkin! I knew you'd show.'

Larkin turned. The man who had spoken bore only a passing resemblance to the cafe owner he'd met yesterday. This man looked like Rayman's flashy twin brother. He was dressed in a long leather coat, buttoned up, with only the top of a roll-neck sweater showing. All in black. He exuded confidence and focus, with a dangerous kind of swagger. Larkin's doubts had grown from chrysalis stage to full-blown butterflies.

'Hello Rayman,' Larkin croaked.

'You didn't disappoint me. Good.' He walked towards the back of the cafe and said over his shoulder, 'Come on, white boy, we got work to do.'

Larkin dumbly followed, the young guy following him. That was it, he was in now.

93

Once past the bead curtain, he found the back room had a kitchen area where food was prepared and stored, a table and chairs, and some weighing and measuring equipment shelved on one side. Larkin knew immediately what that was. He pointed towards it.

'You still dealing, Rayman?'

'Sure am, man. Can't make a livin' servin' up slop round these parts.' His amiable Jamaican accent had been replaced by a much harder East London one. 'You met Kwesi, my lieutenant?'

The young guy gave an imperceptible nod.

'We met,' said Larkin.

Rayman smiled. 'His mother named him Winston but he named himself Kwesi. Wanted something African, take him back to his roots even though he lived all his life round here. Isn't that right, Tottenham boy?'

Kwesi said nothing, just stood impassively. Rayman let out a harsh cackle.

What the fuck have I got myself into? thought Larkin.

'We not messin' about, this is what we do,' said Rayman sitting at the table. Kwesi sat also. Larkin followed suit. 'You go to the door of the crack house.' He pointed at Larkin. 'An' say Lonnie sent you. That's important. Lonnie.'

'Who's Lonnie?' asked Larkin.

Rayman smiled. 'Some junkie. OD'd over there. They'll know. Just sound like you're a junkie, moan a bit. Tell them you're desperate. Sound convincing, they let you in. When you're in there, ask them about the Scottish girl you're lookin' for.' Rayman sat back looking pleased with himself.

'That's it?' said Larkin.

'You think it won't work?' asked Rayman with a twinkle in his eye. He sat back, turned to Kwesi. 'White boy don't trust Rayman! Don't think he can cut it no more!' He leaned forward again. 'Then you better take this.' He snapped his fingers. Kwesi produced an automatic from his jacket pocket and laid it on the table in front of Larkin. 'Take this.' Rayman's eyes were as cold as the gun. 'They won't argue with that.'

Larkin sat back in disbelief. 'Sorry guys,' he said, 'I think you're confusing me with Bruce Willis. I'm a journalist not a gunslinger.' He tried to laugh but the sound died in his throat.

Rayman became deadly serious. 'You want the girl? You do as I say.'

Larkin looked from one to the other. Two stone faces stared back at him. It was too late to walk out now. He reached across and picked up the gun. It felt heavy in his hand, cold, powerful. He could see why some people thought it was an easy way to respect.

He pocketed it. 'Now what?'

Rayman gave a chilling smile. In the kitchen's half-light he looked like a devil who'd sweet-talked a soul into Hell.

'Now we do it,' he said.

Larkin walked from the cafe to the crack house, watching the street all the time. He could feel Rayman's eyes on him without looking back. The weight of the gun was dragging at his side, and that's where he wanted it to stay. When he reached the steel door he banged on it. No reply. He banged harder, hurting his knuckles in the process. A speaker phone by the side of the door spoke to him.

'Yeah,' said a suspicious, monosyllabic voice.

'Here we go,' Larkin thought. 'Oh, man...' he drawled in his best East London druggie drawl, 'I need some gear, man...'

'Whosis,' said the voice, too flat to be considered a question.

A bad Keith Richards impersonator, thought Larkin to himself. 'It's Stevie, man...'

No reply.

'Lonnie sent me...'

'Lonnie,' said the voice, almost betraying curiosity.

'Yeah, I think it was Lonnie ... think that's what he said...' Larkin let his voice deliberately trail off. The speaker phone fell silent. What else could he say to persuade them? 'Come on, man, I got cash...'

'Waitaminnit,' the door said, and lapsed into silence.

Larkin stood there for what seemed like a small eternity until he eventually heard the sounds of bolts being withdrawn and locks released, then the door opened a crack.

'In,' said the voice. Larkin entered.

The place was a tip. Old, ripped sofas on threadbare carpet, a scarred coffee table covered in junk food containers and gear. Coke can pipes, lighters, spoons. All illuminated by a bare, overhead bulb. The one incongruity was in the far corner, a brand new-top-of-the-range TV and video with an expensive-looking CD system beside it.

The guy who'd let Larkin in was wearing oversized jeans, box white trainers and a T-shirt. He was white, or rather his race was Caucasian, since he looked and smelt like he was a stranger to soap and water. He was also, Larkin reckoned, not much older than eleven or twelve. The way he glanced suspiciously over Larkin's shoulder told him there was no one else in. He began to eye Larkin suspiciously.

'Who you?' he asked, slamming the door and nervously fingering the back of his jeans waistband.

Gun, thought Larkin, better move quickly.

'I want to talk to you about someone who used to live here,' he said in as calm a voice as possible.

'You're not after gear!' the kid shouted. His hand went for his belt but Larkin was on him. He grabbed the kid and shoved him against the wall, keeping his right arm firmly across the kid's neck. With his left hand he grabbed the gun from the kid's waistband and pointed it at his face. The kid, cockiness now gone, suddenly resembled the scared child he was.

'Now look,' Larkin began in his most reasonable voice, 'I don't want to hurt you. I'm not the law, I just want some answers to a few questions, then I'm gone, OK?'

The kid nodded hurriedly.

'Good,' said Larkin. 'Now go and sit over there.' He gestured to the sofa. The kid, once released from Larkin's grip, moved shakily towards it and sat down.

The gun felt unpleasant and alien in Larkin's left fist and he didn't like having to do it, but he continued to point it because that was the way the kid had made the play. It may be the only way to make him understand, thought Larkin sadly. Using the gun confirmed his earlier thoughts about it. It did give him a thrill, but also a feeling of disgust. He wanted this over with as quickly as possible.

'There used to be a girl who lived here. Karen. Scottish accent. Remember?'

The kid shook his head.

'Thought not,' said Larkin. 'You probably weren't born then. What's your name?'

'Karl.'

'OK Karl,' said Larkin. 'Think harder. A girl called Karen. Scottish. Yes?'

'You'll have to ask Theo,' muttered Karl, his head aimed at the floor.

'And who's Theo?' asked Larkin.

Suddenly he heard the sound of a key in a lock and turned towards the front door. It opened and there stood the huge, mixed-race guy with the pit bull that Larkin had seen the day before. He was still dressed for a summer's day, still exposing skin. It was hard to tell who looked the fiercest.

'Theo!' shouted Karl, relief all over his face.

That answers one question, thought Larkin.

Theo ignored Karl and stared straight at Larkin. 'You'd better have a good reason for bustin' into my house, you motherfucker, or you're dog-meat.'

Oh fuck, thought Larkin.

Larkin knew he had to think quickly and act even faster. Weighing up his options he swung the gun on to the dog.

'That bastard comes near me and *he's*

dogmeat,' he snarled, with a toughness he didn't feel.

Theo and the pit bull stopped in their tracks.

'Sit over there.' Larkin gestured to where Karl was. Theo, eyes burning with anger and hatred, perched himself on the edge of the worn-out sofa, body erect, like a firework waiting to explode. The dog stood beside him, eyes never leaving Larkin.

'You're makin' a big mistake, man,' said Theo.

'We'll see,' Larkin replied. 'Now that I've got your attention, though, I want to ask a couple of questions. Karl says you're the man with the answers, Theo.'

Theo stared at Karl, mentally snapping the boy's bones. Karl looked from one to the other, not knowing who to be the most scared of.

'I'm sorry man,' Karl was almost in tears. 'He said he was a friend of Lonnie's...'

Theo looked sharply at him, as if he'd been slapped. Then gradually, a look of slow understanding crept over his features. He sat back, relaxing slightly. A bitter smile curled the edges of his lips and he managed to dredge up a short phlegmy laugh.

'Fuckin' Rayman,' he said.

Larkin was taken aback. 'What?'

'You're from him, ain'tcha? He put you up to this, fuckin' foolish old cunt.' Theo's confidence seemed to be rising with every word. He puffed his chest out, rippling his pecs in the process.

Larkin was thoroughly confused. This wasn't what he had expected. He tried not to let it show, though, since he was still the one with the gun, the one in control. But not for long if he didn't do something about it.

'I don't know what you're talking about,' spat Larkin.

'Yeah you do,' Theo replied. 'Rayman. He's doin' it again. I bet he gave you some bullshit, got you riled up, stuck a shooter in your hand an' sent you here.' He sneered at Larkin. 'What he do? Give you his poor old Jamaican shit? You been 'ad, man.'

Despite the gun, Larkin felt his grip on the situation slipping. He gave it one last go. 'I don't give a fuck about that. Just tell me about the girl. She was Scottish. Name of Karen.'

'I din't have no Scotch girl. You got the wrong man.'

Theo sat, arms folded, thinking he was in charge now. Larkin decided something drastic was needed to refresh his memory. He pointed the gun at the floor between Theo's feet and fired.

His legs jerked up, trying to dodge the bullet and the splinters. The dog sprang back, barking as it went. Karl covered his eyes and screwed his eyes tight shut. The noise of the blast was deafening in the small space. Larkin's ears were ringing like he had been to a Metallica concert.

'Don't fuck me about!' Larkin shouted, probably too loud because of the ringing. He knew he would have to move quickly in case the noise alerted the police, although he doubted they would venture into this area. 'Tell me!' he shouted.

'That Scottish bitch was sent by Rayman,' Theo blurted out. 'To fuckin' Trojan Horse the door open, just like you. Her an' that other whore, they tried to rip me off. It got nasty, the cops came, an' I had to fight to get my name back.' He sounded sullen and sulky now.

'Why does Rayman want to get in here?' asked Larkin.

Theo looked at him like he had two heads. 'Whassamatter with you, you thick or somethin'? I got all the trade in this area. I got the dealers, the suppliers. I'm the man. He's nothin', he's history. He wants my business!' Anger was welling up inside Theo.

'Listen,' said Larkin, his own anger rising as he realised how he had been used. 'I don't care about you and Rayman. I just want to know what happened to the girl. Tell me, then I'm gone.'

Theo fidgeted in his seat. Either his attention span was wandering and he was getting bored, or some tiny living creatures from the sofa were trying to make their home in his clothes. Even the dog was looking restless. 'How the fuck do I know? Whores like that, junkie whores, come and go all the time. After the police came I never saw them again.'

Larkin stood for a moment, weighing his options. That looked like all he was going to get. 'OK. I'm going to walk out of this door, then I'm gone. Out of your life forever, right?'

Theo just sat there. 'Fuck you, man.'

Larkin turned to the door and undid the locks, all the time keeping an eye on the two men and the dog. Especially the dog. It looked like a muscle-formed spring, coiled and ready to go at any second. He opened the door to leave, but got no further. For there stood Rayman and Kwesi, all razor smiles, both holding two of the meanest twelve gauge-pump-actions he had ever seen, both itching to use them.

'Well, Stephen, my man, how's it going?' said Rayman, crossing the threshold.

'You fucking used me!' snarled Larkin.

Rayman gave out a laugh. 'Used you? You white liberals always ready to listen to a poor black man with a sob story.'

'I'm not a liberal,' growled Larkin, anger and fear fighting for prominence.

'So you say,' he laughed again. 'But you listened. An' you believed me.' He turned to address Theo. 'I'm in charge now, boy. You're history.'

Hatred burned in Theo's eyes. 'The bosses'll get you.'

Rayman gave out another cold laugh. Mr Cheerful. 'The bosses don't scare me. They'll do business with me. Like they used to with you.'

The two men stared at each other. Theo and his pit bull against Rayman and his human pit bull. Larkin decided to leave them to it and quietly made for the door.

'Where you goin'?' asked Rayman without turning his gaze away from Theo. 'Don't you wanna know about your girl?'

'Theo told me. You were her pimp, right? You got her stoned, made her come on to Theo, and when he was distracted tried to muscle in on his patch. But it didn't work. Is that what happened?'

Rayman shrugged. 'Sounds about right.'

'So where is she now?'

Rayman gestured with his left hand. 'Vanished like the mornin' mist...'

Larkin looked at Theo and Rayman. They were standing in the middle of the room, eye to eye, toe to toe, squaring off to each other, lost in their own private grudge war. Karl sat on the sofa, eyes darting between the two, wishing he were somewhere else.

Larkin reckoned they were no longer a threat to him so he made his way to the door, holding onto the gun just in case he was wrong. He moved past Rayman, who didn't remove his eyes from Theo. He laughed.

'A pleasure doin' business with you boy. Drop by anytime.'

Larkin looked at him, wanting to say something – anything – just to have the last word. Nothing came. Karl looked up as Larkin reached the door. His expression was one of wonder that Larkin was able to walk out so easily, mixed with envy and fear because he couldn't do the same.

Too late, mate, thought Larkin. You're in it for life. However long that'll be.

He clashed the heavy steel door shut behind him as he left.

Larkin stood outside on the street, looking from right to left, shaking from rage, anger and adrenalin. The road was deserted. He swore under his breath and turned left. Glancing down at his quivering fist, he was amazed to see Karl's gun still in it. He looked round for a place to dump it and, seeing a litter bin that was still standing, headed towards it.

No, he thought, if I dump it there, some kid might find it. And then, on the heels of that thought, another one: some kid already had it. I took it off him.

In the gutter was a drain with a broken grille. Perfect, he thought, and dropped the gun down it. He heard the satisfying plop, then took the other gun, the one Rayman had palmed him, out of his pocket and sent that one down too. As he stood up to go, he caught a glimpse of movement from the corner of his eye, something that made his heart skip a beat. Theo's pit bull coming towards him at full pelt.

It was too late to retrieve either gun, so he turned and ran. But it was no good, the dog had his scent and was after him, a relentless missile of slavering muscle and bone, bounding along at breakneck speed.

Larkin ran as fast as he could. His legs raced, his heart pounded and his lungs had a sharp menthol ache as breath went in and out. He gave a quick glance over his shoulder, checked that it was still gaining. It was. His attention elsewhere, he didn't notice a chunk of gutted engine debris on the pavement in front of him. He hit it with his foot, stumbled, tried to right himself, but it was too late. His balance lost, he went over.

The dog was still bearing down on him and even if he made it to his feet, there was no way he could outrun it now. He lay on the pavement, his mind racing. He was done for. Suddenly he saw a whole rusted wheel hub, minus the tyre, lying to his right. Just as the dog was almost on him, he grabbed it.

The pit bull leapt, jaws open, primal blood lust in its eyes. Larkin quickly brought the wheel hub up, groaning at the weight, and caught the dog on its neck. He heaved with all his strength, putting his rage at Rayman and Theo into it, and propelled the dog high in the air, over his head.

Larkin dropped the hub and turned sharply. The dog landed on its back, looking more surprised than anything. It started growling, readying itself for another attack. Larkin was on it fast. He swung the wheel hub, catching the pit bull as it charged on the side of its jaw. It went down and he heard something crack, accompanied by a reluctant whimper. The injury didn't keep it down for long though, and it soon righted itself, ready for another charge.

Larkin was running out of options when suddenly from around the corner came the screech of tyres. He looked up to see a Saab, his own car, come hurtling towards him, Andy at the wheel, driving like the hordes of Hell were pursuing him.

Larkin got to his feet, the dog still running towards him. Andy sized up the situation immediately and drove the car straight for the pit bull. He mounted the pavement and with a dull thud, machine and canine connected. The dog was thrown up in the air, coming to land against the concrete wall of one of the tower blocks.

Larkin ran round to the passenger door and dived in. With another squeal of tyres, Andy spun the car around and they were off. He gave a cock-eyed smile to Larkin as he drove.

'Cavalry to the rescue!' he shouted, laughing.

Larkin just stared at him, panting, shaking. 'Where the fuck have you been?' He was furious. 'All you had to do was wait in the street and pick me up when I came out.'

Andy knew that Larkin was in no mood to argue. 'I couldn't get parked!' he said indignantly. 'If I'd stopped anywhere round there the fuckin' wheels would have gone, wouldn't they? I'd 'ave ended up on bricks. So I just circled round.'

'You're so fucking unreliable! D'you know that?'

It was Andy's turn to be angry now. 'Unreliable? Unreliable? Who just saved your fuckin' life back there? Ay? Ay?' He stared at Larkin, taking his eyes off the road, and narrowly missed an oncoming car. 'If it wasn't for me you'd be half a fuckin' pound of badly wrapped mince by now.'

Larkin fell silent. Andy had a point, but he wasn't prepared to admit it yet. They sat like that for a while, until Andy asked Larkin how it had gone. He told him.

'I was used, Andy, fucking used.'

'And we're no further forward.'

Larkin sighed heavily. He was coming down from the adrenalin, the post-rush blues were kicking in. The truth of the situation was beginning to sink in. 'Nope. A dead end.' And then in a smaller voice, 'We've lost her, mate.'

They drove back towards Clapham in silence.

The Land of the Blind

By the time they had reached the High Courts of Justice, Larkin had had enough. He told Andy to pull in and started undoing his seat belt. Andy, his expression puzzled, had done as he was asked and, to the accompaniment of car and bus horns, allowed Larkin to get out.

'I just need to walk for a bit,' Larkin shouted into the car above the din. 'Sort my head out. Think. I'll see you at home later.'

Andy, protesting loudly and looking perplexed, had driven off, leaving Larkin standing alone on the pavement.

On the way back from the Atwell Estate, Larkin had found the silence in the car to be interminable. His initial anger at being used had subsided and the enormity of his task, of finding Karen with his one slender lead gone, was just sinking in. He had deluded himself into thinking it would be as easy as walking into Theo's place. But now she could be anywhere, she could be nowhere.

He didn't want to face Moir with the news of the dead end, not just yet. He wanted to go home with something positive, another strategy in mind. To do this he needed to be alone, and walking was one of his best ways of thinking.

He looked at the Law Courts, the sandblasted, white stone façade giving an appearance of either innocence untarnished or too much whitewash. Larkin didn't dwell on it. Instead he pulled his jacket around him and headed down The Strand.

It was the commuter hour and all around him suited hordes made their way, heads down in single-minded determination, to their tubes, trains and homes. Swirling amongst them were tourists, gaudily dressed, as if in defiance of the late winter weather, and others, the hip and the wannabes, out for a night on the town. The shops of The Strand were a curious alternation of London exclusive and tourist tat: designer dresses and accessories next door to plastic policemen's helmets and postcards of painted breasts. The neon signs of the theatres glowed in the dusk; clarion calls to the faithful, they offered escapism and enlightenment in varying degrees and combinations to the middle class. They also offered air conditioning, plush seating and a warm ambience; an environment where even the most difficult, uncomfortable idea could be safely digested and discussed in comfort. The grand hotels, all polished gold signs and liveried doormen, looked more like theme parks to an age of vanished elegance than functioning places for travellers as they played host to hordes of brightly anoraked Europeans and Americans.

At first glance, it looked like a typically prosperous West End street. But as doors closed, it told a different, more truthful story. In the doorways lay the homeless, huddled up inside filthy blankets, lying on stained, damp cardboard. The lost boys and girls: dirty, defeated, literally hopeless, their hopes, fears, addictions and struggles rendered insignificant when placed against the scale of the overbearing buildings. It was hard to tell if they were dead or alive as February laid its bite on them.

Larkin could remember a story he'd reported on a few years ago when the community-minded shopkeepers of The Strand tried to club together and pay for street cleaners to hose down their doorways at hourly intervals during the night, as a disincentive to homeless people to sleep there. When questioned on this, they claimed it was 'bad for business', but didn't elaborate on who would be using a closed shop in the middle of the night. Eventually, wiser, or at least more circumspect, heads had prevailed and the scheme hadn't gone ahead. But the thought had been there. And, Larkin didn't doubt, was probably still there now.

They sat now, some begging for change, some just staring, a couple sucking on a home-made Coke can crack pipe, while the rest of the pavement traffic wilfully ignored them. The commuters were oblivious to them, oblivious to everything but their need to get home. They strode with blinkered vision, making their way to a dinner that was more habit than necessity, followed by a night slumped in front of *Eastenders*, Chris Tarrant and *Peak Practice*, all in glorious cathode ray narco-vision; a banal comfort that was beyond those in the doorways. The young, hip, well-dressed crowd circumvented them with practised ease as they hopped from bar to restaurant to bar. Two separate cities existing side by side, the second a fallout from the first. The seen and the unseen. The Land of the Blind and the Kingdom of the Invisibles. The gulf between them looked huge but, as Larkin had seen before, it wasn't. A few bad business decisions, a couple of personality flaws and you could easily slip from the top world to the bottom one, where it was harder, if not impossible, to get out.

Karen could be here, Larkin thought. She could be under one of those blankets right now and he would never know. He could spend days, months, looking for her and she would have been here all the time.

A sudden impulse gripped him, one he had to restrain himself from carrying out. He wanted to rip the blankets off each person, see if she was there; and if she wasn't, interrogate each and every one of them to find out what they knew about her. But he didn't. Instead he just kept walking, kept thinking, and realised he was no nearer to finding her.

His walk took him down to the Embankment and over Hungerford Bridge to the South Bank. The bridge was primarily a railway track over the river with a footpath to one side. At each end of the walkway sat a beggar holding out a cup for change, a little guilt tweak for the well-heeled off to the National, NFT or the Festival Hall. It seemed to Larkin, as he tossed a few loose coins into a cup and became the recipient of desperate, but rehearsed, 'thanks', that he was crossing over a privately run toll bridge.

The view from the bridge of the Thames, with its twinkling waterfront buildings stretching far past St Paul's, looked quite spectacular. It made London seem like a pleasant place to visit, but in a strictly look-but-don't-touch way. For, as the beggars at either end reminded you, you might not want to live here.

As he crossed the bridge he had wondered why he had picked this route to walk home, but once he had reached the other side, realisation had struck him. Apart from the theatres, cinemas, art galleries, TV studios and concert halls, there was something else the South Bank used to be famous for. Cardboard City.

The roundabout in front of Waterloo Station was, when Larkin was last in London, an underground shanty town housing hundreds of homeless people. It existed on several levels and strata, with walkways, access routes and service roads running through it, all of which had been colonised. Cardboard, plastic and tarpaulin had been turned into lean-to bivouacs stuffed with grubby old sleeping bags, blankets and newspapers. Lighting was weak: occasional diffused sunlight, the odd unbroken fluorescent tube, or one of several bonfires that dotted the area, made from old pallets, cardboard or anything else to hand, providing an unstable and dangerous source of both light and warmth.

The inhabitants were all filthy, with

matted, long hair, all wearing a uniform of army surplus, cast-offs and skin diseases. When Larkin had first encountered them a few years ago, they had stared at him with suspicion, unease and, in most cases, outright hatred. He hadn't stayed long.

It had been, quite literally, an underworld. A city beneath a city. Larkin had felt like an outsider, someone from the land above. It had reminded him of HG Wells' morlocks or the stories he had heard about Mole People – subterranean tunnel dwellers in the disused tube lines and sewers of both London and New York. He had always regarded the stories as urban myths, but after seeing this place, he wasn't so sure. The people here were marginalized from the surface world. It wouldn't take much to set them on the next leg of the journey, the descent.

He could remember the feeling he'd had when he'd returned above ground. The weak London daylight had never seemed so bright, the smog-choked air of Waterloo had never appeared so fresh. But at least he had been able to walk out of there. For the denizens of Cardboard City it had seemed as if the only way out, one way or another, was down.

But that was then, this was now. He had come this way again because he didn't want to return home without a plan to help Moir find Karen. He was hoping this place would provide inspiration, direction. There was a slim chance Karen could be living here, or that someone would know her whereabouts. He knew it was an idea born of futility and desperation, and he began to realise how anxious parents felt when they came down south from some repressive northern town looking for their missing offspring, who had run away to make their fortune in London. He, like them, would ignore the official figures, the ones that tell of over thirty thousand people going missing in London alone every year, and instead remember St Jude, keep walking, and tell themselves they would be the lucky ones.

He was, of course, to be disappointed. Not only was there no one to help him, but there was no Cardboard City. The whole area had been razed, and in its place were whitewashed breezeblock and hardboard hoardings camouflaging a newly emergent, half-completed building advertising itself as an IMAX cinema. The place had been reclaimed for the surface.

Larkin wondered what had happened to the inhabitants of Cardboard City. Perhaps they had been dispersed, sicked up into the upper world of doorways and pavements, dwelling forever in the peripheral vision of citizens' eyes. Perhaps they had begun their descent to the lower depths and were now

Mole People; not just passing from the surface to below, but from the land of reality to the land of urban myth. Perhaps, without shelter or means of support, they had just died.

Larkin knew he would find no answers here. His walk had yielded no inspiration, no plan, nothing. Just a reminder of the enormity of his task. He would have to go back to Clapham, talk to Moir and decide what their next plan of action would be. With dragging feet, he made his way to the tube at Waterloo.

Of course, had he known what, or rather who, was waiting for him at Faye's house he would have been in even less of a hurry to get there.

Camden Town

Larkin sat at the table in the small, grey room, staring first at the wall, then the barred window, and finally, the closed door. He sighed, drumming his fingers on the table. He was alone as he had been for the last three quarters of an hour or so, and, twitchily, was beginning to wish he smoked, just to give himself something to do.

He knew what the police were doing to

117

him. Making him sweat. Leave the bastard alone long enough, ran the famous interview technique, and they'll confess to anything. Even murder. He tried to kid himself that it wasn't working, but his shaking hands and quickening pulse suggested otherwise.

Much more of this, thought Larkin, and I'll be owning up to topping JFK.

He stood up and moved to the door, pressing his ear to it. Nothing. Beyond the door was silence. He hoped they hadn't gone and left him there for the night. It was a stupid notion, knowing how police stations functioned, but, alone in a claustrophobic room, his mind was playing tricks.

He sat down again, stretched out his legs and tried to relax. Try to think of something else, he commanded himself, you still don't know what this is about. He tried focusing on his search for Karen and what he intended to do next, but he couldn't concentrate. Instead, forcing his heart to beat normally, he replayed the events that had brought him to his present predicament.

On reaching Faye's house, he found they had a visitor. He was sitting at the kitchen table, mug in hand, talking to Moir, Andy and Faye. Moir also had a mug in front of him, Andy and Faye were working their way through a bottle of red wine. As Larkin entered they all looked up.

118

'Here he is now,' said Faye. She tried to sound nonchalant, but the graveness of her expression stopped her from pulling it off. Larkin began to feel uneasy.

The man stood up and introduced himself. 'Detective Sergeant Irvine,' he said, showing his warrant card. His accent was Scottish and, to Larkin's ear, a little like Sean Connery. He was about six foot tall, with good bearing, dressed in tweeds, with brogues on his feet. He looked more like a country squire than a policeman. 'I'm afraid there's been a murder,' he said without any preamble, 'and I'd like to ask you a few questions about it.'

Larkin's heart skipped a beat. 'Who?' he said, finding a chair and sitting down.

Irvine opened his mouth as if to say something important, then changed his mind. He looked at the others round the table. 'I think it would be best if we talked somewhere a little more ... formal.'

'Are you arresting me?' Larkin asked, trying to keep the sudden panic from rising into his voice.

'No, I'm not. But I don't think here is the best place to talk about this. Would you mind coming down to the station please?'

'Do I have a choice?'

'You do. But it would be easier if you came with me.'

'Don't worry Stephen,' said Moir. 'You're

not in any trouble. You'll be OK.'

'Thanks,' Larkin replied. He looked at Moir as he did so. There was something different about him, something he couldn't put his finger on. Never mind, that could keep. 'Come on, then,' he said, hoping he looked as confident as he sounded. 'Let's get this over with.'

Irvine thanked Faye for the coffee and Moir for the conversation. He just nodded at Andy.

They got into Irvine's car and headed north.

'Where are we going?' asked Larkin.

'North Bridge House, Camden,' Irvine replied.

'Camden?' asked Larkin. 'You're a bit off your beat, aren't you?'

'Yeah. But the crime isn't. I was just going to pop round, ask you a few questions, but I got talking to Mister Moir. He told me a few things about you I thought my boss should hear.'

Thanks a lot, Henry, thought Larkin. 'I'll bet he did.'

Irvine's face cracked a smile. 'Don't look so worried. You're only helping us with our enquiries.'

'Yeah, right,' Larkin replied. 'So who's been murdered, then?'

'I think it's better if you hear it from my boss. He'll tell you when we get there.'

Irvine took the scenic route along Millbank, past the Houses of Parliament, up Whitehall. Perhaps it was a new tourist policing initiative for the Met, thought Larkin. As he drove, he spoke.

'I was talking to your friend Mister Moir. Terrible business with his daughter. He's got you doing the leg work, I hear?'

'Yeah,' said Larkin, not wanting to give too much away.

'You had any luck finding her?'

Irvine's apparent sincerity immediately put Larkin's guard up. 'No. Not yet.'

'Well, I said to him, if there's anything we can do to help, just give us a call.'

Larkin looked suspiciously at him. 'Why would you do that? Because he's on the force?'

Irvine laughed. 'Not so much that. He's a fellow countryman. And you do what you can for your folk.'

Irvine seemed genuine and honest, not qualities Larkin normally associated with policemen, and he didn't know how to take him. But he'd been fooled before, so, rather than say something he would regret later, he clammed up for the rest of the journey and just enjoyed the view.

Like hospitals, Larkin had always hated police stations. And for the same reasons: once he went in, he doubted he'd come out.

121

If he went to hospital for a check-up he was afraid they'd find something terminal. Likewise, if he went to help the police with their enquiries there was every chance he'd be banged up for the same charge. As an investigative journalist with an interest in such matters, he'd seen it happen plenty of times.

Larkin had now sat so long he was seriously contemplating screaming aloud just to get attention, when he heard a sound behind him. The door. Here we go, he thought, steeling himself, the rubber hose gang are coming to get their confession. Quickly composing his features, he focused on the wall ahead. He'd decided to play the studied nonchalance card for all it was worth.

'Sorry to have kept you,' said a lilting Irish voice. 'I was under the impression I'd gone home for the evening. Some chance, eh?'

Despite himself, Larkin turned. The pleasant-sounding voice belonged to a genial-looking Irishman, quite short for a policeman, crisply dressed and with an affable air that didn't disguise the intelligence in his eyes. He crossed to where Larkin sat and extended his right hand.

'Detective Inspector Kennedy. How you doing?'

Larkin shook his hand. 'Stephen Larkin.'

'And a representative of the Fourth Estate,

I believe, eh? I'm on good terms with some of your associates.' He gave a short laugh, chiefly for his own benefit. 'Or one, at least.' He sat down facing Larkin. 'Have you been sitting here all this time? Have they not offered you a drink?'

'Nope.'

Kennedy looked appalled. 'They haven't? I'm sorry, what will you think of us? Can I get you some tea?'

'I'd prefer coffee,' Larkin replied.

Kennedy leaned forward, eyes twinkling conspiratorially. 'Believe me, not in this place you wouldn't.'

'Tea's fine, then.'

'Okey doke, I'll get that sorted out. Not be two ticks,' he added, and was out the door, leaving Larkin alone again.

Larkin was, to say the least, surprised. He'd expected strong-arm tactics, not a friendly approach. Don't read anything into that, though, he thought to himself. He still hadn't been given a reason as to why he was here and, until such time, he would regard everyone and everything with suspicion. He wasn't about to be taken in by one of the oldest tricks in the book.

Kennedy returned, resumed his seat. 'Tea'll be along in a minute,' he said with his disarming smile. 'Now to business. I'll bet you're wondering why you've been dragged along here.'

'Yes,' Larkin replied, unable to keep the exasperation out of his voice.

'Sorry about all this cloak-and-dagger stuff,' said Kennedy genuinely, 'but it's a rather delicate situation.'

Larkin waited. Eventually, Kennedy spoke.

'Jackie Fairley, head of the Finders Keepers Agency and someone I know you were acquainted with, is dead,' he said.

'What?' said Larkin, looking stunned.

He could feel Kennedy's eyes on him all the time, gauging his reaction. He must have been satisfied that Larkin's shock was genuine, for he continued, 'That's what my detective sergeant didn't want to say in front of your friend. We found her body this morning on a patch of waste ground just behind King's Cross station. Now, she was one of the good guys and we want to close this one quickly. When we checked her diary at her office, the last entry was you.' Kennedy sat back. 'So, what can you tell us?'

Larkin sat there, dumbstruck. 'Not a lot,' he said eventually. He told the detective why he had called on her. 'On behalf of a friend of mine.'

'This would be Mr Moir?'

'Yeah. We're looking for his daughter. Finders had been checking on her. With no success, I'm afraid.'

Kennedy nodded, as if confirming what he already knew. 'And how did Jackie Fairley seem to you?'

'Fine. It was the first time I'd met her, so I had nothing to compare it to.'

'Not agitated? Nervous?'

Larkin shook his head. 'No.'

Kennedy shook his head sadly. 'A good woman, Jackie Fairley. The force served her badly. But she had a passion for her work. Best thing she could have done, setting up that agency. Did it all by herself.'

'Yeah,' said Larkin, 'I didn't have a chance to know her but she seemed like she was on the right side.'

The tea arrived. Kennedy poured, nodded and sat back, knowing that was all he was going to get. He looked tired, as if the investigation was a burden of personal sadness to him, as if, no matter how many times he investigated violent death, he would never quite understand what would drive a person to do such an act. His sympathies would always be with the victim.

'Can I ask you a question?' said Larkin.

'Go ahead.'

'How did she die?'

Kennedy gave a sardonic smile. 'Is this for publication?'

'No. Just for me.'

'Old curiosities die hard, eh? Well, she didn't go easily. Her office was ransacked, stuff all over the floor, ripped apart, the works. Judging by the state of the office, that's where they did what they did to her, too. Dumped the body afterwards.' Kennedy shook his head, his mind on what must have been a horrific sight, his imagination filling in the rest. 'Whoever they were, they knew what they were doing. They made sure she suffered before she died. It was a methodical, professional job. I think they wanted her to tell them something.'

'Why her?' asked Larkin. 'Would this have anything to do with who I'm looking for?'

Kennedy shook his head. 'We just don't know. The line of work she was in she could have trodden on anyone's toes. A vindictive pimp, angry at having one of his girls taken away, some equally annoyed drug dealers, anyone. The people she mixed with weren't pleasant.' He sighed heavily. 'I knew her a little, admired her. Her work made a difference. She gave a voice to the victims. Unfortunately, that's what she became in the end.'

Larkin said nothing, just nodded in silent agreement.

Kennedy stood up suddenly. 'Well, thank you for coming in, Mr Larkin.'

'That's it? I can go?' asked Larkin rather incredulously.

'Certainly.' Kennedy smiled. 'Did you think we were going to arrest you?'

Larkin gestured around the room. 'Stuck in here for what felt like hours on end...'

Kennedy looked sheepish. 'I must apologise for that. DS Irvine doesn't have the keys to my office, and the canteen was closed.' He smiled. 'It wasn't intentional.' He stuck out his hand and Larkin took it.

Another first, thought Larkin.

Larkin reached the main security door and said goodbye to Kennedy, asking to be kept in touch about any further developments. As he walked through to the front desk, relieved at actually being able to leave, he was surprised to find Moir sitting on one of the chairs, overcoat bundled around him, looking like he'd settled in for the night.

'What are you doing here?' asked Larkin, surprised.

Moir stood up. 'Waiting for you.' As he spoke, Larkin detected a gleam, almost a rekindled fire, in the man's eyes that he hadn't seen there for a while.

'You OK, Henry?' he asked.

'Fine. Get in the car and I'll tell you on the way home,' Moir replied, almost smiling.

Larkin, wondering how much more confusing the night could get, did as he was told.

They drove through Camden, Moir in the passenger seat, Larkin driving. The area was a huge bohemian melting pot, a libertarian village within a city, buzzing and vibrant. The pavements teemed with midweek revellers alive to the beats of several different drummers. They made their way dressed in oversize utilitarian clothes, not a million miles different from the oversized uniform of their homeless counterparts, but the vibrant, sudden flashes of colour gave away their monied status. Cars, pubs and clubs all thumping out tarmac-shaking, ribcage-rattling rhythms. Music, energy, creation, disposable income. It was a positive, life-affirming vibe and Camden thrived on it.

'So,' said Larkin, negotiating his way through a throng of people unaware of where the pavement ended and the road started, 'what have you got to tell me?'

Moir, trying, and failing, to suppress his excitement, told him.

He had decided to follow Larkin to the police station, just to make sure he got home all right. Andy had reluctantly agreed to drive the Saab and on arrival been told to wait by the desk. Irvine had emerged and invited them in.

'That was when Andy said he'd find his own way home,' Moir said.

Larkin smiled. Andy hated police stations even more than he did. Besides which, Larkin knew for a fact that Andy would have been carrying at least two different kinds of illegal substances about his person. Andy had left Moir with Irvine and disappeared into the night.

'So, over a cup of tea, your man and me got talkin',' said Moir. They had talked in general of their lives in the police, their upbringing in Scotland. All in the light tone of equals discussing work. Eventually, the conversation reached specifics, namely Moir's reason for visiting London.

'I told him about Karen, how we were no nearer to findin' her.'

Larkin said nothing.

'Oh, I know today was a dead end,' Moir said looking at Larkin. 'Andy told me. But thanks for tryin' though.'

Larkin nodded, keeping his eyes on the road.

Moir had told Irvine something similar. Irvine asked if there was anything he could do to help. 'I said no, we'd tried everything. She was only on record the once, and that was a dead end.' Irvine asked if she could be using an alias.

'And that,' said Moir, barely able to contain his excitement, 'is when the penny dropped. All this time I've been lookin' for Karen Moir. But she had another name. A name she would only use out of spite.' Moir smiled. 'Her stepfather's name. Shapp.'

So they had punched the name Karen Shapp into the computer and come up with a match straight away. 'Thank fuck she wasn't called Jones,' Moir said, almost laughing.

'Good work, Henry,' Larkin said smiling. The name might have been another dead end, but Larkin didn't mention that. For now, Moir had hope. And, although it might have just been false, to Moir it seemed better than no hope at all.

'I've got an address in Kentish Town,' Moir said, his features clouding slightly. 'We can check it out tomorrow.'

'OK, then,' replied Larkin.

They drove on in silence after that, until a question formed in Larkin's mind.

'Why did they have her on file? What was the charge?'

The cloud that had been moving over Moir's features darkened and spread. 'Soliciting. The place is a well-known knockin' shop.' He sighed. 'You never know, it might not be...' His voice trailed off, unable or unwilling to complete his thought.

'We'll see tomorrow, Henry.'

Moir nodded. His earlier good mood seemed to be dissipating fast. 'Aye.'

Larkin stole a glance at Moir as he drove. He didn't want him to sink back into depression. 'You look different, Henry. I can't put my finger on it, but you look different.'

Moir reddened slightly. 'New clothes,' he said. 'Faye took me shopping today. Said I looked disgraceful.'

That was it, thought Larkin. New clothes.

Moir still had on the same old overcoat, but underneath was a new sports jacket, polo shirt in what looked to be wool, dark trousers and shoes. The wardrobe, alongside Moir's continuing reacquaintance with the bathroom, made him seem almost presentable.

'I'm astonished,' said Larkin. 'I've never seen you look so good.'

'It's Faye,' Moir mumbled, tongue tripping over his embarrassment, 'she made me.'

'She's a good woman.'

'Aye,' said Moir. 'She is.'

Larkin didn't reply. The heartfelt tone of Moir's voice had surprised him. He thought it best if he didn't say anything more about her. He tried to change the subject, but was all out of diversionary topics of conversation. He just wanted to get home, have a shower and let his head hit the pillow. It had been a long, draining, day and he was tired. But the night was bringing on his old, familiar hollow feeling, an emptiness that was still gnawing at him. He would have to ignore it, live with it. There was nothing he could do about it at the moment.

He thought of Jackie Fairley. Although he'd only met her once, he had taken to her, admired her, as Kennedy had said. Her death was a loss. If he'd still had some faith, he would have offered up a prayer for her, as it was he just wished she was well, wherever she was. Thinking of her led him back to Faye. Would she still be up when he got back? And if she was, what, if anything, would happen? What did he want to happen? Would she, however temporarily, be able to banish the emptiness, the loneliness?

He didn't know the answer to any of those questions, so he drove in silence. Moir didn't seem to want to talk either, so they sat, each one lost in his own private, but tangentially intersecting, thoughts, all the way back to Clapham.

Back in the house, Moir went straight to bed. Larkin had his shower. Being tired but unable to sleep, he went into the kitchen to make himself a coffee. As he waited for the kettle to boil, he noticed what was on the draining board. The wine bottle Faye and Andy had been drinking from earlier was there, along with another one. Next to that sat a drained gin bottle. Faye's way of coping with her own emptiness, her own loneliness, thought Larkin. It made him want to hold her all the more.

Coffee in hand, he made his way up the stairs to his room. As he did so, he paused on the landing outside Faye's room. He could just make out the faint sounds of her deep breathing. She was asleep, alone.

With no option, he decided to do the

same, and walked slowly up the stairs to the attic. His feet hit the bare boards as he went, and each time left a small, hollow slap in his wake. The sound didn't reverberate, didn't echo, and it wasn't long before the house returned to darkness, and stillness, for the rest of the night.

The Love Shack

Larkin walked along the pavement, alert the whole time, yet trying not to look it, not to look conspicuous. A north London street just off Kentish Town Road, it consisted of old, terraced Victorian and Edwardian houses, some undergoing, or having undergone, renovation, some in a state of misplaced modernism, having gone the pebbledash and UPVC windows route, and the others allowing, or even actively encouraging, entropy to take its course. It was an ordinary street, quiet enough not to attract attention.

The address he wanted was about halfway along, next to a house that sat firmly in the precinct of the gentrification police: UPVC windows were being torn out and replaced with wooden sash ones, pebbledash was being ripped off, brickwork restored. The work was being done with care and pride and it made the house Larkin was after look even shabbier.

37 Priory End Lane had discoloured red brick, old rotting window frames that looked like they hadn't been painted since the Suez crisis, and a replacement front door; solid, well-secured, windowless. No light could enter. Yellowed net curtains hung at the windows and they, along with an inch-thick coating of urban grime, obscured the view inside.

Larkin reached the house, paused to check it was the right one, and clocked an old, dowdy-looking pub on the next corner. He made his way across the road, and entered.

The pub, called ironically enough The Hope, was the kind of place where career alcoholics took their dreams to die. The décor obligingly reflected that. It had just gone eleven and there were only a handful of drinkers in the place: a few old men with ravaged faces and wasted bodies, close to celebrating their Golden Weddings, fifty years of being locked into a loveless marriage with alcohol – and a decidedly uncomfortable-looking Andy Brennan. Larkin bought a pint at the bar, withstood the landlord's openly hostile stare, and went to join Andy.

'Nice place,' said Larkin, pulling up a stool so uncomfortable it could have been used as a form of punishment in a Catholic monastery. 'Earthy ambience.'

'Fuckin' dive,' Andy grumbled. 'You see the look you got off that landlord? You'd think he'd be glad of the business. I mean, when his regulars peg it, he'll be out of a job, won't he?'

'Not like you to be so fussy.'

'Yeah, well I've got my pride.'

Larkin laughed. 'No you haven't.'

Andy was about to answer back but Larkin silenced him.

'Never mind that. We've got work to do. What's been happening?'

'I've been watchin' that place. Number thirty-seven. I've watched them come, an' I've watched them go. An' yeah, you're right. It's a knockin' shop.' He took a swig of beer, sighed. 'Fuck, Henry must want her back pretty bad to put himself through this.'

Larkin nodded. He had phoned Andy on his mobile first thing in the morning and asked if he was still around Camden. Andy had started to make excuses for the disappearing act he'd pulled the night before – 'Got talkin' to this stunnin' bird an' before you know it I was back at her place givin' it the old heave ho' – but Larkin waved them aside. He told Andy to stay where he was, gave him the address Irvine had provided them with and set him to work on surveillance. Andy had phoned back with his location and Larkin had arranged to meet him.

'How d'you reckon we should play this, then?' asked Andy.

'I think it's best if only one of us goes in. I'll do it.'

'And what'll I do?' asked Andy in not so mock aggrievement.

'Wait here,' said Larkin, lips curling into a smile.

'Here?' squawked Andy, indignation rising, 'with Cheerful Charlie over there givin' me the evil eye all the time?'

'It's a perfect surveillance spot. You can see the house, keep an eye on the street and give me a bell on my mobile if there's anything I should know. And you're here for back-up if I need you. Plus,' Larkin added, the smile back again, 'you're always telling me what a born and bred London boy you are. Well these are your people. This is your culture. Sit here and bond.'

'These aren't my people!' Andy spat, distaste on his tongue. 'I'm a south London boy. That's my manor. It's like askin' you to go to Sunderland, innit?'

'This place has got much more class than anything in Sunderland. And anyway, you're not a south London boy, Andy. You're a farmer's son from Hampshire.'

'Fuck off,' Andy said, arms crossed, mumbling into the table. 'You're just pissed off 'cos I scored last night an' didn't wait around for you.'

'You think there's a lot of skill involved in getting a girl so drunk she agrees to have sex with you?' Larkin stood up. 'And you're not getting any younger, you know. All you'll be getting soon are sympathy shags.'

Andy started to reply but Larkin cut him off. 'Just stay here,' he said, 'and keep your eyes peeled.'

Earlier that morning Larkin had emerged from his room, made his way downstairs and found Faye and Moir sitting at the kitchen table together. As soon as he entered they stopped talking, words falling off in mid-sentence, and looked at him, smiling politely. Too politely. Something didn't feel right, thought Larkin.

'Morning,' he said.

They both replied.

'Henry's been telling me about the new lead,' said Faye. 'Sounds promising.'

'We don't want to build our hopes up,' Moir replied.

'Henry's right,' said Larkin. 'It could be something, it could be nothing.' He poured himself a coffee and sat at the table.

They outlined their plans for the day. Moir had intended to accompany Larkin to Kentish Town but Larkin had dissuaded him from that idea. If Karen was there, he might not want to see the condition she was in, and she might not want to talk to him yet. He'd call Andy, ask him to help instead. Faye then volunteered to spend the day with Henry, do something together, keep him occupied. Moir's eyes seemed to light up at the thought, and he gave an involuntary smile to Faye, which she returned.

There was something flowing between them, Larkin thought, some kind of exclusive bond he wasn't part of. Moir smiling was an unusual sight in itself, like he was using muscles his face didn't possess or at the very least was only rediscovering the use of. Like watching stone wrinkle and crack open. Larkin excused himself, took his coffee to his room, and phoned Andy.

He walked up the stairs feeling strange. He was happy that the two of them were getting along, but there was a much deeper feeling lurking around inside him. Something with a lashing shark's tail, basking below the surface. Jealousy, perhaps? He didn't know, and didn't have time to dwell on it. Instead he sat on the bed, dialled Andy's number, waited for him to answer, and started with the insults.

As Larkin approached the house, he saw the door open. His first thought was to hide, not be seen, but he soon discarded it. Instead he moved quicker and reached the front gate just in time to see a nondescript middle-aged man wearing a cheap suit and a look of self-revulsion step over the threshold, blinking as the light hit him, pulling his fly shut. Larkin moved briskly up the well-rutted front path.

'Hold the door,' he said.

The man held the door open, studiously avoiding eye contact, then hurried off once he saw Larkin had it. Larkin entered, letting the door close behind him.

The hall looked, depressingly, just as he had expected it to. Woodchip-covered walls bulging and discoloured, lino cracked, worn and perishing. Despite a masking of cheap air freshener, the place smelt of damp, decay and something more unpleasant and all-pervading. Larkin knew what it was, he'd come across it before. The stink of humanity at its worst.

He heard sounds from down the hall, the echo of heels clacking on floorboards followed by a retching sound. He followed it.

At the back of the house, off to the right, was a room that could once have been the dining room. Now a double bed took centre spot, covered by a faded, stained, purple terrycloth candlewick with a junk shop bedside cabinet beside it. On the cabinet was an open packet of condoms, an aged tube of KY and a grubby, sticky-looking black vibrator. A Calor gas heater stood in the corner, an old disembowelled armchair

139

beside it and a threadbare rug on the floor. Against one wall was an old wardrobe that had never seen better days. Thin, cheap curtains were drawn at the window, stopping any light from entering. They had been that way a long time; dust had gathered in the folds.

In another corner of the room was an old porcelain wash basin, and bent over that was a young, miniskirted girl, coughing a last mouthful of vomit down the sink. Larkin watched as she straightened up and reached for a bottle of mouthwash. It looked like a move she'd practised many times. She flung her head back, gargling with a capful, and Larkin chose that moment to knock on the door.

The sound startled the girl and she turned quickly, swallowing the mouthwash as she did so. Larkin got a good look at her.

Her hair was almost blonde, long and swept over to one side, her make-up looked like the work of an over-enthusiastic child mimicking an adult. Her clothes – mini-skirt barely covering her backside, slingbacks with impossibly high spike heels, blouse exposing both flat-chested cleavage and midriff – all looked like they'd come from the racks of Tart Express. There was no air of sexuality about her, she just looked tired, worn and used. Larkin's stomach gave a sour lurch as he put her age at no higher than fourteen.

Her eyes, teary from vomiting and probably something more, were now wide with fear.

'Sorry to startle you,' said Larkin, as affably as possible, 'but the door was open. I just came in.'

Her fear subsided slightly. 'You're early,' she said in a broad, but wary, Yorkshire accent. 'I'm not expectin' you for another fifteen minutes.'

Larkin gave what he hoped was a disarming smile. 'Sorry. D'you want me to wait?' He could see she was scared, so rather than worry her even more, he decided to play along, pretend to be her punter.

She quickly sketched a smile that didn't reach her frightened eyes and flung it in Larkin's direction without making eye contact.

'No, since you're here, you may as well stay. Welcome to the Love Shack.' She sounded as genuine and convincing as a Channel Five game show host. She walked round the bed towards him. 'Sorry about that before.' She gestured to the sink. 'Had a bad curry last night,' she lied.

Larkin nodded and thought of the man he had just bumped into, the one fidgeting with his zipper. He'd put something down her throat, but Larkin doubted it had been curry. 'Right,' he said, colluding with her in the lie.

'Let's get it sorted out then,' she said,

sitting on the bed, addressing her chipped, painted toe-nails. 'Money before the honey, as they say. I've not seen you here before. This your first time, then?' She reached out, grimacing more than smiling, and began to inexpertly stroke his arm.

He tried to come back with an answer, but a sudden thought lodged itself, stubborn and unwelcome, in his mind. No, Larkin thought to himself, it's not. There was a time, just after his wife died, when he didn't want to be close to anyone, couldn't stand anyone to be near him. Conversely, all he wanted was to put his arms around someone, to hold them, and be held in return. It had been his absolute nadir. He had wrapped himself in booze and pills for a while and that hadn't worked, but one bleak night he had been so lonely, so lost in a haze of memory and alcohol, that he had found a prostitute who the bottle convinced him looked like his dead wife, and gone back to her place. He had wanted sex, wanted his body to feel pleasure again, wanted the warmth of a woman next to him, wanted intimacy. He had paid her, stripped, then collapsed on the bed, calling his wife's name, sobbing, begging to be held. The woman, a hardened professional who had had enough maudlin drunks to last a lifetime, had held him until he had passed out, put him to bed, and gone off to work somewhere else. The next morning he had woken up twisted with self-revulsion, got up and left; but not before the prostitute had extracted full payment from him for staying the night. He had never visited a prostitute since that night. Until now.

'Look,' Larkin started hesitantly, trying to keep his voice as unthreatening as possible, 'I'm not a punter.'

Fear returned to the girl's eyes. She backed away to the corner of the room. 'What you doin' 'ere, then?'

'Don't worry, I'm not going to hurt you,' Larkin continued, although the girl didn't look convinced. He kept his voice slow and calm. 'I'm just looking for a girl who used to live here. Work here, I don't know. All I know is, this is the last address I've got for her. Her name's Karen. Her surname was probably Shapp. Scottish.'

The girl just stared at him.

'I don't mean her any harm. I'm not the law, I'm not a social worker and she's not in trouble. I'm a journalist. But I don't want to do a story about her. I've been sent by her dad to see that she's all right.'

The girl looked straight at him. She's so young, he thought with a twist of anger. Too young to be coping with situations like these.

'I think you'd better leave,' she said, walking purposefully towards the door. 'I'm waitin' for a client an' 'e'll be 'ere any minute.'

Larkin followed her. 'Please. I just need to talk to you.' She kept walking. 'I know you're busy, I'll pay for your time.'

She stopped and turned. At the mention of money she had suddenly, instantaneously mutated from girl to hardened tart, eyes lit by a feral glow.

'How much?'

'Whatever you were charging your client.'

'Seventy quid?' she said, looking like she'd just hiked the price by at least twenty.

'Done.'

'And you just want to talk?'

'Yeah, I just want to talk. But it might be a bit inconvenient here, if your next client turns up, so shall I take you to lunch?'

The girl's eyes brightened. 'Where?'

'Wherever you like.'

'Can we go to McDonald's?'

'Certainly can.'

She smiled, looking, for the first time, like a teenage girl.

Andy's face, pressed up against the pub glass as Larkin sped past in the Saab with the girl in the front seat, had been a picture. Larkin didn't want him along, as he thought he'd have a better chance of getting the girl to open up on her own.

As they sat at the moulded plastic table, the girl, who had given her name as Tara,

144

was enthusiastically dipping lumps of processed battered chicken into a tub of red gloop that had never seen a tomato in its life. Larkin had before him a cup of coffee, quarterpounder and fries. He wasn't particularly hungry, but he reckoned if he joined her in eating she might relax more. He was going to have to tread carefully as it was.

Tara had thrown a bright yellow puffa jacket over the top of her working gear, and it went some way to making her look like a generic teenager, admittedly one who was inexpertly vamping around in her big sister's clothes. Her eyes, though, they gave her away. They spoke of a world-weariness that she shouldn't have had at thirty-five, never mind fourteen.

'So where you from?' Larkin asked.

'Huddersfield.' The last of the chicken disappeared into her mouth.

'Do your folks know you're down here?'

She sucked the sauce from her fingers, munching all the time. 'Ha'n't got no folks. None to speak of.'

'So how did you end up here, then?'

'You brought me for me dinner.' She laughed like it was the funniest joke she'd heard in ages. Perhaps it was. 'D'you want them chips?' she said.

Larkin slid the cardboard container across the table and she started to dunk them where the chicken had left off.

'So how did you get here?' Larkin asked again.

Tara answered, addressing the cardboard. 'Ran away from the children's home. Had to. Care worker kept shaggin' me. I were just a kid then.' Her words, depressingly predictable, were delivered in a detached monotone, as if she was talking about a distant relative, one she'd lost contact with years ago, one she'd never really got to know. 'Anyway,' she said, looking up. 'I thought you wanted to know about that other lass, not me.'

'OK, then,' said Larkin. 'Karen. Did you know her?'

'Might've. Dunno. What's she like, again?'

'Scottish. Dark-haired. Thin. About nineteen.'

'Were she 'angin' around wi' that other lass? That Hayley?'

Larkin thought. Rayman had mentioned another girl being with Karen. 'Could be.'

Tara screwed her face up, deep in thought. 'Yeah, that were her. Bit miserable, stroppy, like.'

Takes after her father, thought Larkin.

'So where did she go?' he asked.

Tara shrugged. 'She left. Girls come and go there. Les is always bringin' new ones in. Some don't last that long.'

'Who's Les?'

Tara gave him a look as if he'd failed to

146

pick Boyzone out of a lineup. 'Les? Les looks after us. Les is great. None of the girls would have a roof over their 'eads or money to spend if it weren't for Les.'

A genuine philanthropic soul, thought Larkin. He'd come across Les before, or one of his clones. All the kids who've had cruel childhoods, either in care, foster or biological homes, want to escape to somewhere else. Most of them pick London. As soon as the bus pulls in, there's Les, or someone like Les, waiting with a smooth tongue and a comfortable car, telling them no one understands them or feels their pain except him. He's sorry for them so he'll take them under his wing, sort them out, give them a chance. He'll take them home, or to one of his rented properties, install them there, soften them up at first, give them the easy life. Make them feel safe. Then comes the bottom line. It costs to stay here, and they have to start paying their way. He'll claim they owe him for drugs, alcohol or just living expenses. Next thing they know, they're turning tricks, and the proceeds are being handed over to him, kept in line by a few well-placed blows; ones that hurt but don't show, don't stop the girl from working. Trapped, with no escape. The only way out is to escape if they can, or wait until he's finished with them, by which time they may be no use to anyone, least of all themselves.

He looked at Tara, sitting there happily working her way through his fries. She's just at the first stage, he thought. She's coping, but the poor kid's about to discover the price of things.

'So how many girls are at the house now?' asked Larkin, keeping his face as neutral as possible.

'Three,' Tara answered through a mouthful of fries and ketchup. 'But the other two aren't there at the moment. They're out with Les somewhere.'

'Are you happy there? Doing what you're doing?'

Tara stopped chewing, fixed him with a suspicious look. 'What d'you mean? Are you sure you're not one of them fuckin' social workers? Or one o' them religious nutters, tryin' to get me to pray for me sins?'

'No, I'm just asking.'

'Yeah,' she said defiantly. But she spoke with a kind of hardened detachment, almost in the third person again. 'Yeah I am. Anyway, I thought you wanted to talk about Karen?'

'OK, tell me about Karen.'

She shrugged again. 'Not much to tell. When I moved in, she was already there. Stropped around for a bit, did a few punters, that was it. Didn't mix much, didn't talk to anyone apart from Hayley. They were always together. Only time Karen ever smiled.

Whisperin', like they were plannin' some-thin'.'

'What was this Hayley like?'

'She were alright. Nice girl. Blonde hair. She were from Wales, I think.'

'And when did they leave?'

'Just after I moved in. So I didn't know them much.' She looked around suddenly, as if the other diners were listening. 'But I don't think her an' Les got on. I think she ran away when Les's back were turned. Les were fuckin' furious.'

'Any idea where she went?'

Tara thought for a moment. 'No ... I mean, Les tried to find her an' all. Said her an' Hayley'd done a runner wi' some money owed to Les.' She shuddered involuntarily. 'Les were really out o' sorts that night.'

I can imagine, thought Larkin. I can also imagine who he took it out on.

'So you've no idea where I could find her? Anything at all?' He was coming to the conclusion this was yet another dead end, and steeling himself for that fact.

Tara was frowning again. Face contorted, brow furrowed. She could frown for England, thought Larkin. 'No.'

He sighed. That was that.

'D'you want that burger?' Tara pointed to Larkin's untouched quarter-pounder.

He didn't.

'What d'you order it for, then? You're

mad, you are.'

'I think I must be.'

Tara munched, Larkin watched her. He was assessing his short-term future when Tara said, 'Mind you, I don't know if this is any help at all like, but Hayley used to have this mate.'

Larkin's heart skipped a beat. 'What? Where?'

Tara looked up as if the thought had just occurred to her. 'D'you know, I never thought of it until now.'

'Where?' Larkin tried to hide his impatience.

'Well, she were a Paki, like, but all right, you know? An' she used to come an' visit 'er. Les didn't like that, so there were a stop put to it. Wouldn't let her come round.'

'Why didn't Les like this girl?'

'She were always tryin' to get Hayley to live with 'er. I think she were on the game an' all. For 'erself, like. No pimp.'

'And where did she live?'

Tara beamed. 'I know that one. She said. She were always bangin' on about what a beautiful flat she 'ad. Fuckin' borin' if you ask me. Flats an' that. As long as I've got enough money to enjoy meself, I'm 'appy.'

'Where?' Larkin restrained himself from reaching across the table and throttling her.

Tara smiled. 'You're impatient you, aren't you? Walthamstow. Cleveland Avenue. I should know, she said it enough times. Dunno what number, though.'

Larkin was almost beside himself. 'Thank you, Tara, you've been a great help.'

'Don't get too excited. I think Les's already checked it out. Couldn't find either of them.'

'Nevertheless, thank you.'

Tara looked at her watch. 'Fuckin' 'ell, I'd better get back. I've got another punter comin' soon.' Her features suddenly darkened. Fear crept into her eyes. 'An' Les'll be in, wantin' to know where I've been.'

'Don't worry about Les,' said Larkin. 'I'll square things with Les.'

Tara looked at him, dread and apprehension bubbling under the surface.

'How d'you mean?'

'I'll tell Les I've just been having a chat with you and that I paid for your time.'

Larkin smiled, but Tara continued to look at him, her expression saying she was far from convinced that Les would be happy.

In the car on the way back to the house, the mobile rang. It was Andy, informing Larkin that there was company waiting back at Tara's house. 'Big number, leather jacket,' was as much of a description as Andy, from his vantage point, had been able to see. It was enough, though. It was the kind of reception Larkin had anticipated.

He parked the car and walked to the front gate with the girl, expecting trouble. He knew a pimp like Les wouldn't keep one of his girls unattended for long. He was mentally prepared and even looking forward to this; a couple of self-righteous punches into a sleazebag pimp would do him the world of good. Unleash a bit of pent-up frustration and strike a blow for the good guys. He had it all planned; walk in, wait for Les to start, then strike so quickly Les wouldn't know what had hit him. It was perfect except for one thing, something he hadn't anticipated. And the unanticipated was exactly what happened.

Behind Closed Doors

'Where the fuckin' 'ell 'ave you been?' squawked an unpleasant, guttural voice as soon as Tara had opened the door.

Larkin and Tara moved down the hall towards the back room and the source of the voice. Larkin's fists were clenched, his senses heightened. His body had slipped into fight or flight, geared up. He looked at Tara. Fear seemed to have gripped her whole body. She moved reluctantly, awkwardly, as if the lino had turned into treacle and she was sinking.

Big man Les, thought Larkin. Getting off on terrorising teenage girls. It pushed his anger a notch or two higher.

'I ... I've been busy, Les...' Tara spoke hesitantly.

'You 'ad a fuckin' punter! What d'you expect me to do? Service the cunt myself?'

Tara began to tremble even more. She opened her mouth to speak but no sound would emerge.

They rounded the hall and entered the back room. Larkin stopped in his tracks. Stunned. This wasn't what he had been expecting.

Sitting in the disembowelled armchair was a woman. Big, wearing jeans, leather bike jacket, DM boots and a white T-shirt, but still a woman. Hair cropped skinhead close, and from the way she held herself Larkin doubted there was much fat beneath her clothes. Her expression described mean, hard stone, fringed by psychotic anger. She looked as threatening and potentially dangerous as a Sumo wrestler.

Les pointed to Larkin. 'Who the fuck's this?' she asked in her guttural, forty-Players-a-day rumble.

Tara, shaking, sounding in fear of her life, found her voice. 'He's called Stephen Larkin. He's...' Her voice trailed off.

'I'm looking for Karen Shapp,' Larkin said. He'd recovered from the initial shock

153

of Les being a woman.

'What d'you want 'er for?'

Woman or no woman, she was a pimp. 'None of your fucking business.'

Les stood up, with surprising speed for her size. 'You stand here on my property, with 'er, also my property, and you tell me it's none of my business? You're a bloody cheeky cunt an' I'll fuckin' 'ave you for that.'

His anger was up. 'Give it your best shot.'

Les moved across the floor to where Larkin stood. He braced himself, squared off and ready to fight, but the shot came so quickly he didn't see it. Les had swung her right arm as she was walking, making it one fluid motion, the momentum carrying her first to connect with Larkin's left cheek. Taken by surprise, his head snapped backwards and his body followed, hitting the floor with a thud.

'Whassammatter?' Les said, standing over him, leering. 'You never fought a woman before? Well let me tell you, cunt, we're more fierce than men, 'cos we get straight down to it. None of that macho posturin' bullshit your sort feel they 'ave to go through. So you gonna get out now? Or d'you want some more?'

The inside of Larkin's head was like a cosmic meteor shower and Guy Fawkes night all rolled into one. It was some punch. Luckily it had landed just above his jaw, so that wouldn't be broken. It might have rattled a few teeth loose though. His lungs were starting to reinflate, the fall having knocked all the air out of them. Slowly, he struggled to a sitting position. Les was still in front of him, waiting for him to stand so she could knock him down again. Tara had retreated to behind the bed.

'Look,' he gasped, playing for time as he climbed laboriously to his feet, 'I just wanted to talk.' He stood now, grasping the bedside table for support. He needed a weapon, anything to fight back with. 'I'm no threat to you, I'm just looking for her. I understand she's not here any more.'

'That's right,' said Les, tension easing out of her body as she sensed she had the upper hand and that Larkin would be no more trouble. 'Little tart tried to fuck me over. I showed 'er, right enough. I–'

The description of what she had done was abruptly cut off, because Larkin had regained enough composure to launch a counter attack. He grabbed the vibrator off the bedside table, trying to ignore the way his fingers and palm stuck to it, and swung it with as much force as he could muster. It landed with a twanging noise on the bridge of Les's nose, hitting so hard the batteries dislodged themselves and went flying across the room. Les cried out in pain and rage, her hands flying to her injured face, but she still stood. Larkin pressed home his advantage, flinging the vibrator on the floor and jabbing a straight left to her already injured nose, putting all his strength behind it. He felt knuckle connect with cartilage and bone; something cracked but he couldn't tell who or what. Following up before she could respond, he shoved both fists into her chest, catching her square in the centre of her ribcage. Her centre of gravity unbalanced, she went down with an even bigger thud than he had.

'I've never hit a woman before,' said Larkin, standing over her, flexing his damaged knuckles. He gave her a swift kick in the ribs. From the noise that escaped her lips, it sounded like it hurt. 'But I'll make an exception in your case. You're a piece of shit, picking up young girls, terrorising them, forcing them to work for you, you–'

Les swung her leg up sharply, DMs connecting with Larkin's balls. He doubled over, the pain almost inducing nausea. She shambled up, blood from her split nose turning her skin and teeth into a malevolent red mask.

'Found your weak spot, didn't I?' She was breathing heavily. 'What you do your thinkin' with.'

Larkin made a fumbled grab for her, pain clouding his vision, but she was too quick for him. She headbutted him, sending him sprawling once more.

Les moved in to finish him off. She raised her fist above his head, preparing to bring it down with as much force as she could summon. Larkin couldn't move. He was too dazed to pull himself out of the way. All he could do was groan and wait for lights out.

'No, Les, don't!'

Les turned to see where the sound had come from. Tara, all but forgotten in the fight, had moved to the side of the bed. Her eyes were streaked with tears and she was terrified, shivering so much she looked in danger of shaking herself apart.

'Don't hurt him, Les, please. Just let him go.'

'Stay out of this, tart!' Les shouted.

'Please, Les. 'E just wanted to know where Karen was. 'Er dad sent 'im. I told 'im I didn't know, I couldn't 'elp 'im. 'E's goin' away. Honest.'

Les dropped her fist and stared at Tara, her face impassive.

'Look,' Tara said, dipping into her jacket pocket, ''E paid me. I made 'im. Look.' She fanned out the bills that Larkin had given her, waved them in Les's face.

The sight of money seemed to placate her. Tension seeped from Les. She wiped some of the blood off her face, leaving a glistening red streak up the arm of her jacket, and pocketed the notes. She turned and looked at Larkin.

'Get up.'

Larkin was already doing so.

'Get out. And if I see you here again botherin' my girls, fuckin' with my business, I'll fuckin' kill you. An' that's a promise.'

Larkin slowly struggled to his feet. His head was spinning, his balls and face were aching as he looked at Tara and said through laboured breaths, 'come on. You're coming with me.'

Tara's eyes widened.

'She's mine, you cunt,' Les spat. 'Didn't you understand?'

'I'm talking to her, not you,' Larkin retorted painfully. 'Let her speak for herself.'

Les almost laughed. 'You've got balls, I'll give you that.' She turned to Tara. 'He thinks he can just waltz in 'ere an' make off with you. Tell him. Tell him who rescued you, sorted you out.'

'You did, Les,' said Tara in a tiny voice, head pointed at the floor.

'An' who loves you?'

'You do, Les.' She spoke it like a reluctant mantra.

'An' who looks after you an' takes care of you?'

'You do, Les.' It sounded like something Les had forced the girl to repeat until she had convinced herself it was true.

Les turned back to Larkin, eyes shining.

'There's your answer. Wanna make something of it?'

Larkin just stared at her. He looked at the girl. 'Tara?'

'No, I'm stayin' 'ere,' she said quietly, after a long pause.

'So fuck off out of it,' said Les to Larkin. 'C'mere,' she said to Tara. Tara did as she was told. Les sat on the bed, Tara came and sat on her lap. Les looked at Larkin and began to speak, stroking Tara's hair all the time.

'Tara did well to get paid from you. But she was a naughty girl to talk to you in the first place.' Les's expression changed. The stone anger was subsiding, being replaced by what seemed like a maternal look, but one that also included a kind of twisted arousal. 'Now, I love all my girls,' Les continued, 'I'm like a mother to them. Praise them when they've been good, punish them when they've been wrong.' She looked up from Tara, straight at Larkin. 'Now get out.'

'One last time, Tara,' said Larkin. 'Come with me. You'll be free from all this.'

Tara looked between the two of them, her face see-sawing with conflicting emotions. With a great sigh she let her head drop, condemned, accepting the inevitable. 'I'm staying here. This is where I belong.'

Les stared at Larkin, triumph in her eyes. 'Now get out. It's time for Tara to take her punishment. Shut the door after you.'

Larkin stared at Tara, imploringly.

'Just go,' she said. 'Please.'

Larkin, having no choice, turned and left the room.

As he walked up the hall and through the front door into the street, he heard the first sound of flesh striking flesh. His hands shook, his stomach heaved in bitter, impotent rage. He stumbled out of the house, clashing the door behind him.

He made his way up the quiet street to meet with Andy. As he walked he looked at all the other houses. Prim for the most part, well-tended, lived in. Front doors firmly shut. He knew what inhuman, unjust acts were going on in one of them, and wondered how many other atrocities went on as an unreported way of life, shrouded by suburban banality, hidden behind the respectability of a closed front door.

Part Two

Lockdown

Time clicked on, slowly, inexorably. Hours, minutes, days, the same rhythm... There, then gone. There, then gone. There, then gone.

She lay on the bed, eyes wide open. She knew she should be doing more than staring at the ceiling, the four walls, numb with boredom. There were diversions, they'd given her things: a TV, a computer, books. But they'd also taken things away: sunlight, freedom, space.

Time was ticking away, wasting away. She could feel it disappearing. Each beat of her heart was a second less of life. There, then gone. There, then gone. Since she had fewer seconds than most, less time shored up in her body, she felt she should be doing something more with what she had left. But as she looked round the room she knew her options were limited.

She picked up the remote, pointed it at the TV. Afternoon drivel spewed out. She surfed: a faded actress hawking her memoirs on a chat show, a quiz show, an Australian soap, an ancient episode of Ironside, *an advert for life insurance. She watched the last one. An ageing television presenter spoke to the camera, said in reassuring tones how anyone could apply without a medical. While he spoke, small graphics appeared underneath him: Insurance does not cover death by cancer or AIDS. She flicked the TV off, focused once again on the ceiling.*

She was allowed out, but only at certain times, for certain things. She understood that. The room wasn't exactly brimming with amenities. She sighed. There, then gone. There, then gone.

A sudden panic began to rise in her throat, thumping her chest, heaving to be let out, escape. She wanted to scream. She held it in. She wanted to roll on the floor, throw herself off the walls, tear her hair out. She restrained herself. She wanted to smash up every piece of furniture in the sparsely furnished room. She didn't.

Slowly, her breathing fell back to normal. The panic subsided, caged once more. There, then gone. She lay perfectly still until she was in complete control of herself again, sure of her movements, then stood up, crossed to the desk, and calmly started up the PC.

She needed a reminder, she told herself.

The machine warmed up. She logged on, inserted the CD-Rom into the hard drive, moved her fingers over the keys, clicked the mouse until an image began to appear on the screen.

She watched.

She thought she would be inured to it by now, hardened. But she wasn't. The images moved, the sound issued from the speakers and tears began to make slow, silent progress down her cheeks.

Yes, she thought, this reminds me. What I'm doing, why I'm here. Reminds me of the pain, the uncertainty, the risks. This reminds me of how important it all is.

She forced herself to watch, eyes wet, riveted to the horror before her.

Time passed She didn't notice.

The Reconstructed Room

'What d'you reckon then?' sighed Andy, his voice bored and fidgety. 'Shall I get a clipboard and we do a door-to-door?'

'And ask what?' replied Larkin, no less edgily. 'We're looking for an Asian prostitute, can you help us?'

'Just a thought,' replied Andy grumpily.

Cleveland Avenue in Walthamstow told the by now familiar tale of London living. A street in what was once a satellite village, now subsumed into urban London. The city was like a vast, living organism, thought Larkin. Spreading out, expanding its boundaries, colonising rather than destroying. Dragging its inhabitants along with it, taking in new ones all the time.

The houses were large, turn of the century, split into flats and bedsits; every last centimetre of space squeezed and wrung out to appease the voracious city's need to house its inhabitants. Occasionally a whole house would appear belonging solely to one, obviously monied, couple or family. It must be hard not to resent them, thought Larkin.

There were no trees in the street – not enough space – but the overgrown hedges compensated for this. Roads that were never designed for cars now had them planted in kerbside rows, leaving only a thin, one-way route in the centre. Larkin and Andy had managed to find a space in a permit-only zone and there they sat, one eye on the street, one on the lookout for wardens.

Andy sighed again. He looked at his watch. 'It's two thirty. Maybe she's out at work.'

'Maybe she's in at work,' Larkin replied.

They both slumped back into silence.

Larkin's earlier anger had peaked, troughed, peaked again and now sat, like his physical injuries, emanating a low throb. On the back burner, waiting for something or someone to turn the heat up.

They had spotted several Asian women moving down the street, but none seemed like the one they were looking for. Most of them modestly, but colourfully, dressed in saris, had their friends and kids with them. If one of them was a teenage hooker she was heavily disguised.

'Clock that one,' said Andy suddenly.

Larkin looked where Andy indicated. Coming down the street was a girl, late teens, early twenties, wearing a short fur coat tailored at the waist, spray-on black leggings and spike heels. Her hair was long, straight, silky and black, in a style that looked both simple and expensive. Her skin was coffee-coloured and her lips crimson, deep and full. As she walked, she exuded sexual confidence, even to the point of over doing it: her exaggerated walk stopped just this side of Monroe-esque. But it did the trick, because men were looking at her, and not just Larkin and Andy. She was swinging a couple of expensive, designer-label carrier bags.

'Reckon that's her?' asked Andy.

'I'd be more surprised if it wasn't,' Larkin replied.

They gave her time to reach her door, then left the car and crossed the road.

The key had turned and she was about to cross the threshold as Larkin appeared behind her and spoke.

'Excuse me,' he said.

She turned. She wasn't Indian, Larkin thought, but she was definitely Asian. Strategic and, in places, heavy make-up had allowed her to make the best of what were, at close range, rather plain features. Her eyes darted between Larkin and Andy, sizing them up.

'Sorry love,' she said in heavily accented English, 'I don't do threesomes.'

'We're not punters,' said Larkin quickly, although from the way Andy's eyes were touring her body he wasn't so sure. 'We just want to ask you a few questions.'

Her face darkened. She noticed, as if for the first time, Larkin's facial injuries. 'Are you cops? You don't look familiar.'

'We're not cops,' said Larkin. 'We just want to talk to you. We're looking for someone and we think you can help. A girl called Karen. And her friend Hayley.'

At the mention of the names, the girl's eyes dilated with fear. She grabbed the front door, pushed, and attempted to hurl herself inside. Larkin quickly stuck his foot in the way to stop it closing, his arm wedged against the frame, forcing it back.

'Leave me alone!' the girl shouted. 'Any nearer and I'll scream rape!'

'Please!' replied Larkin exasperatedly. 'We just want to talk!'

'I mean it! I'll scream rape!' she shouted, struggling with the door that Larkin and Andy were forcing open.

Larkin managed to position half his body over the threshold. Suddenly he felt a sullen thumping through the thin wall at his back.

'Shut your fuckin' noise up out there!' the voice shouted.

'Piss off!' shouted the girl in return. 'Mind

your own fucking business!'

The next noise to come through the wall was the abrupt, shrieking wail of a baby.

'Now you've woken the baby, you bitch!' shouted the voice. 'I'll have the council on to you, you whore!'

'Please can we come in and talk?' asked Larkin in as reasonable a voice as possible. 'I promise we mean you no harm.'

The girl looked between the wall with the howling baby and the two of them. Reluctantly she loosened her grip on the door, allowing it to fall back to the wall.

Larkin and Andy exchanged glances, stepped in to what was a very dingy, dusty hall. At one side was an old pushchair, next to it a rusty bike. There were two doors: one that led to the ground-floor flat with the wailing baby, the other to the upstairs flat. The girl turned her key and the heavy wooden door opened. She made her way upstairs, Andy next, appreciatively following the swing of her backside, then Larkin. The door swung firmly shut behind them.

She led them up a bland stairway – oatmeal carpet, beige-coloured walls – and down a similarly decorated hallway. Dotted on the walls were occasional, oddly impersonal, prints and hangings. It gave the impression of complete neutrality, neither raising nor dashing expectations.

'That's my working room,' she said,

pulling closed a door, but not before Larkin had glimpsed the décor. It was overly frilly, overly girly. Like her walk it was a caricature. 'We won't be going in there,' she said.

She led them to the front room. This was different. It was large and tastefully furnished: stripped wooden floors, kelims, dhurries, ethnic and exotic hangings, ornaments and furniture, a huge comfortable-looking sofa with mismatching armchairs. A TV and sound system in one corner, muslin-draped bay windows overlooking the main street. Larkin knew he was going on only a preliminary impression, but the room seemed like a retreat, a deliberately designed relaxation zone. It was evident, even on first glance, that a lot of care and love had been invested in the room's creation.

'Sit down,' the girl said, still wary.

Larkin and Andy sat on the sofa. The girl popped her bags on a chair, discarded her fur to reveal a clinging silk blouse, buttoned low to give a generous glimpse of firm, pushed-up breasts. Larkin wasn't exactly immune to the effect she was creating but Andy, he noticed, was so engrossed, his eyes should have been on CGI sticks.

The girl removed a bottle of red wine and a single glass from a heavily carved wooden cabinet. She poured herself a drink without offering the other two any and placed herself in an armchair. In doing this, she seemed to relax, dropping the self-consciously feminine gestures. In fact she now seemed clumsy, almost neutered. She picked up the phone and balanced it on her lap.

'One wrong word, one thing I don't like and I'm making a call.' Her voice, although heavily accented, was direct enough to be perfectly understood.

'No problem,' said Larkin, as breezily as possible.

'Nice place you got here,' said Andy, pulling his eyes away from her breasts and looking around the room.

It was the right thing to say. Despite her fear, the girl was pleased. 'Thank you,' she said, pride creeping into her voice, 'I did it all myself, it is my own creation.' Then suddenly, her voice snapped back to its previous clipped, brusque tone. 'So tell me what you want with me.'

'We're looking for a girl called Karen,' Larkin began in what was becoming a very practised speech. He gave her a truncated version: the reason why, the scene with Rayman. He left out Jackie Fairley and ended with a selective account of his run-in with Les. Finished, he sat back, waiting for the girl to speak.

'So,' the girl said, swivelling her gaze to favour Andy. 'Do you enjoy staring at my tits?'

Andy coughed, reddened. Larkin couldn't stop a smirk from creeping over his features.

'Good,' she said, taking a sip of wine, her feminine gestures restored. 'That's what they are there for.' Then back to Larkin. 'You had a fight with Les, yes? You try to take a girl for free?'

'I tried to stop a girl being beaten up,' Larkin said, his anger bubbling up again.

'Oh, hero man!' said the girl. 'Which one?'

'Tara.'

The girl nodded. 'She will not leave. She is too fond of the...' she made a smoking gesture with her fingers.

'Weed?' asked Andy.

'Crack,' the girl said, barking the word with sharp onomatopoeia. She took another sip.

'Do you have a name?' asked Larkin. 'Something I can call you?'

She smiled. It wasn't particularly warm. 'You can call me ... Diana.'

'OK Diana,' Larkin began, 'I've said we're not here to hurt you. All we want to know is where Karen and Hayley are. That's all. Tell us and we're gone.'

'What makes you think I know?' She crossed her legs, bouncing one off the other. Andy's eyes followed, tennis-fashion.

'If you do know please tell us. We won't hurt her.'

Diana smiled, thinking for a moment.

172

Eventually she placed her glass on the floor, the phone back on its table. She stood up slowly. It was like watching a snake uncoil. She pointed a hand towards Andy.

'Come.'

Andy looked pleasantly startled, as if Christmas had arrived unexpectedly early. He looked towards Larkin, who shrugged.

'Come.' Diana was smiling, this time with an approximation of warmth.

Andy stood, took her hand, and exited the room. Larkin watched them go down the hall, enter Diana's entertaining room. Her walk had returned with a vengeance, he noticed.

Larkin sat there trying not to listen, but not being able to help himself. Muffled voices were replaced by muffled fumblings. Five minutes became ten and ten was about to become fifteen when suddenly Andy's raised voice was heard.

The door opened and Andy burst out backwards, buttoning his trousers, pulling his trainers back on.

'Fuckin' 'ell,' he said, ashen-faced, as he sat back next to Larkin, continuing to button himself up. 'Fuckin' 'ell...'

Soon Diana emerged, adjusting her breasts, smiling as if she was a higher form of life. She walked across the room, swinging her hips in languorous sensuality, and resumed her earlier seat.

'Well,' she said, as if she had been triumphant in battle, 'I believe you are telling the truth.'

'And how have you worked that one out?' asked Larkin.

Diana smiled smugly. 'I know how to find out if a man is lying to me. And he,' – she pointed to Andy – 'is not lying.'

'Good,' said Larkin. Andy's head had dropped. He couldn't look at either of them. 'But what have you done with him?'

'Ask him yourself.'

'Andy?'

At first he didn't move, then his head suddenly jerked up. 'She's a fuckin' fella!' he shouted, rage and shame vying for space on his face. 'A fuckin' fella!'

'No!' Diana barked, pride and anger in her voice, 'I am a woman!'

'No you ain't, darlin',' said Andy, 'I've seen for meself.'

'Perhaps not here,' she said, pointing to her groin. 'Not yet, but I am here,' – she moved her hand over her heart – 'and I am here.' Her other hand pointed to her head.

'OK, you've made your point,' said Larkin. 'Now can we get back to what we came here for?'

Diana's face became a closed book. 'I have nothing to tell you. I do not know where they are.'

'But you have seen them? You did help

them after they ran away from Les?'

She might as well have been carved from stone. 'I cannot help you.' She stood up. 'Please leave.'

Andy was quickly on his feet, making for the door. Larkin wasn't so fast.

'Please—' he began to implore.

'No. I cannot help you. It is unfortunate for your friend. But I cannot help you.'

'Can't or won't?' asked Larkin.

'Goodbye.'

Larkin reluctantly made his way down the stairs after Andy, Diana escorting them off the premises. At the door Larkin turned to her.

'Look,' he said, scribbling Faye's number on the back of his business card and passing it to her. 'If you think you can help call that number. Please. We just want to see she's all right.'

Diana's stone-like mask almost softened for a second.

'Goodbye,' was all she said, and closed the door.

Andy set off for the car.

'Wait,' said Larkin.

Andy stepped back on to the pavement. 'What?'

'Let's walk this way.'

They set off down the street towards the shops.

'Why are we doing this?' asked Andy.

'Because she lied to us,' Larkin replied. 'She knows something, and since she's the nearest thing to a lead we've got, we're going to have to watch her. So I don't want her to know what kind of car we've got.'

Andy nodded, head down studying the paving stones.

'So,' said Larkin, once he realised nothing more would be forthcoming from Andy. 'What happened back there?'

'I don't wanna talk about it,' he mumbled. 'I've never been so humiliated in all my life.'

Larkin smiled. 'I don't believe that for one minute.'

'Oh, fuck off,' grumbled Andy.

They stopped short of the main street, crossed the road on the right and walked slowly round the block to where they'd parked the Saab. They climbed in and had the car ready to go when a minicab pulled up directly outside Diana's flat, blocking the street.

'Look,' said Larkin.

As they watched, Diana emerged, fur coat back in place. She scoped both sides of the street, checking for Larkin, Andy or anyone else. Instinctively the two of them ducked beneath the dashboard.

Satisfied that no one had seen her, she climbed into the minicab and off it went.

'Follow the money?' Larkin asked Andy.

'Follow the money,' Andy replied.

Leaving a couple of beats to allay suspicion, Larkin put the car into first and, as inconspicuously as possible, began to follow.

Homeless

'Shagged,' sighed Larkin, flopping down on the sofa. 'Put the kettle on, Andy.'

Andy turned towards the kitchen then stopped, hesitant. 'Yeah, I... D'you fancy somethin' a bit stronger?'

Larkin nodded. 'Sure.'

'I'll open some wine. Red,' Andy stood there, unmoving, a perplexed look crossing his features.

'You OK?' asked Larkin.

'Yeah...' He was struggling towards something. 'I shoulda known. I shoulda known... She didn't ... smell right.'

Larkin barely suppressed a grin. 'Surprised you'd let a little thing like that bother you,' he said. 'Or maybe it wasn't such a little thing, I don't know. Anyway, she was a lot better looking that most of the women you manage to beg to sleep with you.'

Andy opened his mouth to reply but

couldn't find the words. He reddened, turned and left the room, re-emerging with a bottle of wine and two glasses. He wordlessly set them down on the floor, poured, handed one to Larkin. As he stood up he announced, 'I'm gonna take a shower,' and left the room.

Larkin, alone now, sipped his wine. Thoughts roaming, he tried winding down.

Although he had put on lights and heating, the house still felt empty, lacking in warmth. Missing that vital spark. He knew what that spark was. Faye. The house needed her. Larkin was looking forward to seeing her again.

He took another mouthful, thought back over his day. It seemed to him that there was a subconscious link, a thread, uniting all the people he'd met and the situations he'd encountered. Of wanting to belong, looking for acceptance, finding home. Tara putting up with abuse, coping with dependency; Diana with her reconstructed room, her reconstructed identity.

And then there was Karen. Although he didn't yet have any concrete results, Larkin believed he was moving closer to finding her. He couldn't say how, it was just a feeling.

A sudden thought struck him, sending a frisson down his spine. What if she'd gone back to Edinburgh? Gone back home. His mind speedily worked over the possibilities and calculated the odds. Slim. Very slim. Everything indicated she was running away, not going back. There would be no sense in her going back. He doubted she could ever go home again. That was a feeling he was familiar with.

He thought of his own childhood home, a small town just outside Newcastle called Grimley. Apart from a work-related visit which had resulted in Andy and him slugging it out in the British Legion, he hadn't been back there in years, hadn't wanted to.

Home. He wondered if there would ever be anywhere he could call home. Perhaps this would be the house. Although he hadn't known her long, he knew he liked Faye. A lot. Probably more than he could admit to himself. The murderous end to his marriage had left him unable and, for the most part, unwilling to face commitment again. Could things be different with Faye? He didn't know. And he didn't want to think about it; it was a path of speculation he couldn't afford even to look down yet.

The wine was finished and Larkin went into the kitchen in search of another. He had settled himself back on the sofa and was idly flicking through channels, not stopping long enough on each one to get involved, when Andy re-emerged, dressed and wearing enough aftershave to keep Boss going for a whole year.

'Going out? Off to reaffirm your fragile heterosexuality, then? Have casual sex with some woman too drunk to remember her own name?' asked Larkin with a smile.

'Piss off,' replied Andy, blushing, and left.

Larkin wasn't alone for long. The key turned in the lock and he heard Faye and Moir's voices. They made their way to the front room.

'Hi, Stephen,' said Faye pleasantly. She was wearing a long, woollen overcoat and fake fur hat, and was busy unwrapping a long scarf from around her neck. Larkin caught flashes of cleavage from underneath as she did so. The effect was both simultaneously erotic and homely.

'You on your own?' she asked, with what Larkin might have only imagined was a trace of guilty embarrassment.

'Yep. Just me.' He pointed to the wine bottle. 'I've just opened this if you want to join me.'

'I'll go and get a glass,' she said, seemingly happy to have found a decent exit line.

Moir entered next, mumbling greetings and dropping himself into a chair opposite Larkin. He sat there with a look of apprehensive expectation on his face.

'So how was your day?' asked Larkin.

'Fine,' replied Moir impatiently. 'Faye took me to an art gallery and we had lunch in Chelsea. How 'bout you?'

'I'm sorry,' said Larkin. 'My hearing must be going. I thought you said art gallery there for a minute. And Chelsea?'

Moir reddened, his gruffness returning. 'It was just somewhere to go, for fuck's sake. Now what happened to you?'

Larkin smiled. 'Thought we'd lost you there, Henry,' he said. 'New clothes, lunch in Chelsea, not the Henry we know and love.'

Moir's eyes flashed fire. 'Just tell me what the fuck happened,' he rumbled ominously.

'That's more like it,' said Larkin, and proceeded to apprise him with a truncated version of his exploits. At some point Faye entered, handed Moir a coffee, poured herself a glass of wine and perched on the arm of Moir's chair. Larkin decided not to notice.

'So then we followed her,' he said.

'Where to?' asked Moir expectantly.

'I'm not sure.' Once the minicab containing Diana had left the street, Larkin and Andy had given chase in the Saab. They had stayed a few cars behind and, despite not being familiar with the roads and having to make a few intuitive leaps as to lane structures, had managed to follow without being detected.

The minicab eventually pulled up outside a huge, old Victorian house in Hackney.

Diana got out, cast a quick glance either way and entered the building. Larkin and Andy, hidden just around the corner, managed to avoid being seen. The minicab pulled away. Diana had been absorbed into the house and it now stood still, silent and imposing in the encroaching dusk.

'What now?' asked Andy.

'I don't know,' replied Larkin. 'That house looks different from the kinds of places we've been to so far. I don't think we can just barge in.'

'I know what you mean,' said Andy. 'How about we do a bit of a stake-out?' he said, smiling. 'We could be like Starsky an' 'Utch.'

'Yeah,' said Larkin. 'All we need is the junk food and the white stripe down the side.'

'An' I wanna be Starsky,' said Andy.

'Piss off. You've got blonde hair. You can be Hutch.'

'No way! He was the borin' one! Let's have a quiet night in? Not with you, mate. I wanna be Starsky!'

And that was how they sat for the next hour or so, watching the house, keeping the boredom at bay by discussing the comparative merits of Seventies American detective series. As the time wore on and nothing happened, they used up the popular ones and had to resort to the increasingly obscure.

'Now, Longstreet,' said Larkin, 'he'd have been crap at surveillance work.'

'How come?'

'Because he was blind,' explained Larkin. 'The car chases were pretty good, though.' He sighed, looked at his watch. 'In all the time we've sat here, no one's gone in or out. Shall we call it a night?'

Andy nodded. Agreeing to resume watch the following morning, they had made a note of the house's location and headed back to Clapham.

Larkin finished speaking and sat back, refilling his glass.

'So,' said Moir, frowning and rubbing his chin, 'you've got no idea what this place is?'

'None at all,' replied Larkin. 'Could be the most important thing I've yet come across, could be a dead end. Hopefully we'll find out more tomorrow.'

Dinner followed. Since no one had had the time or opportunity to prepare anything, it consisted of a Chinese take-away. Larkin was happy to eat anything as the wine had sent his head reeling. Faye was happily quaffing, but Larkin noticed Moir hadn't touched a drop. He'd had coffee while listening to Larkin and Coke – Diet Coke at that – during his meal. Larkin thought it best not to mention it.

After dinner they adjourned to the front

room and watched some vapid, inconsequential television. It was just what Larkin needed after the day he'd had. He now knew why soap operas and game shows were so popular. Escape and release, passive and vicarious. Moir, he noticed, still wasn't drinking.

Eventually Larkin had to go to the toilet. On returning to the front room he managed to walk in on the end of a comet's tail of conversation between Moir and Faye. On sighting him they immediately stopped and coaxed smiles onto their faces. This is becoming a very annoying habit, thought Larkin.

'Well,' said Moir, standing up. I'm going to bed.' He glanced at Faye. The look would have spoken volumes if Larkin had been able to translate it.

'OK,' said Faye, weighting her look with equal, yet different, meaning. 'I'll see you in the morning.'

Moir didn't move. His eyes remained locked with Faye. Larkin thought he'd wandered into the final of the World Staring Championships.

Eventually their gazes unlocked and Moir made his way past Larkin to the door. 'Thanks,' he said, turning as if in afterthought. 'Thanks again. For today.'

'Don't mention it,' replied Larkin.

'Tomorrow...' Moir mumbled. He looked

at the floor as if expecting to find the correct words there. 'Tomorrow if you need … me … I'll be there.'

'We'll see,' said Larkin. 'Good night, Henry.'

Moir left the room. Larkin resumed his seat on the sofa and refilled his wineglass.

'Is there some left in that bottle?' asked Faye.

Larkin said there was.

Faye crossed over to re-fill her glass. A glass which, Larkin noticed, was already over half full. Instead of returning to her seat, she sat down next to him. Subtle, thought Larkin. I don't think.

'So,' said Larkin, because he felt he had to say something, 'you had a good day, then?'

Faye nodded. 'Yes. I know Henry's got his problems, but when you get to know him, he's good company.'

He's probably different with you than he is with me, thought Larkin. 'I noticed he wasn't drinking tonight,' he said.

'No,' replied Faye. 'I think that's one of his problems. He's trying to address it.'

'Good for him.'

They lapsed into silence, the only sounds their lips on their wineglasses.

Larkin knew he had to ask the next question. Even if he didn't want to hear the answer. 'So,' he said, 'what was all that about before?'

'Oh,' Faye replied, reddening. She lost eye contact with Larkin in making her reply. 'I think you could say Henry and I were ... defining the parameters of our relationship.'

'So you're having a relationship?' Larkin asked, too quickly to stop himself.

Faye looked at him, this time catching his eye.

'I'm sorry, it's none of my business,' he said, backpedalling.

'No,' said Faye, 'I'll tell you. But it's not what you think. I like Henry. A lot. But he's not...'

'Damaged enough?' Larkin finished for her.

Faye reddened again. 'I know how it must look,' she said, 'and I can understand the way you're feeling. I was going to say, Henry's not my type. But at the moment he needs someone. I'm there for him.'

'He's very fond of you,' said Larkin.

'I know,' she replied. 'But ... I can't explain it to you. It's different.'

Larkin nodded. He said nothing.

'Anyway, Stephen, it's getting late.'

Larkin made to stand. Faye stopped him by placing her hand on his thigh.

'What I meant was...' She addressed her hand. 'The other night. It doesn't have to be a one-off. Not if you don't want it to be.'

He felt his cock stiffen involuntarily. There was something about this woman, some chemical thing perhaps, that made him immediately horny. Yes, he wanted her. He wanted her badly, like a craving that couldn't be satisfied, and he wanted her now. He looked at her, her exquisite body, her beautiful face, and their eyes locked.

'What about Henry?' he asked.

He saw her eyes. And that's when he realised. His own lust had stopped him hearing it in her voice, but nothing could obscure it in her eyes. She looked like her arm was being twisted behind her back, as if someone or more to the point, some compulsion, was forcing her to ask him to bed. Her expression was divided between lust and a painful need. Larkin couldn't work out which percentage was which, but he could guess.

'Henry's in the future,' she whispered, eyes dropping. 'You're here. You're now. I want you tonight.'

'Ah, that's it,' said Larkin. 'Me for tonight. But it's something bigger with Henry, isn't it? Something you don't want to rush into and maybe spoil. But you've got needs and I'm here to take care of them. Is that it?' He kept his voice as steady as he could, gasped out between longings for Faye.

She said nothing, just kept her head down, moved her body closer, grabbed him harder.

'No Faye,' he said, in a voice that took every ounce of self-control. 'No.' There was so much more he wanted to say, so much more he could have said, but it would have done no good.

Faye nodded and immediately withdrew her hands. She stood up, tipped her head back and drained her wineglass. Larkin was treated to a close-up of her body, curved, beautiful, bounteous. His erection was straining, his fingers were tingling at the thought of touching her. It would be so easy to give in, relent and grab her, devour her beautiful body, say fuck the consequences, fuck the morning-after mutual shame session... So easy... All he had to do was reach out his fingers...

She put down her glass and silently left the room without looking at him. He heard her mount the stairs, make her way to her room. Once he heard her door close he breathed a sigh – of relief or loss and despair, he didn't know – and sat back.

He picked up his glass and took a long, deep comforting mouthful of wine.

No, he thought, with a bitter tang of regret, no matter how comforting, how pleasant it is to stay here, this place will never be my home.

Candleland

The playground was deserted, made bleaker by the cold grey February sky, the trailing fog that seemed in no hurry to disperse. The swings, slides, climbing frames and round-abouts looked thin, old and skeletal. It felt abandoned, a framework for a park that would never be finished, never be substanti-ated. Now decrepit, rusted with broken promises.

Larkin and Andy sat on an old brick wall scarred with graffiti, pulling their jackets around them to keep out the damp, chill air. The park they were in probably had a name in some file in some town planner's vault but, to them, it was just a barren piece of land, a compulsory purchase order in waiting. Still, it afforded a good view of the house opposite, and that was why they were there.

They had left the house in Clapham early, Andy protesting that he'd just got in, Larkin saying that was fine, whatever Andy had scored and taken would keep him buzzing for a few hours yet. Larkin had wanted to get an early start because he knew the traffic would be bad crossing London and, since they didn't actually know what went on in the house Diana had disappeared into, thought it best to get there as early as possible.

Moir had been in the kitchen when they'd left. Dressing-gowned, drinking coffee. Hair stuck up on end either from uncomfortable pillows or haunting, disquieting dreams. He half-heartedly invited himself along, making good on his promise of the previous night, but Larkin declined the offer.

'We don't know what that place is yet,' Larkin had said, 'wait till we know more about it.'

Moir's reaction was either one of disappointment or relief, Larkin couldn't tell which. Probably both.

Larkin was also leaving to avoid a confrontation with Faye. Judging from the resolute silence coming from her room, she was doing the same thing. As he crossed the hall to leave, however, he glanced up at her room. The door which had been fractionally open was suddenly pulled shut. OK, he thought, if that's how it's going to be, that's how it's going to be.

They had arrived just before nine, stopping off for take-out coffees from a cafe they'd passed, the East London urban streets oozing with rat-running, car-driving commuters. The street the house was on was full of large

Victorian houses, mostly flat conversions, across the way from a nondescript park.

The house they wanted was the one on the end. Large, redbrick, with a surprisingly well-maintained front garden.

Larkin had parked the car a couple of houses up. They watched. Nothing happened for about twenty minutes, then the front door opened and a figure emerged. Mid-twenties, medium height, slim, pretty and black. Wearing white jeans, boots, overcoat and scarf. A large bag hung from her shoulders.

'Know her?' asked Larkin as she walked past the car.

'No, but I wouldn't mind,' replied Andy.

Larkin smiled. 'Didn't you score last night?'

Andy became sullen, reached for the styrofoam cup of coffee. He took a sip, replaced it on the dashboard. The movement covered his mumbled reply.

'Pardon?' asked Larkin in an amused tone.

'I said I didn't, right?'

'What, not even your old standbys?'

'There was none o' them there!' Andy said, his voice high-pitched with indignation. 'The only one there was this old slapper who's had more rides than Lester Piggott.'

'And why did that stop you?'

Andy looked at Larkin in exasperation, as if he was trying to explain Darwin's theory of natural selection to a bunch of Southern redneck fundamentalist Christians. He shook his head, sipped his coffee.

They sat in silence for a while after that, watching, drinking coffee. Eventually Larkin spoke.

'Well,' he said, crunching up his cup, 'nothing's happened and if that girl comes back and sees we're still here she might get suspicious. Fancy a walk in the park?'

Andy didn't, but went anyway.

Sitting on swings no child would touch, a plaintive, rusty squeak accompanying their idle movements, Larkin and Andy waited and watched.

They watched a man cycle past. For some reason the man looked familiar, but Larkin couldn't think why. He scrutinised the cyclist: middle-aged, wearing jogging bottoms, dun-coloured cardigan and generic trainers, trimmed but thinning grey hair, controlled paunch. Ordinary mountain bike. Larkin couldn't get a good look at his face and the fog didn't help. As they watched, the man pulled up to the house, dismounted, pushed the bike round the side. They waited. He didn't re-emerge.

'Know 'im?' asked Andy.

'I don't know,' Larkin replied. There was something familiar about him, but he couldn't work out what. The man made him feel slightly uneasy, but he didn't know why.

If he were Spider Man, his spider sense would have been tingling.

'I don't know,' Larkin said again. 'Maybe if I'd got a good square-on look...' He sighed. 'Never mind,' he said, and filed the man away in the back of his mind, a niggling itch beneath the cap of his skull.

'I think we've learned all we can from sitting here, don't you?' asked Larkin.

'Yup.'

'Shall we pay them a visit?'

Andy laughed, watching his breath turn to cloudy vapour. 'I thought you'd never ask. I'm doin' meself permanent damage sittin' on 'ere in this weather.'

Larkin jumped down on to the balding grass. 'Then let's go. You never know, they might have the kettle on for us.'

Larkin rang the bell. They waited but not for long: the door was opened by a young man, mid to late twenties, medium height, cropped hair and goatee, wearing a loose, well-pressed checked shirt falling over equally well-pressed stone cargoes. Boots.

'Yes, can I help you?' His voice wasn't unfriendly, just professionally curious. Wary.

'Yeah,' said Larkin. He was at a disadvantage here and he knew it. Going on first impressions, though – the house, the man in front of them – told him his best option was to play it straight. 'I don't know that you can,' he said. 'My name's Stephen Larkin, this is Andy Brennan.'

Larkin gestured to Andy, who nodded. The man's eyes lit up slightly on Andy's nod, but Larkin caught it. The man was gay.

'We're both journalists although we're not here in that capacity. We're doing a job for a guy called Henry Moir. We're trying to find his daughter.'

'Really.' The man's attitude hardened. 'And who might that be?'

'Her name's Karen. We think she's either using her real name or her adoptive one. Shapp.'

Another change took place on the man's features; surprise, fear? Larkin couldn't read it.

'What makes you think she's here?'

'I don't know that she is. We've been looking for her. The trail led here.'

'How?'

'We followed this bird Diana here,' said Andy. 'She a friend of yours, by any chance?'

The man looked from one to the other, sizing them up, coming to conclusions.

'Wait there,' he said, and slammed the door in their faces.

Larkin and Andy looked at each other.

'I think we struck a chord,' said Andy.

'Or hit a nerve,' replied Larkin. 'Anyway, I think you're in there.'

'Do me a favour,' said Andy wearily.

Larkin smiled to himself. 'Twice in two days. I think someone's trying to tell you something.'

Andy turned, face burning. 'Now leave it! It's not fuckin' funny! Any more o' that, an' I'll 'ave you!'

Larkin laughed. 'Careful what you say. That phrase has got a different meaning in Newcastle.'

Andy stepped forward, looking like he was about to do some damage, but at that moment the door was reopened by the same young man. He gave a small blink of surprise when he saw the two of them squaring up to each other.

'Come this way,' he said, stepping aside to admit them.

The hallway was a cross between homeliness and functionality: rugs and ornaments versus cork noticeboards and small filing cabinets.

Larkin looked down the hall, catching a glimpse of a kitchen. Again the pattern was the same; comforting chairs and tables with commercial-sized stainless steel cooking utensils. It was as if the place was trying to be a home but doing so on an institutional level.

He also caught a glimpse of the cyclist in the kitchen – a fleeting look at the back of the man's right shoulder. No help whatsoever, just that vague niggle. He filed it away and followed their crop-headed host.

The man opened a dark wooden door, letting them in to a room that might once have been a small sitting room or study but was now a small office. The walls were lined with filing cabinets and shelving. Larkin checked out the books: child psychology, child development, social studies, legal procedure, current affairs. There were government papers and reports and also, incongruously, what appeared to be a complete set of Dick Francis paperbacks. A well-used Bible took pride of place near the desk. On a lower shelf was a portable CD/radio/cassette player surrounded by tapes and CDs. Larkin clocked the titles: The Best of Otis Redding, Aretha Franklin, Queen Of Soul, Marvin Gaye – What's Goin' On. Time warp taste, but good taste. On the desk was a PC and printer, next to that a small CCTV monitor.

Behind the desk sat a man. Middle-aged, shaven-headed, powerful-looking. He wore grey suit trousers, the jacket of which was slung over the back of his chair along with a plain wooden walking stick, green checked lumberjack shirt and red braces. His face gave nothing away.

'Thanks, Darren,' the man said, his voice like sandpaper over chrome.

Their guide excused himself and, with an

unreciprocated little smile at Andy, left the room.

'Sit down, please, gentlemen.' The voice had unreconstructed East End authority. It was used to being obeyed. They did so.

'Now then,' he said, pointing at Larkin, 'my little birdie tells me that you are Stephen Larkin, and you–' he pointed at Andy, '–are Andy Brennan. My name is Mickey Falco. What can I do for you?'

Larkin launched into his spiel once again, keeping it brief. Mickey Falco listened intently and impassively. Larkin reaching the end, stopped talking. Silence.

'Jackie Fairley,' said Mickey Falco eventually. 'Poor, poor Jackie Fairley. She was a diamond. One in a million.' His sorrow seemed genuine.

'Yeah,' said Larkin. 'So we hear.'

Mickey Falco looked him straight in the eye. They were intelligent eyes, like a fox's. 'Who'd you 'ear that from?'

'The police. I spoke to them. They're still investigating.'

Mickey Falco shook his head. 'Old Bill, bless 'em, will never solve it. I'm sure they'd make the effort for one of their own, but they wouldn't know where to look.'

Larkin was about to press him further on that when he spoke again.

'Now. You reckon I know where these girls Karen an' Hayley are, that right? What gives you that idea?' Mickey Falco asked.

'Nothing,' replied Larkin, 'apart from the fact that we're sitting here talking about it.'

Mickey Falco gave a small smile, exclusively for his own benefit. 'D'you know what "here" is, gentlemen?'

They both shook their heads.

Mickey Falco settled back in his chair. 'Then I'll tell you. This is Candleland. We're a refuge. A safe house. If kids, young adults, are in trouble, for whatever reason, and they ain't got anywhere else to go, they come here. Or get brought here. Problems with parents, pimps, pushers, if they've been abused, victimised, runaways, whatever. We take them in. And we try to help them. Not sayin' we work miracles, mind, just sort them out, turn them round, point them in the right direction and let them toddle off.'

'And has Karen been here?' asked Larkin.

'She's been here. They've both been here,' Mickey Falco replied.

'And are they here now?' asked Andy.

Mickey Falco studied the two men intently, as if he was trying to X-ray his way through their bodies and read the intentions of their souls. Larkin didn't flinch, kept his gaze fixed. Showing he had nothing to hide.

'Karen,' began Mickey Falco, his mind apparently made up. 'Karen had got herself into a spot of bother when she came to us.'

'What kind of bother?' asked Larkin,

sitting forward.

'Her and her mate Hayley ... offended someone.' He stopped talking, searching for the right word. 'Someone ... influential.' Mickey Falco kept his eyes fixed on Larkin and Andy, gauging, measuring their responses all the time.

'Who?' asked Larkin.

'You ain't got any idea?'

''Course we don't,' replied Andy. 'Did you miss that bit about why we're 'ere?'

Mickey Falco smiled as if Andy's response amused him.

'Gentlemen,' said Mickey Falco, 'now, there's something I haven't asked you. And it's important. If, or, I dunno, when, you catch up with Karen, what you gonna do then? What's your plans for her?'

Larkin was beginning to get irritated. 'We don't have any plans for her. All we want to do is let her know her father is concerned about her and that he wants to meet with her. Beyond that, it's up to the pair of them.'

Mickey Falco said nothing, just nodded absently, as if reaching a conclusion within himself.

'Well, gentlemen,' he said eventually, 'I think that's as far as we can go today.'

Larkin and Andy looked at each other. 'That's it?' said Larkin.

'That's it,' said Mickey Falco. 'Time for you two to skedaddle. Mickey's got work to do. Now, I hope I've made it clear that the location of this refuge is a secret,' he said, leaning forward, 'and I want it to remain so.' His eyes hardened, turning to bright, glittering ball-bearings of metal. 'But I don't suppose I have to tell you gentlemen that again, do I?'

'We found it easily enough,' said Andy, trying not to be unnerved by the stare.

'No you didn't,' replied Mickey Falco. 'You had no directions. You were just following someone's trail. You didn't know where it would lead.'

Larkin nodded to himself. Yeah, he thought, that seems to sum up my visit to London so far.

'Now,' said Mickey Falco, handing over two pieces of paper, 'if, and I stress the if, we are to talk again, I've got to get you two checked out. Names, addresses, phone numbers, work contacts, the whole lot, please.'

'Photos?' asked Andy.

'Got them,' said Mickey Falco, showing them two colour ten by eights. 'CCTV hidden behind the front door. Digital camera hook-up. Expensive but necessary.'

'I'm impressed,' said Larkin.

'Good. So you should be.'

'So if we go along with you on this,' said Larkin, waving his piece of paper, 'will it be worth our while talking to you again?'

'Depends, depends, depends. On if you are who you say you are,' said Mickey Falco. 'On whether we think we've got something we can tell you. It's not a game. We have to protect ourselves.'

Larkin, reluctantly, nodded. He picked up a pen from the desk and, like Andy, began to fill up the paper in front of him.

There was something about Mickey Falco, something that didn't immediately compute. There was the obvious fact that he was running a refuge with everything that entailed, yet there was something more. They'd seen glimpses of a much harder nature, like he had a titanium skeleton, unbreakable. Larkin knew this was a man to tread warily round, respect.

'Stick your phone number on there where I can contact you,' said Mickey Falco.

'And when will that be?' asked Larkin.

'If and when I reckon you're cleared,' he said in an offhand way. He took his stick from the back of the chair, leaning heavily on it. 'Thank you for your interest, gentlemen, I'll get someone to see you out.' He pressed a buzzer on his desk.

'One thing,' said Larkin, standing. 'Candleland. Where does that name come from?'

Mickey Falco smiled. 'Are either of you two Catholic?' he asked.

They shook their heads.

'Didn't think so. Well,' he said, pulling himself up to his full height, which wasn't much, 'you probably know the practice? Lighting candles for departed souls? Now I might be something of an iconoclast, but the way I see it, the souls don't have to actually be dead, just lost, missing, disappeared, whatever. And that–' he gestured with his free arm, '–is where we are. Candleland.

'You see,' he said, voice gaining the precise authority and oratory of the street preacher, 'Candleland is a wasteland. The land of the missing and the dispossessed. It's all around us. But the citizens don't want to acknowledge it's there. Just bumble about their lives, refuse to believe it exists. But somebody has to face up to it. Somebody has to be here to help.' The words sounded incongruous in the man's East End accent – incongruous but truthful. 'And we're a candle, a beacon. We let them know there's somewhere they can go.'

Larkin smiled to himself. He thought of Jane Howell, a woman he'd left behind in Newcastle. She was now doing the same thing. 'Good,' he said.

'An' it's also the title of Ian McCulloch's first solo album,' said Andy.

Mickey Falco regarded him as if he'd just sprouted an extra head. 'Pardon?'

'Ian McCulloch. Lead singer with Echo and the Bunnymen. First solo album.' He looked between the two, reddening. 'They've reformed now.'

'Glad to hear it,' rasped Mickey Falco.

There was a knock at the door.

'Come in.' The door opened behind them. 'Well, gentlemen.' Mickey Falco made his way slowly round the desk, leaning heavily on his stick. He shook hands with them. 'I'll be in touch with you. Ralph here'll show you out.'

Larkin turned to go and was confronted by the middle-aged cyclist he'd seen earlier. The man stepped back suddenly, shock on his face, as if he'd been physically struck. He had recognised Larkin.

Larkin scrutinised him, mentally searching for the right file.

Then click. The tumblers moved into place, the long-closed door of his mind opened and the buried memory leapt up at him. He had never buried it that deeply in the first place; it was a shallow grave memory.

His legs went weak, his heart tumbled into sickening somersaults. He now knew who the man was. How the hell hadn't he sussed him earlier?

It was Ralph Sickert. The murderer of his wife and son.

Battlefield

Larkin just stood and stared. He couldn't move, he was rooted to the spot. No words, no coherent articulation came into his head, just jump-cut collage images, white noise, static. His body physically aped his mind; arhymetic heartbeat, limbs suddenly shaking. He could feel, hear and, at the corners of his eyes, see the pulse of his blood.

The room dissolved away. Larkin became unaware of everyone – everything – else as his concentration focused narrowly on the other man. Sickert was doing likewise. Time stopped, they stood transfixed by each other like mongoose and snake.

Mickey Falco was the one to break the moment. 'D'you two know each other, then?' The lame question was asked out of genuine curiosity.

At these words, Sickert managed to pull his eyes from Larkin. At the same time his adrenal glands kicked his body into fight or flight and, wisely, he opted for safety. He turned and ran from the room.

Larkin, his body in a similar state but acting at the opposite extreme, quickly followed him.

Sickert ran down the hall to the front door. Larkin was after him, but Sickert had a better knowledge of the layout and locks of the place, plus a headstart. By the time Larkin reached the front door it had been slammed shut, with Sickert on the other side.

Both Mickey Falco and Andy were shouting now, out of the room, but Larkin either ignored or couldn't hear them. The red mist had descended, sharpening his vision to one man, one objective. Shrugging off restraining arms, he fumbled open the door and ran outside.

Sickert was across the road, pelting through the barren park. Larkin, his rage gifting him with immunity from any oncoming traffic, ran into the road. He reached the pavement on the other side, vaulted the low brick wall, and was into the park, also running.

Larkin knew Sickert couldn't outpace him. The cycling couldn't stave off the ageing and it was starting to tell on the man. Sickert's breath escaped in ragged bursts, the cold air turning it to instant clouds. Feet seeming to get heavier and heavier with each step, he began to resemble an old steam train breaking down.

Larkin saw Sickert reach the playground and allow himself a glance over his shoulder. He picked his pace up. He could see Larkin was gaining. Turning back to face the front, Larkin watched as Sickert stumbled on a discarded glass bottle, missed his footing and fell. A swing was directly in front of him and he made a desperate lunge for the chain to break his fall. He missed and sprawled over it, the swing hitting him flat in the chest, knocking all the air out of him. Within seconds Larkin was on him.

He grabbed Sickert by the shoulders, forced him round, face to face, and looped the chain of the swing round both his arms.

Larkin looked at Sickert, but didn't see the old, jowly man in front of him; ashen, unable to run away. No, his twisted eyes saw the City big noise, the amoral, immoral yuppy high-flyer he'd brought down. The man who had lost everything because of Larkin, the man who had forcibly removed anyone Larkin cared about as a consequence of those actions. That was the man Larkin saw when he drove his fist into Sickert's face, shattering the cartilage of his nose, bruising his own knuckles, savouring the pain.

Larkin took another swing, then another. Suddenly, he felt the air supply to his throat being forcibly, violently cut off. His hands sprang to his neck. Some kind of hard, polished restraining device. Mickey Falco's stick.

He felt himself being pulled backwards and fought against it. It got him nowhere, the grip on his neck was too strong. Instead, Larkin went with it, allowed Mickey Falco to pull him off Sickert and down on to the playground's blighted tarmac.

As soon as Larkin was prone on the ground, the cane was released. He gave it a beat, then sprang up, ready for round two. Or thought he did. The sudden lack of air had made him nauseous and lightheaded; he could only manage a slow climb to his knees. He saw Darren untangling Sickert from the swing.

'Leave him alone!' Larkin rasped. 'The bastard's mine!'

Larkin lurched towards the old man, oblivious to everything but his rage. Had he been more aware, he would have heard a swift, rushing sound approaching the left side of his head, but he only felt the painful crack as Mickey Falco's cane connected.

Small starbursts of blackness began to explode in front of his eyes. His body involuntarily stopped struggling and began to relax. He decided to watch as the starbursts increased in size. He found them fascinating and they began to take all of his attention. There was something he was supposed to be doing, but he couldn't quite remember what. The starbursts grew bigger until they blotted out everything else altogether.

Then all he saw and felt was the comfortable embrace of darkness.

'He's back.'

It sounded to Larkin like a voice through the fog. He opened his eyes and found a young, crop-headed man was staring impersonally into them. It took a few seconds for Larkin's mind to click into place, then it all came back to him.

He struggled to his feet, intent on starting round two with Sickert, but a sudden wave of nausea swept over him, buckling his knees, sending him back to the tarmac.

Larkin looked across to the swing. Andy and Mickey Falco were untangling Sickert from his chains, the man's nose now resembling a thrown tomato. For the first time Larkin saw Sickert as he truly was: an old man, pathetic, trembling. No longer a murderer. On realising this, the fight went out of Larkin and his body sagged. He felt Darren's hands on him, helping him up.

'You all right now?' Darren asked.

Larkin nodded.

'You're not going to start again?'

'No,' Larkin mumbled.

Mickey Falco limped over to him. 'All right?'

'You fuckin' hit me,' moaned Larkin.

'Look what you done to him,' Mickey Falco said, flicking his thumb at Sickert. 'Come on now, up you get.' He extended his free arm, pulled Larkin off the ground.

Sickert chose that moment to be escorted past. A flash of tired hatred buzzed behind Larkin's eyes. He stared at Sickert.

'I've paid,' Sickert wheezed in a small voice. 'I've paid my debt.'

Mickey Falco quickly placed himself in front of Larkin, discouraging any attempts at confrontation.

'I've made my peace,' Sickert coughed, his voice rising. 'Have you?'

He stared at Larkin. Larkin stared back, said nothing. Andy led Sickert away.

As they moved towards the house, Mickey Falco and Darren turned to follow.

'I want to talk to you,' Larkin said to Mickey Falco's back. There was no response. Larkin started after Mickey Falco who was walking quickly, throwing out his right leg as he went, leaning heavily on his stick. Larkin caught up with him, put his hand on his shoulder, spun him round.

Mickey Falco turned, eyes like coals. Larkin took an involuntary step back; it looked like the man was about to attack him. If it was the case, then Mickey Falco managed to control it. He fixed Larkin with a flat, level stare.

'What's he doing here?' Larkin demanded, pointing at Sickert.

Mickey Falco said in an even voice, 'Candleland's got volunteers from all sections of the community. Ralph's doing day-release from an open prison with us. He'll be properly out soon.'

'Open prison?' spat Larkin. 'Fuckin' open prison? D'you know what that cunt did to my wife and son?'

Mickey Falco's gaze flinched, but he managed to absorb the shock of Larkin's words well. His eyes were soon steady again. 'Whatever Ralph did was in the past. In the eyes of the law and society he's paid for his crimes. He's now trying to make amends.'

Larkin's anger continued to rise. 'What about in my eyes, eh? What about making amends to me? Has he done that? Has he fuck!'

Mickey Falco seemed to think long and hard. When he eventually spoke, it was in the carefully modulated tones of the mediator. 'I can understand your anger. I can understand your pain. No one's arguing with you about that. But for Ralph, and for us at the refuge, that's all in the past. What it looks like now is an assault on a member of my staff. Now I've got to go and get some medical treatment for him then see if he wants to press charges. Speaking of medical treatment, that was unfortunately a nasty knock I gave you. It might have cracked something or worked something loose. You'd better get that checked out.' He began to walk off, then turned. 'Look, I'm very sorry about all this, mate, I really am. Now,

I have to go. But I'll be in touch.'

Larkin watched the man's retreating back. He wanted to shout something, scream something, anything that would make him understand, make things clear. But he didn't. He couldn't. There were no words, there was nothing he could say.

Larkin stood alone in the playground. His guts, his head churning with conflicting, overlapping emotions. Sophie, Joe, Sickert … the whole thing was never far away from the surface of his mind. It informed both his waking and sleeping life.

He had, in his own mind, devised no end of pain, no end of torment for Sickert. Thinking those things had helped to keep the memories caged. But seeing the man himself, knowing that whatever nasty fate Larkin had devised for him wasn't happening, or wasn't going to happen, had given him a sudden rush of clarity. The lid was suddenly removed from his pressure cooker heart and all the guilt, the self-pity, the whole range of noxious, destructive emotions, over a decade's worth of razor-painful memories came bubbling over.

Larkin turned away from Candleland. The cold, damp, foggy mist was hovering over the park. The daylight hadn't managed to disperse it. He started walking, putting as much distance between himself and Sickert as possible. He knew his car and Andy were also there, but they weren't important at the moment. He had to get away, be alone, think.

Soon, the fog, the distance, had obscured Candleland. Larkin looked round for roads, exits from the barren grass, but could see none. The fog began to turn to drizzle. Larkin, without any idea where he was going, kept walking.

In the Darkest Place

The pub was old, overlooked, hardly visited. Weak, dusty sunlight filtered down in opaque shafts through the grubby high windows, illuminating the cracked lino, made even brighter-looking by the dark, aged wood interior. High ceilings and tobacco-stained walls, the place seemed church or cathedral-like, with torn, vinyl-padded booths and wrought-iron-legged tables replacing pews, an old, scarred mahogany bar standing in for an altar.

A sparse and elderly congregation, there out of habit more than belief: a couple of domino players, continuing the same forty-year-old game, an old man sitting alone, staring ahead, finding meaning and memory in the shadows of the ceiling, a wino in the far corner, lips moving in conversation with invisible companions, occasionally making audible pronouncements on the imminent end of the world and the procedures necessary to be saved. A barman – bored, listless, age indeterminate – dutifully ministered to their needs, needed but not wanted. Like the pub they were slowly dying, no one to replace them when they'd gone.

And there sat Larkin. Alone in a corner booth, large shot of whisky, pint of strong lager in front of him. He couldn't remember how he'd got there, what route he'd taken from Candleland, how long he'd been there, how much he'd had to drink or what time of day it was. He was there, it was now, that was enough.

The wino rose from his seat and, tired of his imaginary companions, decided to address the pub.

'We're livin' in the endtimes!' he shouted. 'Repent! Repent now and be saved! Be baptised in the waters, accept the son and be born again! Escape the flames! Repent!'

A lorry rumbled past, shaking the pub doors.

'It's the Rapture! The Rapture is upon us!'

'Shuddup an' drink your drink,' the barman said in the bored voice of the perpetual straight man. The wino noiselessly sat down, began to address his invisible companions once again.

Larkin ignored it, instead he sat steadily drinking, head throbbing. His mind completely focused on a single pinpoint of rage, guilt and betrayal: Sickert. By putting pen to paper, or finger to word processor, Larkin had destroyed his life. In return Sickert had put finger to trigger and destroyed Larkin's.

Larkin, in what seemed to him a previous life but was only twelve years ago, had been a crusading, investigative journalist. He had taken regular, accurate aim at the amoral, immoral yuppy highflyers of the time and brought them down one by one. Larkin's theory had been that, just as the Nazis had been Hitler's theories put into practice, these were Thatcher's theories let loose on Britain.

Ralph Sickert, an already very rich, middle-aged stockbroker who had embraced Thatcherism with an evangelical fervour, had been one such target. The time was right for a City scandal and Larkin duly obliged by amassing a pile of evidence on Sickert's fraudulent dealings, and publishing them. Sickert's colleagues and acquaintances distanced themselves from him, scapegoated him. He was left completely ruined, bankrupted and blackballed. It drove him, he said at a later court appearance, temporarily insane. Insane enough to grab a shotgun and come hunting for Larkin.

Unfortunately, Larkin wasn't there. He too hadn't been immune to the joys of the Eighties and was, at that time, passed out on some tart's stomach, a head full of Jack Daniel's, a nose full of Bolivian and his balls well drained.

This didn't stop Sickert. He wanted blood, he wanted to hurt, so he took aim at the nearest available target. Larkin's wife, Sophie, and their son Joe.

Larkin put his head down, trying not to think about what had happened next. He noticed his empty glasses were now full. He had been so involved with his memories he couldn't even remember making the trip to the bar. Or trips. He had no idea how much he'd had to drink.

His mind, as it had done so many times since that time, tried to imagine what must have happened. His hand trembled as it raised the glass.

After a few mouthfuls, the throbbing in his head got worse. He screwed up his eyes, trying hard to shift the pain, feeling needles attack his skull. He sat helpless, teeth gritted, as his surroundings warped in and out around him. Reality was uncapped and the pub drained away into a psychedelic barrage of painfully twisted colours.

Fuck Mickey Falco, he thought, fuck Sickert, fuck all of them...

And then he saw her. In amidst the colours, the pain, the noise. Sophie. Sitting on the seat next to him, smiling, bright and alive. Like she'd never been away.

'Sophie...' His hands reached out to her, didn't quite connect. He tried again.

'Sophie, talk to me! Speak! Tell me you're here, you're alive!'

And then another sharp stab to the head, so bad his eyes slammed shut with the pain.

Eventually, it started to subside. Abstracts became solids, solids became shapes, shapes became remembered surroundings. Gasps became regular breathing. Slowly, he opened his eyes. She was gone.

'Hey mate,' Larkin heard a voice say.

He looked around. The barman was addressing him. 'Hey mate, don't you start.' His voice had a weary, imploring quality to it. 'I've got enough with him–' he jerked his thumb at the old wino, '–over there.'

'No,' said Larkin weakly, 'she was there, she was real...'

'Yeah, mate,' said the barman and walked back to his station.

Larkin looked around. It had felt real, she had been there. He shook his head, trying to ease the throbbing. It was no good. Alcohol and concussion didn't go together. But still...

He ordered another drink. No beer this time, just the whisky. She had been there, she had been real. Down in one, not touching the sides. Glass down, another. He had to see her again, had to get her back. Then, suddenly, he knew where to go next.

Down in one again, thump. No more here. He'd need an off-licence for the next part. Larkin lurched towards the door. As he did that, the wino rose to address the room again. The door slammed shut behind Larkin, cutting off the man's rant. It didn't matter, Larkin had heard it before. He knew all about the end of the world.

Larkin knelt, eyes screwed tight shut, bottle cradled in hand. He didn't feel the cold or the rain. He had no idea of time. He wanted Sophie.

He had bought a bottle of cheap, generic whisky, the kind that burned on the way down, and started in on it. She had returned to him briefly in the taxi. Then disappeared again before he could touch her. He had kept drinking then, in his desperate attempt to hold her, bind her to him.

He had practically fallen out of the taxi, almost breaking his precious bottle in the process, and began looking for her.

Eventually, he found what he was looking for. He knew the spot. The last place he'd seen either of them.

He had knelt down, taken another few gulps of liquid, holding down the impulse to gag on the cheap liquor and allowing it entry to his system, hoping it would work its magic. He screwed up his eyes again, working with the pain in his head, willing her to appear before him again.

And there she was, kneeling casually beside him, smiling prettily. He had never seen a face so beautiful. The rain, the cold disappeared; blue sky and warmth was everywhere. He had never known such sudden serenity, such deep happiness. He never wanted it to end.

He stretched out his fingers, gently brushed her face.

And pulled them away with a start. Where he had expected warm skin, he found cold marble. Where he had expected features, eyes, eyebrows, nose, mouth, he found engraved letters.

Tentatively, he touched her again, trying to make out the words. He found the first one:

SOPHIE

That was what he had expected. He touched her face again:

SOPHIE ALICE
HETHERINGTON-LARKIN

Her name. Her full married name. Oh fuck,

he thought, stomach lurching. This wasn't right. Clouds began to gather in the blue sky. The temperature took a sudden, swift drop. He put his head back expecting to feel sunshine. Instead he felt rain.

He touched her again, felt numbers this time, dates. Her date of birth and her date of–

The pain hit him again, warping his reality, twisting his vision. When he opened his eyes it had all gone; the warmth, Sophie, everything. All that remained was the pain.

He was back in the cemetery, kneeling before a headstone, row after row behind him. Thousands of small, discreet headstones. Geometrically straight row after geometrically straight row, a coffined caravan site. Surrounded by decomposing flowers, rotting remembrance. Brief lives, small reminders.

He looked at the stone in front of him:

SOPHIE ALICE
HETHERINGTON-LARKIN

Her dates, and then:

BELOVED DAUGHTER OF
ANNE AND CHRISTOPHER
WIFE OF STEPHEN

And below was the really painful piece:

JOE LARKIN

And his dates of three years, then:

"UNTIMELY RIPP'D FROM THE BOSOM OF HIS MOTHER"

Larkin stared at the stone, at the words, at the earth in front of it; felt the rain on his face, the encroaching dusk. He had been fooling himself, willing Sophie to be there. His desperate mind had known that all along.

But he wouldn't let go: he now tried to see beyond the grass, beneath it. He tried to see into the stone, willing the gold letters to cease being words, to move back through time, reform themselves as flesh and blood, bone and tissue; living, thinking, feeling humans.

Nothing happened. Nothing changed.

He tried again, closing his eyes. When he opened them, they were wet with more than rain. His chest was heaving and he was down on his knees, the cold, grey stone hugged to his chest.

His body convulsed and shook, his hands gripped harder as tears of grief, rage, guilt, everything intermixed and rolled down his face in streams that threatened to become rivers.

'I'm sorry ... I'm ... sorry...' he sobbed.

There was no reply.

'I'm sorry...'

I know. She was back.

Larkin kept his eyes closed this time. He didn't want to open them, didn't want to break the spell. He cried harder.

'I let you down ... I let you both down...'

There's nothing you can do about it now.

'I know! I know! But I want to! I wuh-want to!'

Yes.

'I need to!'

It's too late for that now.

'I keep seeing you ... both of you ... even now I talk to you...'

Don't delude yourself.

'And I see you both ... when it happened ... I can still see it...'

But you weren't there, Stephen.

'I know I wasn't!'

You were with some tart. What was her name again?

The sobbing almost tore Larkin's body apart. 'I can't remember! I never even knew ... I'm sorry...'

It's too late.

'Please, forgive me ... you have to forgive me...'

You have to forgive yourself first.

Larkin tried to speak, but the words were rendered inarticulate by sobbing.

After regaining his composure he spoke again.

'S – Sophie?'

Nothing. Just the rain, the wind in the trees, the distant rattle of a commuter train, the darkening sky above.

'Sophie...'

His body could no longer hold him up and he slid to the ground, hands losing their grip on the gravestone, bottle crooked in one arm.

'Sophie,' he said again, and passed out.

Walking in the Dark

The room was warm, the duvet pulled up to his chin. For a few blissful seconds he experienced a dislocating amnesia, then it all returned, memory hurtling back towards him like an out-of-control juggernaut. He braced himself for the impact but it still hit him with mind-scrambling force.

Sickert. Sophie. Joe. He leaned over the side of the bed and vomited. Thankfully someone had placed a plastic bowl there and he managed to hit it. He heaved six or seven times until there was nothing left to give, then flopped back on the bed sweating, spent.

His stomach felt like it had been used as a rugby ball, his head had Motorhead doing a soundcheck in there and his eyes had been replaced by a psychedelic oil projector lamp. Everything hurt so much, he couldn't tell if his original headache was still there. He blinked, searching for focus.

He was back in the attic room at Faye's house. He could wonder how he got there later, for he was too wiped out to concentrate. It was daylight but beyond that, he didn't know what time it was, what day it was.

All he could think of was Sickert. Even in the short time he'd been awake, Sickert was clinging on to Larkin like a baleful ghost from a nightmare, clinging on, dragged from sleep to daylight. Still with the power to haunt.

Larkin sighed heavily, fragments of memory dropping slowly into place. After the pub things became hazy. There was the cemetery, yes, and then Sophie. Had she been there or had it just been the fact that he wanted to believe powered by alcohol? It had felt so real, he could have touched her.

He remembered he had touched her. Her face, her stone-cold face... No, she was gone. With the cold, harsh light coming through the thin curtains, he knew she was gone.

There was a small creak of hinges and the

door was slowly pushed open. A blonde, cropped head cautiously appeared.

'C'mon in, Andy,' croaked Larkin.

The door swung open fully. 'Thought I heard movement. How you doin'?'

'Never better. You'll forgive me if I don't get up.'

Andy entered, sniffed the air. 'Better out than in, ay? Fragrant. 'Ere. Drink this.'

Andy handed Larkin a pint of cloudy, slightly fizzing liquid.

'What is it?' asked Larkin, suspiciously. The last thing he wanted was another drink.

''Angover cure. Water, vitamin C, vitamin B-complex, spirulina – don't ask me what that is – and the fizz is Alka Seltzer. One of Faye's recipes. Now, down in one.'

Larkin downed the glass, belched. Despite a cloud of swirls, it stayed down. 'Better,' he said, 'but I still feel rough.'

'So you fuckin' should. Found an empty whisky bottle beside you an' it looked like you'd had plenty before that. Probably lucky to be alive.'

'Yeah,' groaned Larkin. 'Lucky. How did I get here?'

'They were closin' the cemetery at Manor Park, found you sprawled all over the place. They took you for a wino at first, then found your wallet with a card of yours in and this phone number on. Gave me a call, Bob's your uncle, 'ere you are.'

Larkin gave a weak nod. 'Thanks, Andy. You're a mate.'

Andy gave a smile, more sad than happy. 'No worries.'

'How long have I been asleep?'

'We found you last night. It's three in the afternoon. You've slept through nearly twenty-four hours. Best thing, really.'

'Yeah.'

'An' you wanna have that head of yours seen to. Come up in a big old lump where 'e 'it you. Faye's 'ad a look at it, doesn't reckon it's cracked or anything, but you should still get it looked at.'

Larkin nodded. They then lapsed into contemplative silence.

'What a fuckin' state of affairs, eh?' said Andy, shaking his head.

Larkin said nothing. There was nothing to say.

'I've told Henry 'e can 'andle things from 'ere on in,' said Andy. ''Is show now. You've done your bit.'

Larkin nodded. 'I want to stay as far away from Mickey Falco and his place as possible.'

'Don't blame you, mate,' replied Andy. 'Oh, by the way, that Diana bird, fella, whatever, she's been phonin' you. Wouldn't leave a message, wouldn't talk to anyone else. Wants you round there ASAP.'

'She didn't say why?'

'Nope. Says she's got somethin' she'll only share with you.' Andy smiled. 'I'll fuckin' bet she 'as.'

'I think you're more her type than me. Why don't you go?'

Andy reddened. 'I don't think so.' He shuddered.

Larkin smiled. 'I didn't realise your sexuality was so fragile.'

Andy looked at him. 'You gettin' up, or you gonna lie there all day?'

'I'll get up. Give me a minute.'

'Okey dokey, I'll see you downstairs.' Andy began to make his way out of the room.

'Oh Andy?' Andy stopped, turned.

'Yeah?'

'Faye and Henry. Where are they?'

'Out. Why?'

Larkin looked relieved. 'I just … don't feel up to facing her … them, yet.'

Andy gave Larkin a look he couldn't read. 'Don't worry, she's out. And Henry. I'll see you downstairs,' he said, and left the room.

Larkin was alone once more. He stretched out, put his head back. Did Andy know about his fling with Faye? Did it matter if he did? He put it to one side. He couldn't think about that now.

Sickert was alive and, until Larkin got his hands on him again, well. He didn't like it, but he had to accept it.

But he knew where he was, he could just

go round one night, catch him unawares...

Leave it, Larkin thought to himself. Get on with it, go round it. Keep busy, keep him out of my mind, he thought. Diana. She wanted to see me.

He closed his eyes, sighed. Just five more minutes. His mind began to uncoil, settle – Sophie. Alive, happy. Joe.

Larkin's eyes jumped open. He didn't want to sleep. He didn't want to go back there, wherever it was. There was nowhere he could escape to, no hiding place. Not even in dreams. He couldn't run away, he had tried running away yesterday. There was no one to run to. He had to go on. Or go nowhere.

He threw back the duvet and got slowly, shakily, to his feet.

It was early evening by the time Larkin reached Diana's street. The sky more grey than white, the air turning from cold to chill. Just a run-of-the-mill February day.

As a disgruntled Andy had reminded him before he left, the Saab had been parked outside Candleland since Larkin had walked off with the car keys in his pocket the previous day. So Larkin had travelled by tube. He stood on the pavement, staring up at Diana's window. No movements, no lights, nothing. Not promising.

He had showered, shaved, found a clean

pair of faded Levis, thick lumberjack shirt and T-shirt, same leather jacket, same boots, but he still felt rough. The alcohol was sweating its way out of him. His hands were shaking, his head was throbbing. Not as bad, though; Motorhead had given way to mid-Nineties Aerosmith – no longer a deafening noise, just an irritating racket. He'd also had another couple of glasses of Faye's hangover cure, and this had left him if not feeling better, then certainly more functional.

Larkin pressed the bell. After a pause the door buzzed open. No voice on the intercom. Larkin again got a feeling of unease. Something didn't feel right. He stepped back from the door, looked up at the window. Again, no movement, nothing. He quickly scoped both sides of the street. Nothing out of the ordinary.

He pushed the door slowly open, letting his eyes adjust to the gloom of the hall. No one there. Warily he entered, closing the door behind him.

The door at the base of the stairs to Diana's flat was open. Larkin stepped inside and quietly mounted the stairs.

He was operating on radar, but it was damaged radar at best. His head was still throbbing and his heart pounding so hard, blood drumming in his ears, he doubted he would hear anything.

He reached the top of the stairs, turned right. Checked for anything out of the ordinary, saw nothing. All the doors were shut. That was strange enough. The alarm bells inside him began to ring louder.

It wasn't too late, he knew that. He could still turn around, leave now. He placed his hand on the doorknob of Diana's living room. I might be deluding myself, thought Larkin. There might be nothing wrong, no need to worry.

There was only one way to find out. He turned the doorknob and entered the room.

As he stepped inside he saw Diana lying still on the floor, debris around her and a huge man dressed as a biker standing over her. He turned and grinned at Larkin.

Larkin opened his mouth to speak, moving forward at the same time, when a sudden sharp movement from behind the door distracted him. Before he could react to this, a hand holding some kind of pad was clamped firmly over his nose and mouth.

His hands reached for the restraining arm but it was no good, the grip was too tight. Although Larkin knew it was the worst thing he could do, he gave an involuntary gasp, trying to draw air into his lungs. Instead he inhaled the chemical the pad was soaked in.

His mouth and nose were invaded by the

smell, like clinical almonds, he thought, then his head began to spin as if he was on a fairground ride. The ride didn't slow down or stop, though, just kept getting faster until Larkin felt himself catapulted into freefall. He let his body relax, waiting for the inevitable impact, but it never arrived. Instead he just kept falling down, down, until the darkness enveloped him.

Crawling through the Wreckage

Larkin opened his eyes. His sight was blurred, light coming at first in frantic rave beats, slowing gradually to a rhythmic pounding. His vision became more distinct with each thump, as blood was sluggishly pumped round his body.

He began to focus: a ceiling, an electric light. He must have been out a long time, the curtain was drawn too. He let his head swing to the left. It hurt as much as his earlier hangover. He felt a numb pain in his arms as he tried to move them. He couldn't. His re-emergent consciousness told him they were pinned underneath his body, tied behind his back, numb from lack of circulation.

As he tried to look round, a dark presence

loomed into vision. He felt himself being roughly grabbed by the shirt front and pulled up.

The face staring at him was big and wide. Goatee beard, swarthy skin. Hair at the sides of the head greased back but bald on top. The eyes looked him over. Stone eyes. Killer's eyes. The man nodded.

'Get up,' he said in a guttural voice.

He hefted Larkin to his feet. It was too much movement too soon and his head began to spin, his legs to buckle. The biker didn't notice.

'Get over there,' the biker rumbled and swung Larkin towards the sofa. Larkin connected and flopped down, unable to move.

Larkin began to take in his surroundings. Diana's reconstructed sanctuary had been destroyed. It had been systematically smashed, shattered piece by piece, artefact by carefully accumulated artefact. The last piece of reconstruction, Diana, lay on the floor in amongst the debris. She, like the room, looked broken. Her clothing was ripped, her body battered, bruised and bloodied. She lay still, her eyes staring open. If it hadn't been for the faint rise and fall of her chest, Larkin would have taken her for dead. Perhaps that's what she wanted; she was naked in the cruellest possible way, but her eyes showed she was in a place beyond modesty or dignity, a place beyond caring.

Larkin looked again at the man who'd flung him on the sofa. He was all in black – leather bike jacket, T-shirt, Levis, motorbike boots. Sitting in an armchair on the opposite side of the room was another man. Smaller than the first, he had sandy-coloured hair quiffed and gelled back, a small pencil moustache. He was wearing a pinstripe double-breasted suit jacket over a violent Hawaiian shirt, black jeans and cowboy boots. His head was tipped back, eyes closed, and his fingers popped and tapped either to what was playing on the Walkman phones plugged into his ears, or something else entirely, something only he could hear.

The biker stomped over to him, hit him on the shoulder. The other man immediately shot up, eyes blazing with anger.

'Don't do that! Don't do that! Never do that to me, never!' His voice was like his eyes and his body. Quick, darting, wired. 'Miles was blowing! Nobody interrupts Miles.'

The biker shrugged, gestured with his thumb. 'He's back, Lenny,' he said, as if he didn't care one way or the other.

Lenny looked at Larkin, flicked off a hidden Walkman switch from inside his jacket. 'So he is,' he said, and crossed the room.

'You're Larkin, aren't you?' Lenny asked,

eyes pinwheeling.

Larkin gave a small nod.

'You took your fuckin' time gettin' here,' Lenny said, then gave a highpitched, snickering whinny of a laugh. 'I think Diana got bored entertainin' us.'

'Yeah,' said the biker. 'You should 'ave a go. You can't tell the difference. Not after a while anyway.'

Diana lay unmoving on the floor, eyes miles away from the rest of them. Larkin could only guess what she'd been through.

'Yeah,' said Lenny, giggling. 'We showed her all our tricks. And me an' Ringo know a few tricks, don't we?'

Lenny giggled again. Ringo gave a flat-eyed nod.

Hell's teeth, thought Larkin. Where the fuck did these two come from?

'So you forced her to call me,' said Larkin. 'I'm here now. What d'you want?'

'The boss'll tell you that,' said Ringo with a dismissive sniff.

'The boss?' repeated Larkin. This was starting to get very serious, he thought. They might seem like idiots, but look what they did to Diana. They're not to be messed with. Larkin could feel fear creep over his heart. He tried to keep it in check. The last thing he wanted to do was expose that emotion to these two.

'So who is this Mr Big?' asked Larkin with

considerably more cockiness than he actually felt. 'Have I wandered into a straight-to-video gangster film by mistake?'

Ringo crossed the room and stood right in front of him. 'Was that supposed to be a joke?'

'I didn't hear you laughing,' said Larkin.

Ringo stared at him with reptilian eyes then, with a speed that belied his size, gave Larkin a walloping kick to the balls.

Larkin doubled up. The pain was too intense even to shout out at.

'Ringo! Ringo! What you doin'?' squeaked Lenny. 'The boss said not to damage him. We need him.'

Ringo shrugged. 'Boss won't notice if there's a couple of bits missin' here an' there.'

'Let's calm down,' Lenny said, in a voice that sounded like he'd been existing on black coffee for the last fortnight. 'We got a job to do.' He turned to Larkin. 'You're comin' with us.'

'What choice ... do I have...' Larkin managed between gasps.

'None,' said Ringo, not spotting a rhetorical question when he heard one. He reached down, pulled Larkin to his feet. 'Now,' he said, and began to drag Larkin towards the door.

He was pulled past the prone form of Diana. 'And what happens to her?' asked Larkin.

Ringo shrugged. 'With a woman,' he began, as if about to impart some philosophical pearl, 'with a woman you just fuck 'er and forget 'er. She wants to play the game, she has to learn the rules.' He almost smiled, so pleased was he with his Wildean wit.

'She needs help,' said Larkin. 'Call an ambulance.'

'Fuck that,' Ringo replied.

'You want me to come, you call her an ambulance.'

'You're comin' anyway, ambulance or not.' He leaned his face in close to Larkin's. It smelled like whatever he'd been eating hadn't been quite dead when it reached his mouth. 'I can make you.'

'No you can't,' said Larkin with more confidence than he felt. 'Because your Mr Big wants me unharmed. If he sees you didn't do that, if I put up a struggle, it won't look good for you, will it?'

Ringo thought about that one.

'Just do it!' snapped Lenny. He dug into his jacket pocket, pulled out a mobile, switched it on and dialled 999. He shoved it against Larkin's ear.

'You talk to them,' said Lenny. 'Then it'll be your voice on the tape. And no funny business.'

'I wouldn't dream of it,' said Larkin, looking between the two of them.

The call was answered, he asked for an

ambulance, gave the address. Lenny broke the connection before he could say anything further.

'Come on,' said Lenny. 'They'll be here soon.'

Ringo dropped Larkin. He hit the floor with a painful thud.

'I'll get the Jag,' said Ringo, moving towards the door. 'I'm drivin'.'

'OK,' said Lenny, shaking his head. 'Do it quickly, they'll be here in a minute. But I choose the music.'

Ringo turned to him, face covered in threat. 'I'm drivin',' he said, his voice a tone of monotonous dread. 'I want Monster Magnet.'

'Fuck!' Lenny danced away as if he'd been physically struck. 'I don't want any of that heavy metal shit! We'll have Miles!'

'I want Monster Magnet.'

'No!'

Ringo's voice deepened ominously. 'I want Monster Magnet.'

Lenny sighed in exasperation. 'OK! OK! Monster Magnet! Just hurry! Get the fuckin' car!'

Ringo, a small smile of triumph on his lips, turned and left.

Lenny sighed, paced the room, shook his head. 'Sometimes,' he said, as if Larkin was his best mate, 'sometimes I feel as if I'm the last intelligent man left on the planet. Know

236

what I mean?'

'Yeah,' said Larkin, from his position on the floor, 'I know exactly what you mean.'

Fuck me, thought Larkin, what the hell have I got myself into this time?

Savage Gardens

Ringo pulled up in a big, old black Jag outside Diana's flat and left it running, smack in the centre of the street. Cars were waiting on either side to get through, but one look at Ringo ensured that there wouldn't be any argument.

Lenny pushed Larkin into the back and jumped into the passenger seat. He plugged his Walkman defiantly into his ears, and with a twitchy, murderous glance at Ringo, sat back. Tinny sax leaked out from his ear plugs, calming him. Ringo slapped some pounding heavy metal into the sound system, forcing the volume up until it stopped fractionally short of ear- and nosebleed level, and, with a grunted attempt at singing along, gunned the car up and away.

'Shoulda blindfolded 'im,' Lenny shouted after a while, above the din.

Ringo shrugged. 'He'll know where we're goin' soon enough.'

Lenny's brow creased and his mouth jittered, as if he wanted to say something but couldn't make the connection between brain and lips. Eventually this passed and he slumped back in his seat, finger clicking along to an unheard melody, keeping whatever sociopathic pearl had been there to himself.

Larkin gazed out of the window. He kept catching glimpses of places he half-recognised, half-remembered from his previous time in London. He was trying to memorise his route, find something to use as a signpost if he had to retrace the journey. If he ever got the chance. Eventually he saw something he couldn't mistake: Tower Bridge and the Tower of London, looming up dead ahead. Larkin immediately got his bearings. Ringo coaxed the Jag to the right and they entered the City.

The streets were dark and all but deserted; empty concrete, steel and glass monoliths overshadowing what few stragglers were left on the pavements. By six thirty the daily commuter exodus, by eight the pubs have closed, by nine the City is a ghost town. Only during the day does it come to life, as besuited drones file in from the suburbs to wrestle with VDU and calculator, keeping the cogs of capitalism turning, making the rich richer, the poor more marginalised. Worshipping at the temples of greed, money and cunning. A square mile of self-exaltation, a near-unstormable fortress dedicated to preserving the status quo.

Larkin knew the statistics. Over a quarter of the country's wealth was concentrated within this one square mile. This was where the country's real leaders, decision-makers, were based. It was also, Larkin knew from experience, where some of the most evil, corrupt bastards he'd ever encountered were to be found.

At the thought of that, Sickert flashed into his mind. Larkin sighed and shook his head. The image was losing its power. He was all cried out; his emotions and feelings spent. He was too tired, too soul-weary to respond with anything but weak indifference. His head was like a de-tuned radio – all he could pick up was static.

The Jag rounded the corner of Fenchurch Street, passing the overground station, turned down a sidestreet, under a railway arch, took a left. Larkin read the name of the street they'd turned into: Savage Gardens.

How apt, he thought.

The car came to a halt outside a large, anonymous building. Heavy, studded wooden doors were set in a white stone façade. Small, blacked-out windows covered with wrought-iron bars on either side of the doors gave no hint of what might have been going on inside. The seemingly impenetrable building looked to be a couple of hundred years old and there were no clues as to its present use.

Ringo switched off the engine, mercifully silencing the stereo, then he and Lenny, in one smooth, synchronised movement, opened the back doors and pulled Larkin out, pushing him up the steps to the front of the building. As soon as they approached, there was a deep, metallic buzz and one of the doors unlatched itself. Larkin was pushed swiftly inside, followed by Lenny and Ringo. Even allowing for them locking the car, the whole exercise hadn't taken more than fifteen or twenty seconds before they were off the deserted street.

Inside all was darkness. Larkin was pushed forward, and once his eyes had acclimatised to the gloom he was able to make out a long hallway. It wasn't as dark as he'd first supposed; muted, diffused lighting rather than none at all. On the walls and ceiling he could discern ornate decorations and carvings, Art Nouveau or William Morris. The floor was polished marble, the woodwork dark, heavy. The place spoke of wealth but only in terms of taste. Larkin could imagine visitors finding the place reassuring; like entering a welcoming cocoon of old money.

At the end of the hall a huge staircase,

carrying on the dark wood and marble theme, coiled itself ostentatiously round an old, cage-type lift. Immaculately, elaborately maintained, the whole area wouldn't have looked out of place in turn-of-the-century Paris. Larkin was prodded into the lift, Lenny pressed for the basement and down they smoothly went.

The lift touched down gently, as if landing on eggshells, and Lenny pulled the cage doors open. They were in a chamber, quite large, decorated in an only slightly more subdued version of the upstairs hallway. Ahead of them was a huge wooden desk on which was placed various state-of-the-art CCTV monitors and computer systems, and behind which was a woman; expensively tailored suit, blonde hair pulled back from her face, glasses. Severely beautiful. She stood up. Piped classical music gently surrounded them.

'Good evening,' she said, in a voice as expensively tailored as her suit. 'You must be Mr Larkin.'

'And you are?'

She ignored him. Her eyes landed on Lenny and Ringo.

'I was speaking to you,' said Larkin. 'And you are?'

'None of your business,' she said, voice as warm as an Arctic winter. She locked her steely gaze on to Larkin, as if death rays

241

would be fired from her eyes, then turned to Lenny and Ringo. 'You're late.'

Ringo and Lenny exchanged glances. Neither spoke, each willing the other to go first. Their fear of her was sudden and obvious.

'That's because I was late,' said Larkin. 'I didn't realise there was a time on my party invite. You got a problem with that, darling?'

The woman stared at him, as if a lower lifeform had miraculously developed the power of speech. She looked like she wanted to crush him, but managed to keep the impulse under control. Just.

'I'll tell Mr Rook you're here,' she managed to force out, then walked away, her spike heels clicking angrily on the floor.

'Well,' said Larkin once the three of them were alone, 'she's got you two scared, hasn't she?'

'Shut it, just shut it,' snarled Lenny, eyes darting fearfully around the room.

'So you only pick on people smaller than yourselves, do you?' asked Larkin. 'Ones that won't fight back? Like Diana?'

Lenny looked like he was about to explode. 'Doesn't matter what size you are when you use this,' he spat, pulling out an automatic from the back of his belt and aiming it square at Larkin's face.

Larkin swallowed, inwardly shuddered. He had looked down the barrel of a loaded gun before and it wasn't something that became easier. He didn't know if this one was loaded or ready to fire, but he didn't want to take chances. He stood stock-still and said nothing, staring at Lenny's unstable, quivering fist.

Suddenly a voice broke through the tension.

'Come on, Lenny, that's not how we entertain our guests, is it?'

Larkin turned. From back in the shadows stepped a man. Small, but carrying himself with a dapper air. He wore charcoal-grey trousers with a needle-sharp crease down the front, black, polished loafers, a light tweed sports jacket and a cream silk shirt, collar over the jacket collar. His salt and pepper hair was slightly receding but well disguised, cut into the sort of mullet that long-haired Seventies rockers tried as a compromise when the Eighties arrived. Around his fingers, wrists and neck and dangling from his left ear were enough gold and gems to provide several children with private educations. But it was the eyes that drew you in. At once open and innocent, yet also hinting at darker secrets, hidden things. The kind of eyes that belonged to iconic rock stars or cult leaders.

He spoke again, his voice East End or Essex with the rough edges deliberately filed off.

'Melissa said you'd arrived. Good evening, Mr Larkin. Charles Rook. Call me Charlie.' He smiled, crinkling his eyes at the corners.

It was the kind of book-learned bonhomie-type gesture that charismatic sociopaths employ. Larkin decided to tread carefully. He said nothing.

'Can I get you a drink?' asked Charlie Rook, as if they were old pals meeting in the pub.

'Why am I here?'

Again the smile. 'All in good time. Come with me and we'll talk.' Charlie Rook gestured down a dark-panelled, dimly lit corridor.

'You think I'm just going to walk down there with you? When I've just seen your two mates there torture someone to within an inch of their life? You're off your fucking rocker, mate.'

A flash of anger twitched across Charlie Rook's face. Just a flash: he had too much self-control to allow his emotions to overwhelm him. 'If that's the case I must apologise for my staff's over-zealousness,' he said, without a note of apology in his voice. 'I assure you it won't happen again. Now,' he said, all best mates again, 'about that drink...'

Charlie Rook's office wasn't so much a culture clash, as a culture bare-knuckle fight.

The elegant, old-money, wood-panelled space had been invaded by a nouveau riche World Of Leather décor. Larkin sat in a huge black sofa that resembled a giant gastropod, a glass of lager, decanted from a can, at his side, hands now untied. Behind an unnecessarily elaborate desk sat Charlie Rook, his cigar and a bottle of lager. On the wall behind him was a collection of framed prints, Charlie Rook and Robert Plant, Freddie Mercury, Elton John, Marc Bolan, David Bowie, Rod Stewart, plus plenty of others, some Larkin didn't even recognise, all in their Seventies heydays.

Charlie Rook caught Larkin looking at them. 'As you can see,' he said, 'I used to work in the music biz.'

'But you don't any more.'

Charlie Rook shook his head.

'So what do you do now? And why am I here?'

By way of reply Charlie Rook gave an elaborate exhalation of cigar smoke. 'Well,' he said, settling back into his chair, making him appear even smaller. 'This place here–' He gestured round the room. '–is what you might call the engine room for that place up there. The City. What we do here drives what goes on up there. Gives it fuel. Keeps it running smoothly.' He gave a smug smile, obviously pleased with his words.

Great, thought Larkin, not only a sociopath

but a bore. 'That's fascinating,' he said, unfascinated. 'But what does it mean in English?'

'Well, my work is ... you might term it ... event management,' he said. 'Someone wants something of a special, and usually sensitive, nature organised. A fantasy made reality. I do what I can to facilitate that.'

A sense of unease and distaste at Charlie Rook's words began to creep over Larkin. 'Like a pimp, you mean,' he said.

Charlie Rook gave another studied, eye-crinkling, humourless smile. 'No, Mr Larkin, not like a pimp. I have a client base. A very rich, influential client base. Lots of top people. And these top people, naturally, have a lot of ... pressure. Stress. And they all have different needs, different ways of release, so–'

Larkin's headache was returning. He cut him off. 'All right, Charlie, drop the bullshit. I get it. You know a lot of rich weirdos who like to get their kicks in weird ways. And you sort something out for them, right? To keep them fuelled. To keep the upstairs running smoothly. Sounds like pimping to me.' Larkin didn't bother to hide the sarcasm in his voice.

Charlie Rook's face twitched, lips suddenly, momentarily bloodless. He pulled smoke down his cigar, making the tip glow angrily red, exhaled. 'Yeah,' he said, equilibrium restored, 'that's it. If you wanna put it like that.' His accent was thickening up. 'Screwed-up people who like doin' screwed-up things for fun. An' I help them. Yeah.'

'So why am I here? What's all this got to do with me?'

Charlie Rook gave a smile. It contained less humour than a Bernard Manning joke. 'Would you like me to give you a guided tour? Show you what goes on here?'

'No,' said Larkin emphatically. 'I want to know why I've been brought here against my will, why an innocent woman is now hospitalised, and when I'm going to be allowed out of that door.'

'You're free to go any time you like, Mr Larkin.' Charlie Rook leaned forward. 'But if you do, you'll never learn what I wanted to talk to you about.'

Larkin stood up, moved towards the door. 'I can live with that,' he said. He reached the door, opened it. In the doorway stood Ringo's massive bulk, so big he stopped any light escaping from the room. Larkin turned back to Charlie Rook.

'I thought you said I was free to go?' he snarled.

Charlie Rook smiled, spread his hands. 'I'm not stopping you. Just walk out. If you can get out.'

Larkin turned, walked slowly back into the room and sank back into the gastropod.

'What do you want from me?' he said in a tired voice.

'At last.' He smiled. 'We're both looking for someone, Mr Larkin.'

A tingle of apprehension made its way down Larkin's spine. 'And who might that be?'

'Oh come on, Stephen, don't mess me about,' snapped Charlie Rook, irritation showing. 'You know as well as I do who it is. Karen Shapp. Or Karen Moir, as you call her.'

'That's where you're wrong, Charlie,' replied Larkin. The use of Charlie Rook's first name made the man flinch. 'You're behind the times. I was looking for her. I'm not any more.'

Charlie Rook sat rapidly forward. 'You've found her?'

'No,' replied Larkin. 'I'm just off the job. Her father's taken over. You'll have to talk to him.'

Charlie Rook's voice dropped ominously. 'I'm talking to you. Now she's got something belonging to me. I want it back. And I want her. And I want you to find them both for me.'

Larkin's head was throbbing, his body was aching. He had had enough. 'I don't care what you want. Fuck you, Charlie.'

Charlie Rook sat back with a start. Something dark and indistinct passed over his face, scuttling quickly like a malignant insect. He obviously didn't like, and wasn't used to, people talking back to him. He leaned forward, eyes taking on a hard, almost metallic sheen. He pointed his cigar at Larkin. The glow looked concentrated but fierce.

'Now listen to me, you little cunt. I've tried to be nice to you, polite, and you've just thrown it back in my face.' The pretence of civility was completely gone now. The man was stripped to his hard, ugly core. 'Well, the gloves are off now. You do what I say, when I say and how I say it. Got that?'

'And if I don't?'

'People who mess with me tend not to be around long. Like Jackie Fairley. Remember her?' He stopped talking, waiting for the reaction. Larkin didn't disappoint him.

'You fucking bastard,' he said. 'You fucking murdering bastard.'

Charlie Rook smiled. It wasn't pleasant. 'That's right, you're catching on quick. Fuck with me, get on my bad side, and you don't walk out of this fucking room alive, my son. Am I making myself understood?'

Larkin swallowed. 'Crystal,' he said.

'Good.' Charlie Rook sat back, control restored. 'This is what you're gonna do. You're gonna find the girl. You're gonna find my merchandise. And you're gonna bring them both back to me. Got that?'

'What is this merchandise?'

'None of your fucking business.'

Larkin tried a different approach. 'So how are you going to make sure I do it?' he asked. 'I could just leave this room and you'll never see me again.'

'You could. Which is why you won't be alone when you do leave.' He pressed a button on his desk. The door was opened almost immediately. Ringo stood there again, grinning.

'Meet your new partner,' said Charlie Rook.

Larkin shook his head, groaned.

Charlie Rook gave a grin that was all razors.

'Welcome to the firm, boy,' he said.

Underneath the Arches

'So what's this one called, then?' asked Larkin, wearily.

'See You In Hell,' replied Ringo, gruffly.

'Lovely.'

'Yeah, it's all about his girlfriend havin' an abortion an' 'im 'avin' to bury it on a rubbish heap, or somewhere, an' then hatin' 'er for it.'

'And they say romance is dead,' replied Larkin.

Ringo frowned but didn't reply.

The music in the Jag was deafening. Larkin was surprised the sub frame of the car wasn't giving out. He sat back in the passenger seat, the noise pounding at his brain, adding to the already insistent throbbing, and tried to tune it out. He sighed, looked out the window.

Ringo sat, legs apart, both hands on the wheel, seat pushed well back. No seat belt. It wouldn't reach across his body. He was taking Larkin to South London, with orders to keep him in protective custody. They had crossed the river and were now headed towards Bermondsey. Old warehouses converted into overpriced loft apartments sat side by side with sprawling high-rise council estates. Same area, same view, different worlds.

They were currently negotiating the arches, the maze-like stretch of road tunnels, built into the redbrick viaducts that support the overground train lines. Apart from road markings, intermittent overhead lighting and graffiti, they didn't look like they'd been touched in a century.

Larkin stared at the white brick wall speeding past. He sighed. He felt nothing, dead. The last few days had overloaded his emotions and he was now beyond tiredness, guilt, sorrow and self-pity. He was burnt out. He sighed again and thought. Perhaps he had something left: rage. A hard glittering, steel ball of rage.

He could feel it sitting there, lodged deep within, growing bigger. Sending out cold snaps of electricity to the rest of his body, sparking, expanding, bringing life. All his recent experiences were being re-filtered, re-formulated and re-defined. The vague, nebulous rage against homelessness, the wasted lives he'd encountered, down to the personal, specific rage against Sickert, Faye's relationship with Moir, even the fucking awful racket in the car.

And now he was going to be used. Exploited by a callous murderer. Larkin didn't see why that should happen. The rage grew, his heart pounded, his hands shook. It wasn't going to happen. One way or another, it was going to end now.

Larkin looked around for inspiration, anything that would help him to escape. And then he saw it. His ticket out of there.

On the floor, under the passenger seat between his legs, protruded the handle of a baseball bat. If he could get that out, do some damage while Ringo was driving, he might just make it. It was worth a try, anyway.

Body humming with adrenalin, Larkin quickly reached underneath the seat and brought the bat out. It looked well used. The business end was chipped, dented and scarred, with what looked like dried blood and other associated matter gumming up the holes.

'Wahey, what's this?' said Larkin.

Ringo turned to him. 'Put that back,' he growled. 'It's not–'

The rest of Ringo's words were violently and abruptly cut off, as Larkin rammed it into the side of his head with as much force as he could manage. Ringo let out a cry of pain as his head recoiled from the blow and smacked off the side window. His hands automatically shot to his head, leaving the steering wheel free.

Larkin reached across and grabbed hold of the wheel with his right hand, twisting it sharply to the left. The car veered.

'No–' gasped Ringo, foot still on the accelerator. He stuck one of his paw-like hands on the wheel, trying to steady it, but the blow had given him double vision. That, and the pain, clouded him. He yanked the wheel to the right, keeping his foot down, inadvertently aiming the car towards the white ceramic brick wall of the arch.

Ringo realised what was happening, shrieked and attempted to regain control of the wheel. Before metal could make contact with stone, he managed to spin it to the left, narrowly avoiding impact.

He hadn't managed to slow the car down, though, so with a high-pitched Diamanda

Galas squeal and a stink of burning rubber, the car flew round a corner on two wheels, narrowly avoiding an oncoming van, and raced down another archway.

Ringo, eyes blinking rapidly, head pounding, now had the wheel more or less under control.

'Stupid bastard,' he said, 'you could have killed us both.'

He reached across with his left arm, trying to pull the baseball bat from Larkin's grasp. Larkin was having none of it. With his right hand he grabbed hold of Ringo's fist, felt the biker's powerful fingers trying to grip his own, bend them back, snap them. With his left hand, Larkin swung the bat as hard as he could onto Ringo's outstretched forearm, connecting with his wrist. Ringo screamed, but didn't let go. Larkin did it again. There was a cracking noise and Ringo withdrew his arm quickly.

'Bastard!' he yelled and stretched his foot out for the brake.

Larkin knew that even wounded, Ringo would best him one on one. He had more of a chance if the car was moving and Ringo was at the wheel.

Before Ringo could stop the car, Larkin lunged at him again, this time going for his balls. His hand now only an anger-driven machine of bone, muscle and adrenalin, he grabbed them and, through the filthy, greasy denim, gave them as hard a twist as he could.

Ringo let out a shriek and, on impulse reaction, stuck his legs out rigid. His right foot hit the accelerator and, with a roar and a pull, the car flew forwards again, speedo needle climbing higher.

Ringo, squirming in pain, tried vainly to prise Larkin's hand off, but his left hand was now useless and his right was needed for steering the car. Larkin gripped harder, twisted all the more.

Neither of them had control of the car now as it swung madly from one side of the road to the other, speed never dropping below eighty.

With his free hand, Larkin wedged one end of the baseball bat under Ringo's groin, the other on the accelerator pedal. He then straightened himself up, gripping Ringo's balls all the time.

Ringo flailed ineffectually at Larkin with his left hand, but Larkin caught it easily and gave Ringo's wrist a sharp twist. Ringo writhed in his seat as if he'd been hooked up to electrodes. His arms waved about uselessly. He looked like he couldn't make up his mind what to do first; get Larkin off, get the car stopped. He seemed to vacillate between the two, pain clouding his reasoning.

'Not much fun when you're on the receiving end, is it you cunt?' shouted Larkin at the top of his lungs.

Another top-register squeal from Ringo, another bitter, acrid smell of burning rubber; the car rounded another corner. They were out of the arches now. On the left side of the road was a council estate, redbrick flats surrounded by threadbare grass and stunted, anorexic trees. A pile of black bin bags at the side of the road loomed up in front of them. Now or never, thought Larkin. One way or another it was going to end.

Letting Ringo's left arm drop, but keeping his other hand gripping Ringo's balls, Larkin opened the passenger side door.

'See you in hell, fucker,' he said, reached up, and gave one last yank at the wheel.

The car pulled violently towards the left, nearer to the grass on Larkin's side, almost mounting the pavement, and bearing down very quickly on the first of a row of kerbside parked cars.

Larkin dived out, into the air, into the unknown. He was aiming for the bin bags, but he honestly didn't know if he would live or die.

He hit the bags, the force of the impact causing him to keep moving, dragging them with him, spilling rotten garbage all over the place, covering him as well as the pavement. He was hoping but not expecting them to absorb and slow down his motion.

The Jag, still at top speed, ploughed straight into the first parked car.

Larkin lay there on the hard-packed, garbage-strewn earth, breathing heavily. He assessed the damage.

He was alive, that much he knew, but he had yet to determine how alive. He tried to move and found nothing but pain down his left side. He rolled over onto his right, struggling to get up. As he put his elbow on the ground to gain leverage, a sudden pain whizzed round his upper body, as if he'd been wrapped in electrified barbed wire. He lay back down again, thinking: my ribs have gone.

He flopped back, gasping, then slowly tried again. This time he managed to make it to a sitting position. His right arm, beyond some pain in his fingers, seemed not too bad. His left arm, hanging twisted and useless at his side, told a different story. One he couldn't think about yet. He laboriously pulled himself up on to his knees, looked over at the Jag.

The front end had been completely concertinaed into a parked Cavalier. Ringo had gone through the windscreen and smashed into the back of the stationary car, spiderwebbing its glass into an artful fractal. If he wasn't dead, he soon would be.

Larkin managed to make it, painfully, to

his feet. As soon as he stood, his body gave way and he was back on the ground again. His left ankle hurt when he applied pressure to it and the pain in his left side seemed, unsurprisingly, to emanate from his shoulder and twisted arm. Judging by the way it hung uselessly at his side, it had been broken, dislocated or, at a worse guess, completely shattered.

He managed to pull himself to his knees, tried to drag himself across to the car. He was amazed it hadn't blown up. Since his knowledge of car mechanics came first and foremost from Hollywood that's what he would have expected. But it hadn't happened. Yet.

Suddenly, there came a mighty sound, like a sonic boom accompanied by an intense heat on his face. The force knocked Larkin onto his back. He propped himself on his right arm, looked up. The Jag was in flames, the fire rapidly spreading to the Cavalier. Sometimes the movies do get it right, he thought.

He made one last attempt to move and couldn't. It was no good; he had been through too much in too short a space of time and his body wouldn't function any more. He knew he should try to get away, hide. The fire would soon attract attention and people would want to know what he was doing there. Too many questions.

But he couldn't move. He couldn't even keep his eyes open, they were that heavy. He closed them. Then there was a sound. Someone talking to him.

He opened them again and saw a face looking down on him. The face was battered but familiar. It was saying something to him, but he couldn't make out what. He was too tired.

Larkin began to slip away. Just as he was passing the last outpost of consciousness he managed to have one final coherent thought. He knew who the face belonged to.

Ralph Sickert.

Part Three

Part Three

The Dream Corridor

The corridor was strip-lit, fluorescent tubes flickering overhead, bad connections. Bare, institutional walls, plain, stark. Lit by random, constant, strobing, the hall seemed neverending.

In front of Larkin was a small boy, about eight or nine, scruffy-looking, with the kind of clothes and haircut that went out two decades ago. He was walking quickly. He turned to look at Larkin and the overhead flicker caught his face. He had a cheeky grin, bordering on insolence. He raised his hand to beckon, to keep Larkin walking, and Larkin couldn't help noticing it was heavily, but raggedly, bandaged. Blood-stained, with only the thumbs exposed. The boy seemed agitated, in a hurry to be somewhere. He beckoned again. Larkin followed.

The boy stopped in front of a set of double doors. Making sure Larkin had caught up with him he pushed one door open, awkwardly holding it back for Larkin to enter. Once Larkin had entered, the boy followed.

The room they entered was dark, cathedral-still. In the centre were two mortuary slabs, side by side, with two sheet-covered bodies lying on them. One adult-sized, one child-sized. Larkin tried not to look at them. Instead he looked at the boy.

'What's with the bandages?' he asked.

The boy gave a cheeky grin. 'Every time I was naughty, or when I said something they didn't like, they cut off one of my fingers.'

He held up his hands, shook the bloody, bandaged stumps. The bandages partially unravelled. 'I said a lot of things they didn't like!' He laughed as if it was all a game, waggled his exposed thumbs. 'But look on the bright side. They let me keep these. They're not all bad.'

'Who are they?' asked Larkin.

'The ones who don't like my words against them.'

Larkin looked away from the boy towards the bodies. He didn't lift the sheet up.

'How did they die?' Larkin asked.

'Words,' replied the boy. 'Wrong words. Wrong place.' He crossed to the biggest body, put the sheet between his mitts. 'Want to see?'

'Will it bring them back if I look?'

'No,' said the boy. 'But it'll prove to you they're gone.'

'I know they're gone. I have accepted it,' replied Larkin. 'What I can't accept is that they've gone and he's still walking around.'

The boy shrugged, held up his stumps again. 'These have gone,' he said, waving his stumps, then waggled his thumbs. 'But these are still here.'

He gave his cheeky grin, laughed, and Larkin woke up.

Candleland Revisited

Larkin opened his eyes, looked around. He was alive, that much he knew, but beyond that, he was disorientated. He didn't know what day it was, what time it was, or where he was. He was lost.

His head felt groggy, his thoughts vague, but he forced himself to concentrate and gather his senses. He was in a bed, but it was either an unusually hard bed, or he'd been there so long his body had gone numb. His head was resting on what felt like a very thin pillow and there was a sterile smell in his nostrils.

He blinked his eyes, looked up. A pale, sloping ceiling met his gaze. From this he deduced that he was in an attic room, but not Faye's. What he could see of the room matched the smell. Clean, bright and airy but impersonal. Another couple of beds occupied the bare-boarded floor space with small, mismatching cupboards at the side of each. Not a hospital, then.

Needing to find out more, he tried to sit up. A sharp, stabbing pain travelled immediately round his torso. It felt like a charge from a cattle prod. Gently, he lowered himself back down again.

Larkin decided to take it slower, one thing at a time. First, a body inventory. Gingerly, he flexed, lifted, tensed and untensed. Apart from his painful torso, he felt a similar sensation of a few hundred volts jolting through his frame in his left ankle and his left shoulder and arm. Both were too painful to move more than a centimetre or so. On his right side he felt, then saw, a tube running from his wrist to an IV bag suspended from a portable metal frame.

On the wall at the right side of the bed was a red switch with a plaque underneath which read: Please Ring For Attention. Larkin pressed it. He felt like some attention.

While he waited for someone to arrive, he tried to think where he might be, how he had got there. He closed his eyes. All he saw was a boy with bloody, bandaged hands, opening a door to... His eyes burst open again. That wasn't a memory, that was a dream, a nightmare. He tried to forget it and force his mind back further. It was difficult, nothing was very clear. He could see flashes of images, hear snippets of sentences, none pleasant but all meaningless, with deep, black pools in between. It was as if he had reached blackout drunk stage while on a very nasty bender.

He remembered pain ... heat ... fire ... rage ... and something else. Someone else.

At that moment there was a knock at the door.

'Yeah?' Larkin managed to croak. His voice sounded rusty, as if his vocal chords had seized up from disuse.

The door opened and in walked Darren.

'Oh, you're back in the land of the living, then?' Darren aimed for flippant but it was clear he was relieved.

Larkin grunted.

'I'll go and get Mickey.' Darren turned and exited, leaving Larkin alone once more.

Not for long, though. Darren soon returned, and with him was Mickey Falco.

Mickey Falco smiled as he entered, puffing and red-faced, and reached for a straight-backed chair. He dragged it to the side of Larkin's bed and plonked himself in it with a great sigh of relief.

'Those stairs,' he said, getting his breath back, 'be the death of me. So, how you feelin'?'

'Confused,' managed Larkin. 'Hurt.'

'Yeah? Well you're lucky to be here.'

'D'you mean here here?' asked Larkin, his voice creaking and drawling like Lee Marvin at the wrong speed. 'Or here anywhere?'

Mickey Falco smiled. 'D'you want anythin'? A drink?'

'Whatever.'

'I'll have the same, Darren,' said Mickey Falco.

Darren nodded and left, shutting the door behind him.

Larkin gestured feebly with his right hand. 'Chest hurts, left arm, left foot. Headache.'

Mickey Falco nodded. 'That's about what we reckoned. We've had a doctor look you over. We have a couple of local ones do voluntary work for us. She said you had bruised ribs, twisted ankle, dislocated shoulder and concussion. Other than that, right as rain.'

'And I'm in Candleland, I take it?'

'You are.'

'How long have I been here? How long have I been out?'

'Couple of days now. You were unconscious when they brought you in. You've been that way until now. Any longer and we'd have been worried, put you in hospital.'

'Why didn't you?'

'Because we thought we could cope with you here. And we didn't want to involve the police, of course.'

'Where was I?' asked Larkin. 'How did I get there? How did I get here?'

'You were in Bermondsey. There was a car crash and it looks like you threw yourself clear. The other guy wasn't so lucky.'

At that, the memory unfolded. Larkin fighting with Ringo in the car, diving out. He remembered lying on the ground, litter strewn around him, in pain, too spent to move. There was something else. Someone else.

'Ralph Sickert!' gasped Larkin. 'I saw Ralph Sickert!'

Mickey Falco nodded, expressionless. Larkin tried to think, couldn't come to any conclusions.

'I don't understand,' Larkin said. He felt tired again. But there was something he had to do.

'Charlie Rook,' he said sitting up. The immediate jolt of pain forced him down again. The quickness of the movement had left him feeling suddenly exhausted. 'We've got to...'

'All in good time,' said Mickey Falco. 'We've got to get you well again first. Then we'll deal with him.'

There was a knock at the door.

'Ah, here comes Darren with the tea,' said Mickey Falco. 'Good, I'm parched.'

Mickey Falco stood up to open the door. By the time he had returned to the bedside with a cup of tea, Larkin was asleep.

When Larkin next came round, some hours later, he was much clearer headed. He called for Mickey Falco. Asked him to explain.

'My name's down as Diana's next of kin,' Mickey Falco said. 'She's got nobody else. So when the ambulance arrived and she was taken in to hospital, they contacted me.'

'How is she?' asked Larkin.

'She's ... a fighter.' Mickey Falco gave a smile edged with sadness. Larkin didn't press the issue. Instead he asked another question.

'So how did you come to be following me?'

'We weren't,' said Mickey Falco. 'When we saw the state Diana was in, we thought Charlie Rook must have had something to do with it. So we sent someone to check out his place in Savage Gardens. Ralph volunteered to go. He saw you being hauled out of there and followed. And a good job for you that he did.'

'So Ralph Sickert ... what? Saved my life?' asked Larkin, incredulously.

'Looks that way,' said Mickey Falco with a grim smile. 'Life's never black and white, is it?'

'But Mickey...' It was too much. Larkin's head was beginning to hurt again. Mickey Falco's words had confused him. 'How do you know Charlie Rook? Why was Ralph Sickert following him? What's going on, Mickey?'

Mickey Falco smiled. 'Like I said, get yourself well again and we'll talk. Till then...' He shrugged, gave a small smile. 'Well, you're older than the ones we usually get, but you're welcome to stay here. Get yourself mended. In fact, I think this might be the safest place for you.'

'Does anybody know I'm here, Mickey? Have you told anyone?'

'No. But your mate Andy came round the day after you'd been brought in. We told him Diana had given you another lead to follow and that you'd gone.'

'Why?'

'In case Charlie Rook was following him. So he couldn't find you.'

'What's going on, Mickey?' asked Larkin again.

'I checked you out, by the way,' said Mickey from the door. 'Word I got was you was OK. One of the good guys.'

'Mickey…' said Larkin.

'Just get yourself well,' Mickey Falco said, and closed the door on the way out.

Two days later Larkin was sitting up. The pain in his ribs had subsided to a dullish ache and he was able to move his left shoulder, even flex his hand. He hadn't chanced standing on his foot yet.

Larkin's initial concerns about his situation were beginning to slip away. He wasn't happy about being kept in the dark, but Mickey Falco seemed on the level; he had a feeling things would eventually become clear. His body also needed to heal and they were doing their best to look after him. So, since he didn't appear to be in any danger, he decided to trust his instinct and go with the flow.

Darren had left a stack of magazines for him by the side of the bed. All lifestyle issues and movie trivia, things Larkin found less than enthralling, but the man had tried and Larkin was grateful. He had also left his mobile phone for him to use, as Larkin had told him he needed to make a phone call.

He keyed in the number, listened to the ringing tone. Faye answered.

He hesitated, then spoke.

'Stephen! Thank God you're alright! We've been worried sick about you. We were ready to go to the police–'

'Don't do that.'

Faye's voice became grave. 'Are you in trouble, Stephen?'

Larkin sighed. 'No Faye, I'm not. I was injured, though–' Faye gasped. Larkin carried on. '–but I'm OK now. I can't tell you where I am, though.'

'Why not?'

'Just trust me, Faye. I've got to stay low for a little while. I haven't found Karen yet, but tell Henry I'm still looking. I might be on to something, but I can't say for definite. But don't worry, I'm OK.'

'When you didn't come back the other night ... well, Andy told me what had happened. Who you'd met. That must have

272

been awful, meeting the man who...' Her words trailed off.

'It's not as simple as that,' he said.

'What d'you mean?' Faye asked.

'I'll tell you when I see you.'

'OK, right.' Faye didn't push it. Her voice dropped when she spoke next. She obviously wasn't alone. Larkin could guess who else was there. 'I thought at first you were staying away because of ... you know.'

'Yeah,' replied Larkin, his voice deliberately blank.

Faye paused, as if expecting more. Larkin didn't speak. All there was between them was digital static.

'But then,' Faye continued, voice conspiratorially low, 'Andy went to check out the place you'd gone to and found–' Her voice began to rise. The concern in it no less heartfelt but much less personal. '– it had been ransacked! The woman who lived there was in hospital fighting for her life, the police were quizzing everyone in the street. Andy didn't hang around.'

'I'll bet,' replied Larkin.

'He went to that refuge place–'

'I know. Tell him to stay away from there. They can't help him.'

'Alright,' said Faye, sounding slightly confused.

'Look, don't worry,' he said. 'I'm OK.'

Faye's voice dropped again. 'Really?' So

much was loaded into that one word.

Larkin sighed. He was nowhere near together enough to give the answer she wanted to hear. One way or another.

'Yeah,' was all he could manage. 'Look, I'll be in touch when I can. But it might not be immediately. Tell Henry not to worry.'

They made their goodbyes, cut the connection.

Over the next few days, Larkin managed to put himself back together, both physically and mentally.

One of the refuge's local volunteer doctors popped in every couple of days to see how his physical injuries were doing. His shoulder was back in place and holding well, his ankle could have pressure applied to it and his ribs were mending nicely. Larkin felt tender and, as the doctor was always reminding him, lucky.

On one occasion the doctor, a young, cheerful Asian man, asked him about the scar in the centre of his right palm.

Larkin smiled wryly. 'That was from where I went poking my nose into something else I was told didn't concern me.'

The doctor smiled. 'Do you make a habit of doing this?'

Larkin gave a sardonic laugh. 'I've made a career of it,' he said.

Mentally, the scars were taking longer to heal.

Once his strength had returned, he tried to get up and move about but found he had no clothes beyond the pyjamas Candleland had supplied him with. Darren was summoned.

'Where's my clothes?' Larkin asked him.

'We had to destroy them,' Darren replied.

Larkin opened his mouth to complain, but Darren got there first.

'If you will jump out of moving cars and go rolling around in rubbish heaps,' he said, 'what d'you expect? They were wrecked. You couldn't have worn them again.'

'What?' Larkin replied aghast. 'Even my leather jacket?'

'Oh come on,' said Darren, getting camper by the minute, 'it was falling apart anyway. You just gave it that final push.'

'But I've had that jacket for years.'

'You could tell.'

'And what about the rest?'

'You mean check shirts and old Levis? Darling, that's so grunge, so 1992.'

Larkin sighed. It felt like he'd just lost a part of himself. His leather jacket was his favourite item of clothing. His body armour. Now it was gone.

'Don't worry,' said Darren, sensing Larkin's unhappiness. 'Give me your sizes and some money and I'll get you some new stuff.'

'Can I trust you?' asked Larkin, warily.

Darren gave him a look. 'What, you think I'll come back with leather chaps and a biker's cap? Credit me with some taste.'

Darren was as good as his word. The next day, Larkin was out of bed, showered, shaved and dressed. The clothes wouldn't have been his first choice but they fitted and suited him well. He had a mixture of cargo trousers, boots, trainers, sweatshirts, T-shirts and a couple of fleeces. Simple, utilitarian, yet stylish.

'There,' said Darren. 'I wouldn't be ashamed to be seen out with you now.'

Larkin looked at him, eyebrows raised.

'Don't worry,' replied Darren, 'I wasn't making a pass at you.'

'Did I say anything?'

'You didn't have to. Honestly, you breeders. Always flattering yourselves.'

Larkin smiled. Darren had a point. He did look good.

Larkin's movements were confined to certain areas of the refuge and bound by certain times. He kept himself separate from the day-to-day activities in the rest of Candleland and took no part in what was going on beneath him. Mickey Falco wanted it that way and Larkin respected that. After all, he didn't want to be seen and they had work to do downstairs. Larkin also imposed restraints on himself. Sickert was somewhere in the building. And, whether he'd saved his life or not, a concept Larkin still couldn't get his head round, he didn't want to see him. The last thing he wanted, and trusted himself in, was a confrontation.

Even though he was able to move his body quite well now, Larkin spent hours in his room, lying on the bed. He was trying to clarify and quantify all the recent events, put them into perspective.

It was night. He lay on the bed, fully clothed, thinking. Apart from the glow of his bedside lamp, the room was in darkness. He was looking around the room, trying to measure the effect of the light. It glinted off and shone on some surfaces, cast dark, impenetrable shadows in other places, was absorbed and not returned in others. There was no black and no white. Just various shades of grey.

The refuge had a steady silence, almost a hum. Although it operated twenty-four hours a day, it usually became quieter in the evening. Larkin preferred to move around the place at night. It had a warm, cocoon-like feel to it. A real safe house. A house that felt safe to be in.

And, Larkin had discovered, Sickert wasn't there at nights.

It was a strange, unsettling feeling to be in

the same house, at the same time, as the murderer of your wife and child, and then to be powerless to do anything about it. Sickert had a siren pull on Larkin and he became conscious of all his actions while he knew Sickert was in the place.

Some nights, after a couple of belts from the whisky bottle, part of Larkin wanted to go down, see him, talk, but when he was sober the thought gave him butterflies. It was like having the long-lost love of his life from an unresolved and perhaps unfinished relationship living separately under the same roof. A lover he desperately wanted to see again, just to reassess, find out if there was still a spark to keep things going or whether to just end things for good and move on.

But he didn't. He stayed in his room and, thanks to Darren, read about Bruce Willis or the latest form and function Soho coffee bar. He was a virtual prisoner upstairs while Sickert was free to move around downstairs. Larkin wasn't blind to the irony.

He thought of other things. Sometimes he would sit and replay the car ride with Ringo. The pain, the rage ... all the pieces of that night had come back to him now.

He had been responsible for Ringo's death. How did that make him feel? If he was honest, nothing. He had searched and searched but he could find no guilt, no remorse. The man had been a stone-eyed professional sadist and killer. And Larkin would have joined his list of victims at some point. Perhaps Ringo had had a side that Larkin didn't see, perhaps he had been kind to animals or generous to children's charities. But Larkin doubted it. Ringo had been a remorseless killer. Irredeemable and not worth crying over. But, Larkin had to admit, he hadn't been born like that, he had been created. The time for tears, for help, should have been then. It was too late now.

As Larkin lay there watching the shadows, imbibing the whisky, drawing from the stillness of the place, there was a knock at the door.

'Yeah?' asked Larkin without moving.

'S'me. Can I come in?' Mickey Falco.

Larkin said that was fine and Mickey entered. He was wearing his usual suit and lumberjack shirt combination augmented by an overcoat and a knotted paisley scarf. He was leaning needfully on his stick, as if drawing energy from it.

'You not gone home yet?' asked Larkin.

'I think it's time to talk,' replied Mickey Falco. 'Diana. She's dead.'

Campfire Tales

Larkin pulled himself upright. 'Aw, no...'

Mickey Falco's whole body seemed heavier, as if a great weight was pressing down on him. He fell into a chair at Larkin's bedside. Without waiting to be asked he took a glass from the bedside cabinet and helped himself to a generous slug from Larkin's bottle, sighed, shook his head. The weight seemed to increase.

'Yeah.' His eyes were wet. 'We lost her tonight. That's where I've been, the hospital.'

'What happened?' asked Larkin, as quietly as he could.

'Her surgery, her medication, the injuries on top of that... It was too much. They said there was some infection, they operated...' He took another swig. 'She slipped into a coma, then...' He shrugged, put his head down. Trying to keep it bottled, trying not to cry.

Larkin said nothing. There was nothing he could say.

Eventually, Mickey looked up, in control again. Just. 'What a life. What a life she had...'

Larkin again said nothing. Mickey took

that as a signal to continue.

'She started off as a boy, but you knew that. A very pretty boy, apparently. Her family sold her to a brothel when she was about nine or ten. She was vague on the date, said she couldn't remember.' He smiled sadly. 'I keep calling her she. Can't think of her any other way.' He sighed. 'From some village at the arse end of Thailand to a Bangkok brothel. Poor little soul.' He shook his head, shuddered as if the memory were his, then continued. 'Eventually she got too old. The brothel owner sold her to another brothel, this time in Germany. Then on to Amsterdam. By this time she'd had enough. They'd confiscated her passport so she couldn't leave, but she managed to persuade this punter, some Englishman who was there for the weekend, to stow her away in the boot of his car on the ferry. That's how she came to England.'

'How did you get to meet her?' asked Larkin, genuinely interested.

'This guy treated her like a slave, made her life hell. She managed to run away, found her way to us.'

Mickey Falco took another drink, found he had drained his glass, topped it up from the bottle. 'She was in a real state. A transvestite by this time, mutilating herself. We referred her to a psychologist, sorted her with somewhere to live, got her started.' He shook his head.

'That's the part that gets me, the bit I can't grasp,' he said. 'She had such a will to live, to succeed. She remade herself. Even changed her gender. Remarkable.'

Larkin thought of her room the first time he'd seen it. He nodded.

'She was one of Candleland's biggest success stories, I thought. She kept in touch, helped others find their way here...' Mickey shook his head again. 'I know she could be difficult, stroppy even, but that was just a front. A defence mechanism.' He sighed, close to losing control again. 'I just can't believe she's gone...'

Larkin nodded and sipped his drink. Hearing about Diana had certainly put his thoughts about Ringo into perspective.

'Anyway,' said Mickey, 'I didn't mean to burden you. I just thought you might want to know.'

'Thank you,' said Larkin. 'I appreciate it.'

The two men sat, casting large shadows around the small room, slowly sipping. Eventually Mickey nodded to himself, control re-established. 'So,' he said, 'how you feeling?'

Larkin gave a faint smile. 'Oh, you know, I've got my magazines, my booze, who could ask for anything more?'

'Yeah, I know it's boring,' said Mickey, 'but it's for the best. I hear the whole thing, the car crash, has been passed off as an accident. Careless driving, traces of cocaine in the car and the body, an' all that. But I've also heard that Charlie Rook's asked some of his tame coppers to look into it.'

'You've heard?' asked Larkin. 'How have you heard?'

'Tame coppers of my own,' said Mickey Falco with a small degree of pride. 'Anyway, in practical terms, it means stay here as long as you like. They'll be looking for you everywhere else.'

Larkin nodded. 'Look, Mickey. We have to talk. About Charlie Rook–'

'Yeah, yeah, I know. And we will.' He sighed. 'We'll have that talk soon. But not tonight, eh?' His face looked pained.

'OK.' Larkin nodded.

Mickey sighed, took a swig. 'So,' he said, 'you healin' alright, then?'

'Yeah,' replied Larkin. 'I can move my arm, put my weight on my foot for long periods and my ribs only ache when I laugh. Lucky I don't laugh much.'

Mickey gave a faint smile. He went on to talk about organising Diana's funeral. It sounded like something he'd had plenty of practice at. Larkin mentioned this.

'Yeah,' replied Mickey, his gravely bass voice rumbling over the word like an articulated lorry. 'More than I care to remember, unfortunately. Occupational hazard.'

Larkin nodded. 'So,' he said, 'since we seem to be in the mood for talking, how did you get this job?'

Mickey laughed. 'You mean I don't seem like the obvious choice to run a place like this?'

'Something like that.'

'Well I'm not. And since we've got nothing else to do and the bottle's still half full, I'll tell you. But I'm warnin' you, it's a long one.'

'I'm not going anywhere,' said Larkin.

So the two men sat huddled in the dark room, warmed and lighted only by the bedside light and the whisky bottle, talking away the night. Mickey told Larkin the story of how he came to be at Candleland, which was also the story of his life.

Mickey explained that he had been born into a family of second-generation Italian immigrants in Dalston, East London. A family used to living on the wrong side of the law.

Mickey smiled. 'I was trouble, I was a tearaway, restless. Couldn't keep still.' He had found his options limited by his background and environment, so he drifted into a life of crime.

'You've got to remember, though,' he said, pointing with his whisky glass, 'this was the time of the Krays, the Richardsons. It was glamorous to be a gangster. It was also a damn sight more lucrative than anythin' else you were offered.'

'You mean the hours were good, the suits were sharp, that it?' asked Larkin.

Mickey smiled. 'Somethin' like that. Anyway, I soon found out that glamour an' reality have little in common. I went to work for this London family – I won't say which one – an' it was a real eye-opener, I can tell you. They were into anythin' an' everythin' they could make money out of.' He leaned forward to emphasise the word. 'Anythin'. Girls, drugs, porn, protection, you name it, they did it. An' they didn't care how they did it. An' I did it with them.' He gave a bitter laugh. 'All that about bein' gentlemen? Only fightin' their own kind? Bollocks.'

Larkin nodded. As Mickey's memory travelled back, so did his accent. Any refinement was stripped away, his tongue became native.

Mickey continued. He told Larkin how he became good at what he did and how successful he was at it, moving quickly up the ranks until he was running a few things.

'But was I 'appy? No. It was violent, sordid, an' depressin'. Not glamorous. Glamour belonged in fuckin' 'ollywood. An' then everythin' changed.' He stopped talking.

'How?' asked Larkin, coaxing him along.

Mickey paused, searching for the correct tone. He found it and continued. 'I won't go into the details,' he said, with no malice in his voice, 'but I was set up, stung.'

The police carted him away, stuck him in a cell and went to work on him. He said nothing, gave up no one.

'When they saw that wasn't workin' they offered me all sorts of deals, immunity if I grassed up me mates, new identities, the lot.' He stopped again, lost in remembrance.

'And did you take them up on their offer?'

'Only the new identity. I said I wanted to be Sean Connery.' He laughed at the bravado of it, but his eyes betrayed a different, darker memory.

'Anyway, when those bastards got the message that I wasn't talking they charged me. Brought me to court, found me guilty, gave me six years.' He sniffed, took a swallow of whisky. 'Could have been worse.

'But prison, that changed everythin' for me. You see, I'd always been bright, always loved readin'. Not somethin' I wanted to let on to my old associates about, but now that I was banged up for twenty-three out of twenty-four hours of the day, it was somethin' I had the time for. Even did a degree. Sociology. An' you know what? I bloody loved it. It made me see everythin', what I'd done, where I came from, the lot, in a whole new light. It confirmed all the things I'd thought and felt, but just buried. For the first time in my life, I felt like I was in the right.

'Now, somethin' else happened to me in prison. Just as profound. I became a Christian.' Seeing the look on Larkin's face, Mickey smiled. 'That's a turn-up for the books, innit?'

'I'd be lying if I said it wasn't.'

'Well maybe not one the Church of England would recognise, but Christian all the same.'

'I've heard a lot about prisoners being born again,' said Larkin. 'And if you'll excuse my cynicism, I've never been convinced.'

Mickey Falco smiled. 'Neither was I till it happened to me. I used to be sceptical. I used to think it was your "Get Out Of Jail Free" card. You know, get God, smile at the parole board, keep your nose clean, an' off you went. But since it happened to me, well...' He smiled. 'Let's just say I'm more of a believer now.'

Mickey declined to go into details of his conversion, because he said it would make him sound preachy. Larkin was grateful for that.

'An' I hate bein' preachy.' Mickey leaned forward, well into his story now. 'Now I know it's not for everyone, but the way I look at it, I needed a new code to live by, an' I found them at the right time. I've stuck by those rules, an' they've been good to me. That's all I have to say about it.'

'I've got to admit,' said Larkin, 'you don't strike me as a typical Christian. You swear, you drink...'

Mickey smiled, gave a look heavenwards. 'The big fella doesn't mind. He knows I'm under a bit of stress.'

Mickey had then become friendly with some Christian volunteer visitors who ran various projects in socially deprived areas. Since his parole was coming up and he was a model prisoner by this time, he was allowed out on day-release.

'Like Ralph Sickert,' said Larkin, edgily.

Mickey looked at him, eye to eye. 'Yes. Like Ralph Sickert.' He didn't bite, just got on with his story. 'Anyway, I worked somewhere not unlike this place and when I was released and came back to London, I started work here, Candleland.'

'So what made you go in for this line of work?'

'Payback,' said Mickey. 'Pure an' simple. I used to be a bastard, I hated what was done to me an' what I did to others. This was a chance to start again. Do somethin' useful. That's why I'm 'ere.'

He stopped talking, poured himself another drink. 'But that's not the end. Because my old associates found out I was back and paid me a visit. They knew I hadn't talked so that was a big plus in my favour, but then I had to convince them I wasn't a threat to their operations, that I had retired and started a new career.'

Mickey's accent, Larkin noticed, had come up to date along with the story.

'They told me no one retires unless it's in a box, but since I'd kept my mouth shut, not turned Queen's evidence, they'd make an exception in my case. But still they had to leave me with something. A warning not to cross them in the future.'

'And what was that?' asked Larkin.

Mickey tapped his right leg with the cane. 'This. Shattered. It healed eventually, but the best I can hope for is to always walk with a stick.'

'And the worst?' asked Larkin.

Mickey's face was blank. 'I don't want to think about that.' He took another swig. 'So anyway, I never saw them again. Most of them, anyway. I'm still in touch with a few. Not above usin' them for a bit of strongarm when the need arises.'

'When does the need arise?' asked Larkin.

'Oh, you know,' said Mickey lightly. 'If there's a problem with a pimp or an abusive parent. If someone needs sortin'.'

'Doesn't that conflict with your Christian principles?' asked Larkin with a sly smile.

Mickey smiled back. 'No. You see, it's all a question of what you believe to be the greater moral good.'

'Dodgy argument,' said Larkin. 'Didn't Stalin say something similar?'

'That's not what I meant an' you know it,' said Mickey. 'It's an everyday problem we all have to cope with. Not just Christians. Not just me. Everyone. Even you.'

Larkin nodded, put in his place. 'And then you were put in charge of Candleland,' he said.

'And here I am now,' said Mickey. 'Loud and proud.' He sat back and drained the last of his whisky.

His accent and intonation, Larkin noticed, was now a mixture of rough and smooth, his two worlds sitting comfortably together, able to straddle both with ease.

'That's quite a story,' Larkin said.

'Yeah.' Mickey rubbed his eyes, yawned and stretched. 'I'm out of it.' He stood up. 'Sorry to have gone on so much. But thanks for listening. I wasn't in the mood for going home.'

'I don't blame you. Anyway, it's been good to have someone to talk to.'

'I'll come back tomorrow night,' said Mickey. 'You can bore me then.'

Larkin smiled. 'Right,' he said. Then his face clouded, became serious. 'Look, about Diana. If there's anything I can do, arrangements, money, whatever.'

'Thanks,' said Mickey. 'But you already

did what you could to help her. She wouldn't have made it this far if you hadn't been there to help.'

'If I hadn't been there in the first place she might have been alive now.'

'Don't blame yourself,' said Mickey. 'You can play that game of "What If" right back to the womb. It won't get you anywhere. We're all responsible for our actions. And you tried to help. Thank you.'

Mickey stuck out his hand. Larkin shook.

'I'll try and creep out softly so I don't wake any of our guests downstairs,' Mickey said. 'But I'll see you tomorrow. An' this time I'll supply the whisky.'

They said their goodnights and Mickey left, looking lighter but still burdened, closing the door in what was, for such a rough-hewn man, a surprisingly gentle way.

Mickey was as good as his word. The next night he was there, bottle in hand. He sat down, twisted the cap, found two glasses and started pouring.

'Make yourself at home, Mickey,' Larkin said needlessly.

Mickey passed him a glass. 'Your turn tonight,' he said.

'Thought I might get out of that,' said Larkin.

'There's this bookshop in Paris,' said Mickey, 'that lets you stay there if you're travelling an' you're skint. All the owner asks is that you tell him your life story. We're like that here.'

'Well,' said Larkin, taking a large gulp of whisky, 'I suppose you could say things are either pre or post your mate downstairs.'

'You mean Ralph?'

'Right.' Larkin started from the beginning. His working-class upbringing in the North East, his politicisation by his left-wing father. His brief stay at college, his early writing career, taking fuel and inspiration from the punk movement. 'I tried the approach they had to music with investigative journalism. You know: destroy, destabilise, bring down the government. That sort of thing. Or at least make people think.' He laughed regretfully. 'It didn't work, of course, but I attracted the attention of people in London with a large chequebook, and off I went.'

'Were you sellin' out?' asked Mickey. 'Is that how it felt?'

'Not immediately. This was the Eighties, Thatcher and all that. I couldn't wait to have a go at her on as broad a canvas as I'd been given. Not that it mattered in the long run.'

'And then you did your piece on Ralph?'

Larkin thought for a moment, deciding how much to reveal. Mickey had been straight with him, he would do the same in return. So he took a gulp of whisky and explained how he became a victim of his own success, the kind of person he was supposed to hate. Shallow, vain, obsessed by money. Coked out of his brains most of the time, more concerned with being seen at the right parties than writing. He gave a short, mirthless laugh. 'I was a monster. I was the enemy.'

He stopped talking, lost in the past. Mickey said nothing, just sat in silent encouragement.

'But,' said Larkin, continuing, 'I still kept writing. If not biting the hand that fed me, then taking little nips at it.'

'And you were married by this time, yeah?'

'Yeah. Sophie was a model. She was so beautiful I couldn't believe she was interested in some working-class kid like me. So I married her. Course, everyone said she only ever wanted me for my money, but I didn't believe them.' He sighed. 'Now we'll never know.'

He knocked back the whisky, poured another one.

'And then there was little Joe. My son. And I thought I was having it all. Wife, kid, hugely successful career, as much booze and drugs as I wanted, women lining up to shag me. Ah yes, the world and its legs were open to me and I just dived right in.'

Larkin stopped for another drink. His hands were trembling. He felt his words were leaving him naked, exposed. He could stop, of course, but he didn't want to. He had to tell all the story, exorcise the ghosts.

'And then there was Sickert,' he said.

Mickey nodded. He knew that part. 'And afterwards?'

'Afterwards?' Larkin gave a small, joyless, snort. 'I fell apart. Completely. Guilt moved in and never moved out. I saw things as they really had been. I'd been a bad husband to Sophie and she was well pissed off with my behaviour by this time. I'd been a crap father to Joe, hardly ever saw him, just stuck him with whichever nanny was working for us that week. And I'd been bad to myself. The booze was taking a toll, the coke was a serious problem. And I'd betrayed my work. My vision.'

'So what did you do?'

'Nothing,' spat Larkin. 'I just let the guilt do its thing. I thought of all the things I'd done wrong, the betrayals I'd made and where they'd got me. Then the guilt turned to self-pity, the self-pity to self-hatred. I hated myself. And I deserved to hate myself.' He paused and thought. 'And Sickert. I fucking hated him.'

Larkin drained his glass. Still, his hands trembled. 'I was like that for years. I dropped out of sight. I lost everything. And I never forgave.'

'Never forgave who?'

'Who d'you fuckin' think? Me,' said Larkin, breath juddering with emotion. 'Me.'

'Is that still the same now, then?' asked Mickey in a quiet voice.

'Course not,' Larkin retorted quickly. 'I'm writing again, aren't I?' he said, trying to build up confidence in his voice. He was shaking. 'It's sharper, more focused than it has been for years. I'm getting a buzz from it and it's picking up attention, getting an audience. Up in Newcastle.'

'So why are you down here, then?'

'You know why,' snapped Larkin defensively. 'I'm looking for Karen. I'm helping a friend.'

Mickey nodded slowly. 'And what else are you looking for?'

Larkin's head shot up, eyes wet and red-rimmed. 'Nothing! I'm not looking for fucking anything! What you on about?'

'Is there something you're trying to get away from, then?' asked Mickey quietly.

Larkin put his head down again, sat hunched in silence. Eventually his shoulders and chest began to heave spasmodically. He was crying.

Mickey Falco made no attempt to interfere. He just sat watching, empathising. Silent.

'Oh God,' said Larkin eventually, his voice hushed and choked, 'I'm really scared…'

He was acknowledging something for the first time.

Mickey said nothing.

'It could all turn to shit again...' said Larkin. 'Look what happened last time...'

'You're afraid of the future, of committing yourself to anything,' said Mickey eventually, his voice full of quiet authority. 'Because you won't let go of the past, yeah?'

'Don't,' said Larkin, quietly.

'You can't stop blaming yourself for what happened to Sophie and Joe? And if you do, try and move on, you'll feel like you're dishonouring their memory, is that it?'

'Leave it,' Larkin said, head still down, voice getting louder.

'We can all change,' said Mickey softly, 'we can all let go. Reinvent ourselves. But it takes guts to do that. You have to want to do it. And you wouldn't be dishonouring their memory. You'd just be breaking free—'

'Well that sounds fucking lovely, Mickey,' snarled Larkin, voice trembling. 'But that's easy for you to say.'

'Yeah,' said Mickey, his voice sharpening, 'it is easy to say. But it's bloody difficult to do. I know, I've done it. I've changed my whole life.'

'Good for you.'

'Yeah, good for me.' Mickey sat forward. 'And there were people in my past, victims of my former life, that I've wronged. But

I've just got to forgive and move on. It's not easy. But it can be done.'

Larkin sat in silence, head bowed.

Mickey opened his mouth to speak, hesitated, then decided to continue. 'Look at Ralph.'

Larkin's head shot up, eyes burning.

Mickey continued. 'He knows what he did was wrong. He's accepted that. But he's trying to change.'

'So he says,' spat Larkin.

'And we have to believe it,' replied Mickey softly. 'Take the other night. He saved your life.'

Larkin stood up. 'So what? So fucking what? He saved mine, took two away from me. Does that make us even?'

'He could have left you where you were,' continued Mickey, quietly. 'He had every right to, considering what you did to him the other day. How you messed up his face. But he chose to help you.'

Larkin paced round the room. It was small, he soon realised he had nowhere to go. 'Big fucking deal. You want me to stop feeling the way I do just cause of that?'

'No,' said Mickey. 'I just want to show you that people can change. Ralph says he's found faith, that he's making a new start. We have to take him at his word, give him a chance. Like someone did with me.'

Larkin sat down. 'Like you think I can do

with myself, is that what you mean?'

'Yeah.'

Larkin bowed his head, not wanting to make eye contact with Mickey. 'It's time you went, Mickey. I don't want to talk any more.'

Mickey stood up, slowly made his way to the door, and left.

Larkin sat on the bed, poured himself another whisky. His hands were still trembling. He took a big mouthful, swallowed and felt the liquid burn.

Mickey's words had left him feeling angry and confused. He clasped and unclasped his still-shaking fists. He took another mouthful and sighed. It was late, but he didn't feel like going to sleep.

Then he noticed something. He wasn't crying anymore.

Larkin didn't see Mickey Falco the next day. He stayed in his room not speaking, not reading. Just thinking.

The day after that there was a knock at the door. Mickey Falco.

'How you doin'?' he asked, limping into the room.

'Fine,' replied Larkin.

'Body healin' all right?'

'Yeah,' said Larkin.

Mickey nodded, pointed to his head. 'What about up here?'

'We'll see.'

Mickey gave a small smile. 'Good. Well, in that case,' he said, looking round the room, 'I think you're well enough now.'

Larkin looked at him. 'For what?'

'Some answers,' said Mickey.

Larkin sat there expectantly.

'Well don't just sit there,' said Mickey. 'Get your coat on.'

'Where we going?' asked Larkin.

'To see Karen,' stated Mickey simply. 'She's waiting to meet you.'

Larkin was speechless.

Mickey smiled. 'Come on,' he said. 'Let's not keep the lady waiting.'

In the White Room

Larkin, dressed in his new olive-green cargo pants, black box-cut sweatshirt, boots and fleece, walked down the stairs of Candleland, out into the street, and was escorted by Mickey Falco into the back of a waiting Transit, where another piece of apparel was added to his body.

'Sorry about this,' the man said, tying a blindfold round Larkin's eyes and slipping an old sack over his head. 'It's not that we don't trust you, we just wouldn't want you

299

having knowledge someone else could get at.'

Larkin shook his head and said nothing. The bag smelt strongly of old root vegetables, mildew and dirt.

'Off you go then, mate,' said Mickey.

Larkin heard him leave the van, close the door, bang the side. The van sped off.

For the first couple of street turnings, Larkin tried to use his limited knowledge of Hackney to keep track of his route, but it was no use. The van was turning, left, then right, then left, going flat out on some stretches, crawling on others. Street sounds filtered in, music from hip hop to indie, cars revving, tooting, screeching, voices raised in anger and laughter. He had no idea where he was, no clue to his direction. He was a passenger in every sense.

Suddenly, the van came to a halt. Larkin had no idea where he was or how long he had sat there. The door was opened and he was pulled out. The hands were neither rough nor gentle, just proficient. He was walked through a door and down a flight of steps, directed to a chair and forced to sit. He heard the sound of footsteps retreating up stairs then a door slam shut. Then nothing. He sat in silence as well as darkness.

'You can take that bag off your head now,' a female voice said eventually.

Larkin did so, slipping the blindfold off also. Light, artificial and bright, flooded his eyes. He snapped them shut again. Slowly, he opened them, allowing himself to become acclimatised gradually.

He was in a windowless basement room, painted completely white. Walls, ceiling and floor. On the floor were patterned Indian rugs. There was a bed, a chest of drawers, a wardrobe and a desk, all in blonde wood, all looking new. The bed had a patterned duvet cover and scatter cushions on it, on the desk there was a PC, hard drive and printer. A small table with a TV and video sat at the end of the bed. On the bed sat Karen Moir.

Larkin looked at her. Small and slim, her posture was erect, contained. Her hair was short, brown and slightly spiked, her clothes a white linen shirt and faded blue jeans. She sat as if deliberately posed, aiming for neutrality, but her eyes gave her away. They were large, round and haunted.

Those eyes locked on to his and didn't waver. They held more than they could express.

'Hello, Karen,' began Larkin awkwardly.

She held her stare.

'I'm Stephen Larkin.'

'I know who you are.' Her voice, Edinburgh-lilted, had a shake to it. 'And I know why you're here.'

Larkin slowly nodded his head. 'Good. So

you know what I'm going to say to you next?'

Something flared across her haunted eyes. 'Yeah. You're going to tell me how sorry my dad is, how he wants to put the past behind him. How he wants to see me.' The shiver in her voice increased. 'Before it's too late.'

Larkin didn't reply. Karen sounded like she had rehearsed this moment for quite some time. He would let her have her say.

'You can tell him from me,' she said, using anger to channel and control her voice, 'that I don't want to see him. I don't need his sympathy. Tell him to piss off back to Newcastle. Tell him he's too late.' Her voice faltered and cracked.

Larkin again said nothing, just reached into his pocket and brought out a card. He handed it to her.

'What's this?' she asked, taking it.

'That's in case you want to tell him yourself. It's where he's staying. And the phone number.'

She tore it in two, flinging the pieces on the bed. 'You've had a wasted trip.'

Larkin sighed, leaned forward in his chair. He knew this was going to be difficult. There were questions he needed answering, things only Karen could tell him, but this was his main reason for looking for her. The rest would have to wait.

'Listen,' he said, 'I don't think you'd have

gone to all this trouble, all this cloak-and-dagger stuff, just to tell me to piss off.'

'Is that a fact?'

'Yeah,' said Larkin. 'That's a fact. And I'll tell you something else.' He was starting to get annoyed now. 'I haven't come all this way, through a whole load of shit, nearly been killed, just for you to do that. Your dad sent me. I'm here now. And we're going to talk about that.'

'Why should I?' Karen spat back.

Larkin could think of a few answers to give her, but held his tongue. 'You work it out. Then you decide.'

'I decided a long time ago I didnae want him in my life.' She stood up, walked to the furthest wall. 'You know why? Because every time I did want him he was never there. He was out makin' the streets of Edinburgh safe, he always told me. Lyin' bastard. He was out drinkin' wi' his mates. Tryin' tae get into the funny handshake club. Get himself fast-tracked.' She leaned against the wall, as far back as she could go. 'Other kids used to say, "It must be excitin' havin' a dad who's a copper, like *Miami Vice*." An' I used to say "Yeah". I never told the truth.'

Karen, Larkin soon realised, was speaking more for her benefit than his. He waited to see if she had anything more to say. She did.

'And then later on,' she said, 'when I needed him – not just wanted him, needed him – he was missin' then as well.'

Larkin let her words be carried off into silence, then spoke again.

'He's changed, Karen. He's a different man.'

She gave a harsh, mirthless laugh. 'Oh we've all changed, haven't we? I mean, look at me. See how much. And I've got a hell of a lot more changin' to go through.'

She broke off, biting her bottom lip, trying to contain what was inside her. She didn't want to let it out, Larkin knew, didn't want herself or him to see it. Her body twitched and trembled as she fought for control, her eyes, jumping with fear and anger, flitted all over the room, darting about like swallows trapped in a barn.

Larkin felt for her. He managed to catch her eyes, steady them with his own calm, emphatic gaze. He spoke, his voice pitched low and soothing.

'What can I say, Karen? Yeah, I know it's difficult, but he just wants to see you, that's all. He knows what you think of him, he just wants to see that you're all right.'

Karen gave out a long, juddering sigh, and with it came the tears.

'I'm not alright,' she said, sobbing, 'I'm not alright...'

She moved away from the wall, slumped back on the bed. As she cried, the tension and rage left her body too. It seemed to be replaced by something far worse, something beyond sadness. She sighed, shook her head absently.

'I just wish … I wish I could just curl up and go to sleep for a long, long time,' she sobbed. 'Years, even. Then wake up and it'll all be over.' She looked at Larkin, eyes wet with pain. 'But it's not going to happen, is it?'

'No,' said Larkin.

She nodded. It looked like the answer she was expecting.

'So what happens now?' she asked.

'That's up to you, Karen.'

She sat in silence.

'There is another reason why I'm here,' said Larkin at length.

Karen nodded. 'Charlie Rook,' she said.

'Yeah, Charlie Rook,' said Larkin. 'Want to tell me what's going on?'

She nodded again, and started her story.

'He killed Hayley.' The words, carrying the gravitas of a final statement, started her crying again.

Larkin sat in the chair, powerless to help.

Karen's head dropped forward and the tears rolled down her cheeks. She struggled to hold it in, face contorting like a wounded animal.

'Nuh – not him personally,' she said. 'But he had it done.' She looked up, face creased in pain. 'Oh, Hayley...'

'Tell me about her,' asked Larkin.

They had met while they were both on the game. Karen was hooked on smack, doing punters to pay for it. Hayley was another runaway. 'Because her dad used to fuck her.' Karen gave a flat laugh. 'I suppose I should be thankful for small mercies. At least mine never did that.'

Then they fell in love. 'And to this day I don't know what she saw in me. I'm just glad she did.' The tears stopped, her face brightening at the memory. 'We totally fell for each other. I was shocked, because until then I'd never been with another woman. Well, apart from work, but I don't count that. But I never thought of myself as gay. Neither had she. Although when you think about it, it's not surprising.'

'Why?' asked Larkin.

Karen gave him a challenging, confrontational look. 'The things punters try an' get you to do ... you have little love left for men.'

Karen's expression changed and she was again lost in a memory. 'She was everythin' ... I told her about the heroin, she'd already guessed, mind, an' she sorted out a methadone clinic for me. She knew Diana. And Diana knew Mickey. Mickey Falco. He helped. It wasn't easy, but I wanted to try my best, you know? I had someone who loved me. I wanted to do it for her.'

'Did it work?' asked Larkin.

'Yeah,' she replied. 'A few backslides, but
… one day at a time. I'm doin' alright.' She
nodded seemingly to convince herself. 'And
she didn't mind I was HIV either.'

'Was Hayley HIV positive?' asked Larkin.

Karen shook her head. 'No. We took
precautions with each other.'

'And with punters?'

Karen stared at him confrontationally.
'You tryin' tae be judgemental?'

'No, I was just asking.'

'Well for your information, I always used a
condom. Which is more than a lot of them
do. Some punters refused and wouldn't
listen to anythin' I said about AIDS.' She
laughed. There was rage in it. 'Last thing
you want is a lecture in sexual health from a
whore, isn't it?'

She looked away. 'I just let them get on
with it. Some of them liked it better that
way. More of a thrill. Like Russian roulette.'

Larkin nodded. He made no comment but
instead asked, 'So how did you come into
contact with Charlie Rook?'

'We got sick of workin' the streets as
independents, dodgin' pimps, not havin'
enough control over the punters, that kind
of thing. And we needed more money.'

'What for?' asked Larkin.

'HIV and AIDS isn't the life sentence it

used to be,' she said. 'They've got drugs on the market, treatments out there so good they're closin' hospices.' There was a large element of self-conviction in her words.

'I know,' he said.

'But it's not the side-effects that are the problem with them.'

'It's the cost.'

'Right,' she said. 'An' the NHS don't make priority cases out of ex-junkie prossies.'

'And that's where Charlie Rook came in.'

She gave a watery smile. 'We met Melissa, his recruiter. Have you met her?'

'The ice goddess? Yeah, I've met her.'

'Cow,' spat Karen. 'She knew we wanted money, said she worked for this guy, real upmarket stuff, he'd look after us, pay us well. We said, yeah. We were interested. So she took us to meet him, he liked us, asked us to work for him. He's got this place in the City. Lot of rich punters.'

'I know,' said Larkin. 'I've been there.'

She gave him a fierce look, and opened her mouth for something to accompany it, but then stopped herself. 'Oh, yeah. Mickey said.'

'It wasn't for pleasure, believe me.'

'Right. Anyway, Melissa does health checks on all the new girls. She helped me fake mine.'

'Kind of her.'

'Wasn't it?' said Karen. 'I should have

known something was up then. But I didn't.'

She sighed, shook her head. 'So Hayley an' me are workin' there, servicin' the punters, makin' good money an' gettin' no hassle when Melissa comes up. She's got a proposition for us. Wants us to steal somethin' from Charlie. Set up a blackmail scam. She knew we wanted money; this way we'd get it.'

'And what did she get out of this?' asked Larkin.

'Charlie's business. The thing she wanted us to steal would have destroyed all his credibility. He would be ruined. Melissa would then step in and take over. We'd get our money. We all live happily ever after.'

'So you said you'd do it?'

'Yeah.' Karen sighed. 'What fuckin' mugs.'

'What happened?'

'We went through with it. Stole what we were supposed to, we found it where Melissa had left it, went to the place Melissa had organised and waited for the call. Never came, did it?' Her voice began to waver. 'We waited for days, still nothin'. But Ringo an' Lenny. They called. I was out shoppin' buyin' food. I had the thing on me. They took Hayley an' I … I ran. I couldn't…' She broke down in tears again.

Larkin looked on helplessly. He wanted to go to her, comfort her. Put his arm round her shoulder, let her cry into his chest. But he didn't. The girl was hurt, damaged, but she'd started to talk to him. He had established a kind of trust with her in a small space of time. He didn't want his actions misconstrued, the trust broken. So he sat there helplessly, watching her break her heart all over again.

'She might not be...' He couldn't bring himself to say the word.

Karen said it for him. 'Dead? Oh, she is. Charlie Rook's got a special place for that. For people who've upset him or outlived their usefulness.' The words were choked out of her. 'Hayley's sleepin' wi' the fishes now, alright. If there are any fishes in that polluted shite.'

'What?' asked Larkin, confused.

'Dagenham,' she said, raising her tear-stained face. 'He's got a place at Dagenham, his father's old scrap metal yard. Backs on to the Thames. That's where they get rid of the bodies.' Her sorrow had tipped back into anger again. 'That's where Hayley went...' She dropped her head again.

'So what did you take?' Larkin asked. 'What was so important?'

Karen looked up, eyes glistening. 'I'll show you,' she said.

She crossed to the PC, started it up, logged on. From a drawer in the desk she took out a CD-ROM and inserted it in the hard drive. Her fingers moved over the keys with practised ease.

'As well as being a pimp, Charlie had this other thing. His bespoke event management service, he calls it,' she said, fingers tapping. 'What it means is anythin' goes. Anything. And that's where the money is. Anythin' and everythin' as long as you've got the money. Anythin'.' She turned to Larkin. 'C'mere, watch this. If you can.'

Larkin looked at the screen. There was what appeared to be an operating theatre, sparsely equipped, with a naked body strapped to the table. The body belonged to a boy, about eighteen or nineteen. He was struggling, trying to snap the thick leather straps.

Into the scene walked a man dressed like a surgeon. Larkin began to get a bad feeling about it.

'Who's that?' he asked. 'Should I know him.'

'No,' replied Karen, 'but I bet you'll have bought something from one of his companies.'

The camera moved in for a close-up of the boy's terrified face. The man dressed as a surgeon roughly held the boy by the chin to stop him struggling. In his other hand he held a large needle trailing some coarse, black thread. As Larkin watched, he pulled the boy's eyelid out and stuck the needle through it.

'Oh fuck,' Larkin groaned, turning away.

'This has got sound too,' said Karen, her voice flat and desensitised. 'I've turned it down, though. He does both eyes, stitches them up, then starts on the body. D'you want to see?'

'No.' If anything, he wanted to be sick.

'There's clubs round here where they do that kind of thing for fun,' she said. ''Course the kick that bastard on the screen's gettin' is from the fact that it's not consensual. I'll find another one,' she said, her fingers clicking angrily. 'Here.'

Larkin gingerly turned back to the screen. He saw what looked like a gym. A boxers' gym with a ring in the centre. Hanging suspended from the ceiling was a girl. Well-built, blonde. A man entered dressed as a boxer. He was middle-aged, flabby.

'Hey,' said Larkin. 'Isn't that–'

'Yeah,' replied Karen. 'The Right Honourable Member himself. Not so honourable now, mind.'

As they watched, the man put his right fist in alignment with the girl's face, drew back and sent it flying. Her head snapped back from the shot. He repeated the action with his left fist. The girl screamed, silently.

'Seen enough yet?' asked Karen.

'Yeah,' said Larkin. 'I have.'

'There's plenty more. Some really famous faces.'

Larkin stared at the screen, frozen on the girl's agony. 'This is...' He couldn't find the word. 'Melissa. Where does she fit into all this?'

'I'll show you.'

Karen's fingers played over the keys again. Menus dropped down, the mouse was clicked, and the screen was filled by an image of what looked like a dungeon: stone walls, shadows, ominous-looking pieces of sharp, rusting heavy metal dotted about. In the centre of the picture, stretched into an X-shape and chained from floor to ceiling was a naked teenage boy. Thin and tired-looking, he couldn't have been more than fifteen. Slightly to the left of the screen Larkin could make out a figure. Old and frail, his back to camera, he sat motionless and blanket-wrapped in a wheelchair, oxygen cylinder at his side.

'Who's that?' asked Larkin.

'You don't want to know,' replied Karen. 'He's too old to do anything, so he gets off on watching. And look who does it instead of him.'

Melissa strode confidently into the picture. She was dressed in full dominatrix gear; leather basque exposing her breasts, thigh-high, spike-heeled boots, severe hair and make up. She walked up to the boy, held his face in her hand and began to kiss him, working her tongue right into his mouth.

313

He soon became aroused by her pretence of passion as his erect penis showed. Melissa reached down for it with her free hand, began working it backwards and forwards. The boy began to writhe, losing himself to her.

She moved her other hand behind her back and drew from a pouch a pair of old, rusted secateurs. The boy, engrossed by Melissa's hand and mouth, was unaware as she positioned the cutters over his right nipple, but he certainly felt the blades being brought together. The boy's head jerked back, screaming soundlessly, as he struggled to pull himself away from her grasp. Melissa held on to his now withering erection and pumped it all the harder. Her face was contorted by a cruel ecstasy as she moved the cutters over his chest, trailing blood, and played them around his left nipple, ready to inflict more damage. The man in the wheelchair hadn't moved.

Larkin turned away. 'Turn it off.'

Karen did so. The black screen came as a welcome relief.

'She doesn't stop there,' said Karen, her voice losing its desensitised tone. 'Not Melissa. You should see what her and her friends do with the baby.' Her voice cracked.

'What?' asked Larkin incredulously. 'How did they get a baby?'

'Same way they get any of them. Through

Melissa. There's two kinds of recruitment: working girls for the vanilla trade and the others for this stuff. Melissa gets them to order. What happens is, someone comes to Charlie Rook with their idea. He gives them a price, they agree, then he sends Melissa out to get what they want. She poses as a health worker, social worker, anything that gets her near to her target. She gets to know homeless kids, gives them money, food, organises shelter, earns their trust, then tells them she can get them work and money. Next thing they know, they're starrin' in one of these. Afterwards, when they're no more use, when there's nothin' left of them, it's off to Dagenham.'

Larkin nodded, understanding. 'And nobody misses them. Because nobody knew they were there.'

'Right.'

'So what about the baby?'

'Bought by Melissa off a heroin addict,' Karen said, struggling to keep her voice even. 'Used, then dumped. Like the others.'

'Shouldn't you go to the police?' asked Larkin, struggling to get his head round the whole thing.

Karen gave a sharp, bitter laugh. 'You wanna see some high-rankin' policemen?' She nodded towards the screen. 'I'll show you.'

'Shit.' Larkin sat on the bed in shock.

'Yeah. And you know what else?' said Karen. 'That bastard Rook reckons he's doin' a public service. Can you believe it? He says that if these bastards weren't able to let off steam in his controlled environment, they'd do it in public. What a cunt.'

Larkin nodded in agreement. 'So what are we going to do?'

Karen looked at him. 'We?' she said. 'You mean you want to do something about this?'

'Of course,' said Larkin. 'But what?'

'My question exactly,' said a voice from the far end of the room.

Larkin turned. At the top of the steps stood Mickey Falco. As they watched he hauled himself slowly down and across the floor until he was in front of Larkin. Larkin stood up.

'How did you get here?' Larkin asked.

'Through the door.'

Larkin looked at Mickey Falco. The older man said nothing, his face as impassive as stone. Suddenly, the penny dropped.

'I'm still in Candleland,' said Larkin.

Mickey gave a weary smile. 'Yeah, Stephen, sorry about all that cloak-and-dagger mumbo jumbo. But as you can see, we're not playin' about 'ere.'

'No.'

'We were listening upstairs,' said Mickey. 'I didn't want to come in till you'd seen that.'

316

Mickey gestured to the computer screen, then crossed to Karen, still seated at the desk. He gently placed his hands on her shoulders.

'Sorry to make you go through all that again, love,' he said.

'That's OK, Mickey,' she said. She looked tired. Worn out by life. She looked at Larkin. 'He had to see it.'

Larkin wasn't so sure, but he took her point. 'I suppose I did,' he said.

'So,' said Mickey, 'now you know the score. You know what we're up against. We can't count on any help with this one, but we've got to do somethin' about it. So.' He looked Larkin square in the eyes. 'What's it to be? You in or out?'

Larkin looked at Mickey, at the screen, at Karen and back to Mickey.

'In. Definitely in.'

The Volunteer

Larkin was standing in the public bar of The Volunteer in Hackney. His heart was beating so fast he was sure it could be heard. His hands were trembling. A camouflage tabloid, open at the sports pages, was spread out in front of him, a barely touched pint at

317

his elbow. Through the mirror behind the bar he had a clear view behind him and at either side of him. It was twenty past two in the afternoon, the day was cold and threatening rain and he was nervous. He stood as still as he could, trying not to let his nerves show.

In his mind, Larkin had already gone over his plan of action and the events leading up to it several times but, like an anxious traveller mentally repacking his case before he reaches the airport, he thought he'd better do it again. Just one more time. So he again played back the last three days. The chain of events since he had met Karen Moir.

Hours after meeting Karen, Larkin was in Mickey Falco's office.

'Here you go,' said Mickey Falco, handing Larkin a mug of coffee. He sat behind his desk. Larkin sat in the chair he'd occupied on his first visit to Candleland. It seemed a lifetime ago.

Mickey Falco filled two glasses with generous slugs of brandy, handed one over and slumped in the chair behind his desk.

Larkin sipped his drink. The room was geared to keep the cold at bay: closed door, central heating, and the warm tones of Aretha Franklin in the background.

Mickey reached down into a drawer and

pulled out a couple of files stuffed with papers.

'This,' he said, 'is the evidence. Look, I'm sorry about you havin' to see all that downstairs. I didn't think you'd understand what we were up against unless you saw it.'

'You wanted me as angry as you, you mean.'

'Something like that.'

'I can understand that,' said Larkin suppressing a shudder. 'But I'm more concerned for Karen. What it's done to her.' He remembered her face as he walked up the stairs. Like a condemned woman, left alone in her cell.

Mickey gave a grave nod. 'I agree. That's why we've got to get this thing sorted as quickly as possible.'

'You got any ideas?'

Mickey took a mouthful of coffee. 'We need to do two things. Set Karen free and make those bastards pay for what they've done both to her and the others. Now, Darren and Karen have spent the last few weeks gathering information on Charlie Rook. Karen on the internet, Darren pounding the pavements and sitting in libraries. This is the result.'

Mickey moved his arm, patted the files.

'We've tried to get as much information on him as we could find. His business, his associates, his clients, his family, everything.

Even what colour toothbrush he has. This is it so far.'

Mickey opened the file. He started with Charlie Rook's father. Jack Rook had been a scrap metal dealer in Dagenham in the Sixties. Even in a trade renowned for skirting the fringes of legitimacy, his exploits had been legendary. A hard man, mean and ruthless.

'A real nasty bastard,' said Mickey, 'brought his son up with the same values.'

The police had always been trying to pin something on him and when one of his business rivals disappeared, having last been seen complaining loudly at Rook's yard, they thought they had him stitched up for murder.

But Jack Rook was smarter than that. No body was ever discovered, and he remained briefed up and silent throughout questioning. Eventually, having no case to argue and not enough for a warrant, they had to let him go. Nothing was proven but everyone knew he'd done it.

'There was a lot of heavy-duty machinery and stuff in that yard. Easy to dispose of a body if you weren't squeamish.'

'And he wasn't squeamish,' finished Larkin.

'Exactly. And it's a case of like father like son. The yard's still there, in Charlie Rook's name, although someone else runs it. He just comes and goes as he likes. Or rather he sends his henchmen, Ringo and Lenny.'

'Just Lenny now,' Larkin reminded him.

'True.' Mickey turned to another page of the file. 'Lenny Lothario, so called because he liked to sample the merchandise a bit too much. Ringo was half Greek, had a mother who was a Beatles fan. She named him. Impeccable choice.'

'Yeah,' said Larkin with a grim laugh. 'Programmed to fail from birth, really.'

'Then there's Melissa,' said Mickey. 'If it's her real name, because we drew a blank on her. Couldn't find a single thing. All we know is she's dangerous. Probably the most dangerous of the lot. The real force behind the operation, we think.

'Charlie Rook's also got connections with the local families. They hire him their heavy boys when he wants something doing. And there's also his so-called legitimate contacts. But we've seen enough of them on the disc.'

Mickey pulled out the second file. 'Now Darren's been following them. The legits have left a paperchase, a hidden one mind, but it establishes links between each one of them and Charlie Rook. This is still a work in progress, though. When we've got enough information together, enough solid facts, we're going to go public. Till then we're still working on it.'

'You've been busy,' said Larkin in admiration.

'Yeah,' said Mickey, 'we have. Even Ralph's been helping us with the last bit.'

Larkin said nothing.

'But what we have to do in the meantime,' said Mickey, 'is make sure Karen's going to be safe. We can't keep her in the basement indefinitely. It's drivin' her mad.'

'What have you got in mind?' asked Larkin.

'A deal. We give them the disc in exchange for Karen's safety.'

'They won't stick to that,' said Larkin.

'I know. But it'll buy us time to compile a full case for the prosecution, as they say. We've got the disc, we just tell them we'll take it to the papers if they don't play ball. They won't argue.'

'You had experience of this kind of thing?' asked Larkin.

Mickey gave a tired smile. 'A little,' he said. 'In a previous incarnation.'

'Why would they agree to it?' asked Larkin. 'If they know we'll be keeping a copy?'

'The way I see it, the disc Karen took was the master and only copy,' Mickey replied. 'Accordin' to what Melissa told Karen, it was Charlie Rook's insurance against his clients. That's why it's so important. Maybe he was plannin' his own little sting.'

'So our copy is insurance against anything happening to Karen?'

'Yep.'

Larkin thought. 'Then we'd better keep Karen well away from wherever this is going down,' he said. 'They may try and nab her.'

'I agree,' sighed Mickey. 'Trouble is, she knows about this. Said if we ever did this, she insists on bein' there.'

'Why?'

'Got a message for Lenny, she says. Reckons he'll be the one doing the handover.'

'But – haven't you tried–'

''Course I have,' said Mickey, irritably. 'But you try arguin' with 'er.'

Larkin nodded. 'True.' He thought for a moment. 'It'll be more than one man, you know. They'll want to come in mob-handed.'

'Well they can't,' said Mickey, raising his finger. 'Only one person from each side.'

'They won't stick to that,' said Larkin.

Mickey Falco gave a grin that showed more than teeth. It showed the cunning gangster he used to be. 'Neither will we,' he said.

'So who's the person from our side going to be?' Larkin asked, already knowing the answer.

'That's what I wanted to talk to you about,' said Mickey.

Larkin raised his eyebrows, waited.

'You're the logical one for the job. I was going to do it myself, but...' He tapped his leg. 'This is a bit of a liability.'

'So you waited till I was all healed, introduced me to Karen then showed me the CD, knowing I'd get angry and want to join up?'

Mickey nodded.

'You used me, Mickey.'

Mickey looked shame-faced. 'Used a little manipulation, might be a better description. I checked you out. I know your past. With your body workin' and your head back together I thought you could carry this off better than me. Especially since it was for Karen. But if you feel you can't and you want to back out, I fully understand.'

'You think flattering my ego's going to help?'

They both smiled. Mickey remained silent.

Larkin thought for a moment. 'What about you, Mickey? How d'you reconcile something like this with your beliefs? It could get nasty, you know.'

Mickey nodded, grimly. 'I know. I've thought it over and over, looked at every possible alternative, prayed for something different...' He sighed. 'It's a risk, but a risk for the greater moral good. And those are the ones worth taking. If it goes wrong, the blame's on me. I'll have to live with it.'

Larkin sipped his brandy. Aretha told her lover he was all she needed to get by.

'You'd better count me in, then,' he said. 'I

don't like being used, but in a way, you seem to have more to lose.'

Mickey nodded. 'Thanks.' His relief and sincerity were apparent. He picked up his glass, raised it in a toast. 'To Karen,' he said.

Larkin raised his. 'And peace and love.'

'An' happy ever after.'

'And all that shit.'

Clink.

Then Mickey told Larkin the plan.

The next day, Larkin stood in a phone box he'd picked out at random, feeding change into the slot. He dialled 141 to preserve his anonymity, then keyed in the number Karen had given him and waited.

'Rook Enterprises.' A woman's voice. Pleasant but efficient.

'Hello Melissa, d'you know who this is?'

'No.' Still pleasant.

'Stephen Larkin.'

The voice on the other end didn't just freeze, it seemed as if ice had formed on the phone box. He had taken her by surprise. He pressed his advantage.

'Bet you thought you'd never hear from me again, didn't you?'

'What d'you want?' she hissed.

'Nothing that you've got to offer, darling. Get your boss.'

'He's busy.'

'He'll talk to me. I want to deal.'

There was a pause. Her animal cunning was almost audible down the phone line. 'Give me your number,' she said. 'I'll get him to call you.'

Larkin laughed. 'You mean I wait here till you pinpoint where I am? Send the boys round? Fuck off, Melissa, get Charlie Rook.'

There was another silence on the line.

'Remember,' said Larkin, 'I've been talking to Karen. She's told me all about what you've been trying to do. Hostile takeover, is it?'

There was nothing but the sound of her breathing. When she did speak, her voice had dropped an octave. 'You can talk to me, Stephen. We can make a deal.'

'I couldn't give a fuck what you've been doing, just get Charlie. Oh, and Melissa? It's Mr Larkin to you. Not Stephen. Now get him.'

There was an angry stabbing noise as Larkin was put on hold. He waited a couple of minutes then a familiar psychocockney voice came on the line.

'Stephen Larkin. Well, well, well.'

'Hello Charlie, how you doing?'

'Well. Considering I've just had a close friend's funeral to arrange recently.'

'Ringo didn't need a funeral,' said Larkin. 'He'd already been cremated.'

There was a sharp intake of breath from the other end. 'You're dead, Larkin.'

'No Charlie, you are. You're just still walking around, that's all.'

Silence on the line.

'How many kids you killed today, Charlie? How many untraceables have taken a one-way trip to Dagenham, eh?'

'You said you wanted to deal.' Charlie Rook's voice was hot, bubbling, struggling to keep control.

'Yeah Charlie, I do. I've got your CD. I've got Karen. You can have the CD back, but not her. That's my side of the bargain. Your side is, you leave her alone. You leave me alone. And you will. Because I've copied the CD for insurance.'

'Fuck off. No deal.'

Larkin smiled. He was enjoying himself. 'Then we go public. I'm a journalist, I know how to do that. Think, Charlie, this is your only chance. After today all bets are off. Are you in?'

'I've got some conditions.'

'No you haven't. It's my way or the highway, mate.'

When Charlie Rook spoke next, he sounded like an underground nuclear test: planet-destroying heat inside, only tremors and cracks showing on the surface. 'Talk, then, cunt. And it better be good.'

Larkin talked, Charlie Rook listened. He didn't like it, but he agreed. He had no option.

Larkin had another call to make, no less important.

He dialled the number. Andy answered. Larkin announced himself.

'Fuckin' 'ell, mate, where you been? You phone to say you're fine, then nothin'! What's goin' on?'

Some things never change, thought Larkin, and Andy's one of them, thankfully.

'I'm fine, Andy. Just had to put myself back together.'

'And have you?'

'I think so.'

'Good, 'cause you need to get back 'ere quick. These two're gettin' on me nerves, an'–'

'I've found her, Andy.'

There was silence on the line.

'Who? Karen? You've found 'er?'

Larkin was about to answer him when there was a commotion at the other end of the line. He heard Andy's voice raised, another, more guttural voice interject, sound of the receiver being fought over, then near-silence. The only sound in Larkin's ear was heavy breathing.

'Hello?' said Larkin.

'It's me. I heard Andy say you'd found her.' Moir's familiar gruff tones sounded dry, uncertain. 'Is that right?'

'Yes, Henry,' said Larkin. 'I've found her.'

There was a huge sigh at the other end. It sounded like a zeppelin deflating.

'How is she?' asked Moir. 'Does she want to... Is she...' His cracked voice oscillated away to nothing.

'Don't worry, she's fine. There's just some things that have to be sorted out.'

'What sort of things? Are you stoppin' me from seein' her?'

Larkin sighed. He had known this was going to be difficult. 'Look, she's in a ... situation. When that's sorted, we'll take things from there.'

The words sent Moir ballistic. He had to be there, he wanted to know what was going on, what Larkin was keeping from him ... and on, and on...

And so, twenty minutes, one huge argument and one very reluctant capitulation later, Larkin, his supply of pound coins used up, replaced the handset and exited the phone box, ear ringing. After that, he needed a drink.

That night, as Larkin lay on his bed in his room, eyes scanning an old paperback, brain too pumped to take in the words, there was a knock at the door.

'Yeah?'

The door slowly opened. There stood Karen.

'Can I come in?' she asked.

'Sure,' said Larkin, swinging his legs off the bed and putting the book down. 'Make yourself at home.'

She carefully closed the door, sat herself in the armchair and gave him an awkward smile. Larkin picked up on it, threw it back at her, with what he hoped was something akin to reassurance.

'Would you like a drink?' he asked, gesturing towards the bottle of whisky.

'No, no thanks,' she said quickly. 'I don't drink.'

'Very wise,' said Larkin. 'You don't mind if I...' He held the bottle over his glass.

'No. Go ahead. I don't mind other people doin' it, I just stopped drinking when I stopped the other stuff.'

Larkin poured, sipped and sat down.

'So,' he said, 'you're taking a risk by coming up here.'

'I got Darren to clear a route for me. I wanted to talk to you.'

Larkin said nothing, just continued to sip from his drink.

Karen looked at her feet. 'The other day, when you came to see me, I was a bit ... defensive, shall we say.'

Larkin smiled. 'I didn't take it personally.' An aggressive mask is often the best kind to hide behind, he thought. Especially if someone had been through what she had.

Karen smiled back, glacier cracking. 'I've

330

been talking to Mickey. He told me what you're gonna be doin'. The risk you're takin' for me. I just wanted to say thank you. I do appreciate it.'

'That's OK,' said Larkin, much more casually than he felt. The fear hadn't kicked in yet, but it would.

'Mickey's told me a bit about you.' She smiled. 'You were very determined to find me.'

'That's me, good old bloodhound Larkin.'

They exchanged nervous laughter. It seemed to relax them more.

'He also told me about Ralph,' she said. 'I couldn't believe it. He's such a sweet guy. Caring.'

Larkin swallowed his drink in two gulps. It hurt going down. 'Yeah?' he said. 'Well he didn't use to be.'

'People change. You said so the other day.'

He was about to answer her when he noticed her lip trembling slightly.

'Hayley used to say that too. She proved it with me.' Karen quickly got herself under control.

The sight made Larkin's anger about Sickert die down. 'I suppose you're right,' he said. 'Look at your dad.'

The ice began to reform. 'Do I have to?'

'He put himself out a lot to find you.'

'He got you to put yourself out, you mean.'

'No, Karen. I wanted to help him. He's a

friend. He'd do the same for me.'

Karen gave a bitter laugh. 'Really? That's not the bastard I used to know.' The mask was moving back into place.

'Then maybe you don't know him at all.'

Karen said nothing. She stared at her knuckles.

'Look,' said Larkin, 'don't take my word for it. When all this is over why not give him a ring? Judge for yourself. I'll give you another card.'

Karen remained silent. Larkin wasn't sure she'd actually heard him. Back to square one, he thought. Then she looked up. And smiled.

'You don't need to give me another card,' she said. 'I've still got the last one.'

'You tore it up.'

'We have a thing called Sellotape.'

They both smiled. Karen stood up.

'Well, I'd better leave you to…' She trailed off, her words becoming awkward again.

'Yeah,' said Larkin standing. 'Thanks for visiting. Anytime you're passing, you know, just drop in.'

She laughed. 'I will. I'll see you tomorrow.'

'You don't have to be there, you know.'

'I know,' she said, 'but I want to be. Thanks again. I mean it.' She walked to the door, let herself out. Larkin heard her feet on the stairs, tentative, slow, then turning to silence. He was left alone.

He walked back to the bed, poured another drink, threw it down in one. He needed to sleep, told himself the whisky would help. He put the light out, undressed, and climbed into bed.

He tried to force himself to sleep but it wouldn't come, so he just lay there staring at the shadows on the ceiling, the shades of grey, until eventually tiredness made a weary truce with his body and he slept.

His dreams were uneasy but at least he didn't remember them.

And so the next day he sat in The Volunteer in Hackney, shoulders bunched in tension as if expecting a bullet between them. Trying to act casual, even confident, but the tightness in his chest, the shake of his hands and the smell of his sweat was giving him away. He drank his pint; easy, slowly, hoping the alcohol would calm him rather than anaesthetise him. There was no chance of either; he had enough adrenalin coursing round his body to power a small town.

He waited, eyes on the mirror, eyes on the clock. Twenty-eight minutes past. Two minutes to go.

He heard the sound of a car pulling up and parking outside. His heart flipped over.

'BMW pulling up,' said the barman.

Larkin nodded his thanks and took a deep breath.

Suddenly the door opened. Larkin's eyes jerked up to the mirror. He looked at the man, made eye contact. He was wearing an overcoat and carrying a shoulder bag, but apart from that he looked exactly the same as when Larkin had last seen him, even down to the Walkman stuck in his ears. Lenny Lothario.

Lenny walked up until he was right behind Larkin.

'Afternoon, Lenny,' Larkin said.

Lenny looked twitchy, but since this was his natural state of being, Larkin couldn't tell if the man was nervous or not. Probably not. Larkin suddenly felt something very hard being poked in his back. He stiffened.

'Know what this is?' asked Lenny, giggling. 'I bet you do. I'm here to get what I want. That disc and then revenge for what you did to Ringo. Don't fuck me about, because from this range I won't miss.'

Larkin tried to swallow, but couldn't. There seemed to be something the size of an apple stuck in his throat.

Oh fuck, he thought.

The Last Chance Saloon Bar

Larkin swallowed, forcing the imaginary apple to go down. He found an adrenalin-soaked reserve of false bravery and spoke.

'Listen, Lenny,' said Larkin, throat dry, 'you fire that thing and you'll be dead in seconds. You don't believe me? Try it.'

Lenny sneered. 'Just gimme the disc.'

'Lenny, I agreed to meet you here for a purpose. Look around you.'

'Fuck off.'

Larkin leaned in close. 'Look around you, Lenny, but don't make it obvious. I'm not here alone. All the men you see sitting round here, reading their papers, eating their crisps and drinking their pints are with me. All eight of them. And they're well armed. One word, one gesture from me and they'll blow you away so quickly you'll be fucking atomised. Go on, look.'

Lenny looked. He saw men dotted round the pub; hard, scarred men. Their jackets were open exposing handguns in easy-access holsters, their folded newspapers concealing the stocks of bigger pieces of ordnance. Their expressions were flat, unreadable. They were waiting for the word.

'We've even got men on the roof,' said Larkin. 'So do we understand each other now, Lenny?'

Lenny, Larkin saw in the mirror, nodded. There was fear in his eyes.

'Put the gun away, then. Sit down.'

Lenny did as he was told. He sat on the barstool next to Larkin. Larkin allowed himself a small sigh of relief. Only a small one. There was still a long way to go.

'Now,' said Larkin, 'let's get this over with, Lenny. Then you're out of my life forever. You want the disc.' Larkin slowly put his hand into the left-hand side pocket of his cargo pants and, aware that Lenny was watching him like a hawk, carefully drew out the CD in its plastic cover. He placed it on the bar top.

'Yours,' said Larkin. 'In exchange for certain assurances.'

Lenny said nothing. He unzipped the shoulder bag and brought out a laptop. He flipped it open, slid the disc on to the tray and started it up. His fingers flicked over the keys. A familiar, ugly image appeared onscreen.

'This is the one,' said Lenny, flatly. He flicked off the laptop and packed it away.

'Now,' said Larkin. 'You've got the disc. Fine. Keep it. But remember that we've got a copy. So if anything happens to Karen, no matter how accidental it might look, this stuff goes public. You got me?'

Lenny nodded. Larkin breathed another sigh of relief.

'Now find the door, go and tell Charlie that.'

'Karen was supposed to be here,' said Lenny, not moving. 'Where is she?'

'Right behind you,' said a voice.

Lenny turned. At a table by the door sat an androgynous figure dressed in thick workshirt, jeans, boots, black puffa jacket, with a woollen hat on her head. Karen. She stood up, crossed to where Larkin and Lenny sat.

'Hello Lenny,' she said. 'You look surprised. Did you think I'd be too scared to face you? I wanted to see you.'

'The boss wants me to bring you with me.' Lenny's eyes were jittering between Larkin and Karen.

'Which boss would that be, Lenny?' asked Karen. 'Charlie? Or has Melissa taken over yet?'

Lenny swallowed, his eyes darting nervously around the pub as if someone was listening. 'How d'you know about that?'

Karen laughed. Larkin could see that she was burning with anger, but she was channelling it, using it. Enjoying it.

'Oh, I know lots of things, Lenny. Lots of secrets. Want to hear another?'

Lenny didn't reply.

'Remember all those times you used to force me to have sex with you?'

'I didn't force you–'

Karen didn't let him speak. 'What, you think I enjoyed it? I did it by choice? No, Lenny. All those fuckin' awful things you used to like. All the stuff you did that made me physically ill afterwards. All those body fluids. Remember?' Her voice began to crack. 'Well, I've got news for you. I'm HIV positive, Lenny.' There was a brittle kind of triumph in her eyes.

Lenny's face, already pallid, became chalk-white. 'You … you can't be. You were tested. All the girls were.'

Karen smiled. It was like an arctic frost. 'Melissa faked it for me. She also gave me the CD. Nice of her, eh?'

Lenny was lost, staring into space.

'HIV, Lenny. And you've got it. That means one day you'll get full-blown AIDS. Then it'll be a horrible, slow, painful death.' There were tears in her eyes. 'Just like mine.'

Lenny looked at her, stunned. 'I might not … it might not have infected me.'

'You think so?' asked Karen. 'Then this will.'

She spat right into his eyes.

Larkin's mouth fell open. That wasn't in the script, he hadn't been expecting that. Neither had Lenny. He reacted as if he'd just been hit with acid, pitching himself backwards off the stool, clawing at his face. He landed in a heap on the floor, writhing and struggling, frantically wiping his face with his overcoat.

Larkin looked at Karen. Her face was shining with the kind of righteous vengeance that only the oppressed overthrowing the oppressor can ever feel.

'Bitch!' screamed Lenny. 'You're gonna fuckin' pay!' He grabbed hold of his Walkman, shouted into it. 'Now! Now!'

Larkin moved quickly. He tore open Lenny's jacket and coat, ripped the Walkman out and examined it.

'Fuck!' he shouted to the men in the pub. 'This isn't a Walkman! It's a transmitter! He knows how many people we've got in here! And he's just called for reinforcements!'

The men dotted round the pub jumped to their feet, guns drawn. They scanned the pub, keyed up, ready.

They didn't have long to wait. Outside there was the screech of tyres, the sound of a car roaring nearer and the squeal of suddenly applied brakes.

Then all hell let loose.

Rifle shots were heard from an upstairs window, aiming into the street. In reply came bursts of automatic weapons fire. The rifle shots stopped. Silence.

Suddenly, the windows of the pub shattered in a hail of rapid fire.

'Down!' shouted one of the men. Most of the men dived for cover, upturning tables and pulling out wall seats, and began to return fire.

Larkin dived to the floor, face down, hands over his head. He knew they would have no effect against bullets, but at least he could shield himself from raining glass.

A couple of the men who didn't reach cover in time were hit; spinning and dancing, the bullets jerking them around, blood paintwheeling from their bodies as they fell.

Larkin was terrified. He had been in some rough situations before, but nothing like this. The noise, the movement, the terror ... this was a war zone, as brutal as it was sudden.

A sudden thought struck him: Karen, where was she? He risked a glance up. Lenny was pulling her along the floor, one arm round her neck, the other with a gun pointing at her head. The laptop was slung over his shoulder and he was slithering along the floor on his back, the heavy overcoat absorbing any glass, his legs powering his movement, Karen clutched on top of him.

Larkin started to crawl, commando-style, towards them. Bullets popped and thudded into the wood of the bar, centimetres above his head. Lenny caught the movement, swung the gun towards Larkin, and fired.

Larkin didn't have time to think. With speed that amazed even himself, he rolled out of the way and under a nearby table, the bullets embedding themselves in the floor where he had been. Lenny noted his new position and took aim again, a look of intense manic glee on his face.

There was nowhere for Larkin to turn to, so he pulled the table down in front of him as a makeshift shield, hoping that Lenny's gun wouldn't be powerful enough to penetrate the wood, but knowing that at this short distance it would blow the table to matchwood. He was trapped.

Karen saved him. Just as Lenny was about to fire, she reached up and grabbed his gun hand. She didn't succeed in wresting the weapon from his grasp or stopping the shot, but the pull she gave his arm sent the shot harmlessly wide.

The glee became equally intense anger as Lenny, with a cry of rage, tightened his grip on Karen's throat and banged the handle of the gun against her head. She gagged, trying to pull her head away from a follow-up blow, legs thrashing wildly. Lenny refocused his efforts on escaping, his legs propelling his body faster along the floor.

Larkin watched from behind the table as Lenny dragged Karen behind the counter, all the way to the door at the back of the bar. Larkin scrambled across to the corner of the bar, following them, but was dissuaded from venturing further by the bullet Lenny fired that splintered the wood at the side of his head. He pulled himself back sharply. By the time he felt it safe enough to chance another look, they had gone.

Larkin pulled himself up into a crouching position and ran behind the bar, head down to avoid stray bullets and exploding bottles. He reached the door at the back of the bar and found a prone Mickey Falco; dazed, blood gathering from a cut over his left eye. Mickey was still wearing his barman's apron.

'They came past here,' Mickey gasped. 'I tried to stop them but Lenny smacked me one with his gun. He's gone, Steve. An' 'e's got Karen an' all.'

'I know, Mickey. That bastard's won,' spat Larkin, slumping down beside him. In the bar the fight was starting to wind down. They would count the bodies later.

'The bastard's–' Larkin stopped in mid-sentence. 'No he hasn't.' Larkin stood up, newly energised. 'I know where they're going. Come on.' He stuck out his hand, helped Mickey to his feet.

They left the pub by the back door and made their way cautiously round the side. What was left of Charlie Rook's team were bundling themselves into a black Merc, paintwork pitted, glass spiderwebbed, with bullet holes. There were a couple of bodies, their own men, sprawled in the road. They were left where they had fallen. Job done, the survivors were getting ready to squeal away.

As soon as they'd gone, Larkin ran and Mickey limped over to where Larkin had parked the Saab. Luckily it hadn't been in the line of fire and so wasn't damaged. They got in: Larkin as driver, Mickey as passenger.

'Where we goin', then?' asked Mickey.

'To where Lenny's taken Karen.' Larkin started the car. 'Mickey, how the hell do I get to Dagenham?'

Where the Wild Roses Grow

'Here we are,' said Mickey. 'Dagenham. City of dreams.'

'Yeah,' said Larkin. 'I've had dreams like this before.'

They had driven out of London on the A13, past the over-developed Isle of Dogs, the squandered glory of the Dome, and out-wards. Dagenham itself could have defined the word depressing. A collection of drive-thru McDonald's, run-down retail parks acned with rust, with boarded-up bingo halls and health-threatening nightclubs, choked by the industrial clouds from the Ford plant and the exhaust fumes from the never-ending stream of M25-dodging juggernauts. Larkin wouldn't have been surprised if the letters DEAD END had materialised in the sky in huge neon letters. To make matters worse, the long-threatened rain had now turned up, throwing a dull, grey tarpaulin over everything.

Mickey directed Larkin to an industrial estate. Even given the fact that it was six o'clock and most people should have left for the day, the whole place looked deserted, if not abandoned. Most of the industry on the estate had long since ceased. They drove down broken concrete roadways looking for the yard. The buildings were all ex-factories, now reduced to crumbling empty shells. Every other site they drove past had a 'For Sale' board pinned to the wire; weathered and faded, they seemed to have been there as long as the buildings.

With no man-made order, nature was re-asserting itself. Weeds pushed through the broken concrete, moon-cratering the once flat surface, while more sturdy plants challenged the remaining structures. The land was being reclaimed.

The place they wanted was right at the end of the road, far away from any remaining inhabited units. As they approached, Larkin killed the headlights and rolled the car to a slow stop.

A high, barbed wire-topped fence, now browned with rust, surrounded the perimeter. Its base was obscured by wild grasses and plants, roses and vines. A huge pair of sturdy iron gates, newer than the fence, stood chained and padlocked, barring any entrance.

'This the place?' Larkin asked.

'Supposed to be,' replied Mickey. 'Looks deserted.'

'That's probably the idea.' Larkin pointed to the gates. 'D'you reckon you could climb them?'

Mickey sighed in anger and exasperation. 'Looks like you're on your own, mate.'

They shook hands, Mickey wishing Larkin all the best, and he left the car. He pulled his fleece around him, trying to keep out the cold and the rain, ignoring the small slivers of wood and glass that rubbed against his skin. He grabbed hold of the gates, pulled himself up with only the slightest twinge of resistance from his recently injured shoulder, and swung over. He landed on the other side and looked round.

A rough road of gravel chips lay ahead of him, a fence on either side. He walked down it. Straight ahead was a large warehouse, old and redbrick, with a rolling door pulled tightly closed at the front. At the side was a newer addition, a flat-roofed breeze-block building, initially painted white, now several shades of grey.

The warehouse faced onto a large yard. It was divided up into several bays separated on three sides by walls made of old wooden railway sleepers slotted into concrete posts. The bays took up the whole of the back wall, itself strengthened by sleeper and concrete walls. A couple were full of metal skips stacked five or six high, some held smaller square metal crates, themselves full of scrap metal. Some bays just had piles of metal in them, either identifiable objects such as old car radiators and engines, or more obscure industrial waste. The rain lent an oily sheen to everything.

There were two cranes in the yard; one a grabber, the other a grabber and shovel combination. There was also a number of smaller, more dangerous-looking machines with long, heavy metal blades attached to a motor. They couldn't have said 'Industrial Accident Waiting To Happen' more clearly if they'd had the words printed on the side.

The furthest wall bordered a path. Larkin saw that it led to an old jetty, the wood green and rotten-looking. Above the rain he heard water slapping against its supports. He presumed the sludge-coloured river was the Thames.

He had a quick look around. The warehouse seemed the likeliest place for activity, even though he could see no light emerging from there, so he moved cautiously towards it.

As he approached he heard a noise: a door opening, footsteps crunching gravel.

He looked round for a hiding place, saw a skip to his left, and jumped behind it.

The sound was coming from the side of the warehouse. Larkin tried to see what was happening but couldn't. There was, however, a skip next to him which he could hide behind and get a better view. He crept slowly behind it and looked round the edge.

At the side of the warehouse were two vehicles: a BMW and a Jeep Cherokee. As he watched, Lenny opened the boot of the Cherokee and pulled out a large, heavy bundle. It was blanket-wrapped but unmistakenly human-shaped. He struggled to get it over his shoulder, knees sagging from the weight, then shut the boot and made his way back to the side door.

Larkin planned his next move. There was no way he could just walk in the place, especially unarmed, so he would have to be more subtle than that. After all, although it seemed like an accurate assumption, he wasn't sure Karen was actually in there. He looked around. Not the main warehouse. The breeze-block annex looked the best bet. Crouching down, he made his way around the back of the skips, moved swiftly over the open space of the yard, and flattened himself against the far wall.

He edged round the side, crouching beneath the windows, aiming for the door. He found it: modern, half-panelled with glass, unlocked.

Larkin was about to turn the handle and enter but stopped himself. Why would it be unlocked? Wouldn't there be an alarm? He cupped his eyes to the glass, looked through the window and got his answer.

On the floor of the office was a man, middle-aged, dressed in dirty old work-clothes, with a ragged, gaping, meaty red hole in his chest, blood pooled beneath him.

Larkin became lightheaded, his stomach flipped and his knees buckled. There was nothing pretty about the body. Taking deep breaths to steady himself, he turned the handle and entered.

The office had the usual trappings: filing cabinets, a PC, phones, chairs, desks and calendars showing pictures of naked women. Everything was covered with several films of grease and dirt. A working man's office. Larkin gingerly stepped in, trying to avoid looking at the mess on the floor.

To his left was an internal window which afforded a full view of the warehouse. He wanted to see but not be seen, so he crouched down underneath, bringing his head slowly up to eye-level, and peered in.

The place was sparsely lit by overhead lights, but Larkin could make out bins containing metal stacked around the walls, touching the ceiling in some places. Scraps of metal and packing materials littered the floor and in one corner was a cropper, its heavy metal razor edge at rest. Next to it was what looked like a car press in miniature. The press had a small space, about the size of a child's coffin, and two very thick sharp plates to handle the work. Industrial tools that Torquemada would have been proud of.

As Larkin watched, Lenny unwrapped the blanketed figure. To his astonishment, it was a very battered Charlie Rook, his wrists handcuffed together in front of his body. Lenny pulled down a hook attached to a length of chain from a ceiling-mounted hoist, fitted the handcuffs over the hook, and hauled him up, slightly off the floor. Any relief Larkin felt at seeing Charlie Rook was tempered by the fact that next to him was Karen, similarly suspended. She looked exhausted and in pain. Larkin looked again at Lenny. The man looked sullen and distracted. Hardly surprising, thought Larkin, the news he'd just received. Next to Lenny, dressed in jeans, boots, sweatshirt and fleece, was Melissa. Her hair was scraped back and her face held such a cruel expression that even from a distance it sent a shiver through Larkin. As he watched, she spoke.

Unfortunately, Larkin could only make out muffled sounds through the glass, so he tried to get nearer. A door set into the wall leading into the warehouse was slightly ajar. He pulled it slowly open and entered.

He was conscious of being visible, so he quickly moved behind a pile of bins and listened.

'–all fucked, Charlie,' Melissa was saying. 'And you fucked it. You've got no vision, no…'

The words trailed off as her temper took over. She became suddenly inarticulate with anger, hands bunching into fists, pummelling the chest of the hanging man. Now we're seeing your true colours, love, thought Larkin. You're a vicious, dangerous psychopath.

Melissa's rage abated and she resumed talking, gasping for breath. 'You see, Charlie,' she said, her voice dripping with pity, 'I had to do it. Had to take over. I've got vision, my sweet. I have to use it.'

Her mood swing was as swift as it was unexpected. It confirmed to Larkin that the woman was unhinged.

'You see,' she said, as if she was a teacher patronising a retarded pupil, 'I gave the disc to the girls. I sent Lenny and Ringo after them to get it back. I had planned on keeping the disc to myself and telling you the girls still had it. But...' She gave a theatrical sigh, turned towards Karen. 'This little bitch got a bit too clever, didn't she?' She squeezed Karen's face. 'And now we have to keep the little whore alive, don't we?' She squeezed harder. 'Don't we?'

Larkin struggled against the impulse to rush forward and intervene. He would have been powerless.

Melissa let go of Karen's cheek. Tears were forming in the girl's eyes. 'But that doesn't mean things have to be comfortable for you. You're going to have to do what I say.'

'And if I don't?' Karen managed through a broken sob.

'I'll show you,' said Melissa, face lit by a sick light. 'Lenny, bring the stuff over here.'

Lenny didn't move, just stared into space.

'Lenny!'

He shook himself from his unpleasant daydream and moved over to the far wall. He trundled a trolley over, stood it beside Melissa. Larkin recognised what it was. The twin cylinders of an oxy-acetylene torch.

'This is what happens, Karen,' said Melissa. She ripped off Charlie Rook's shirt, fired up the torch, and went to work.

The screams were sudden, loud and sickening. Larkin blocked his ears, screwed

351

his eyes tight shut. It was no good, he could still hear it. And he had to do something about it, or Karen would be next.

Unblocking his ears but trying to dislocate his mind, he moved slowly around the wall of the warehouse, using the bins for cover. There was just enough space for him to squeeze through, and he worked his way round until he was flattened against the wall nearest to where the torture was taking place. Seeing nothing to hand that would help, he took another couple of deep breaths and began to haul himself up the stack of bins.

Charlie Rook's screams camouflaged the noise of his climb. Her reached the top, peered down, and wished he wasn't seeing what was happening in front of him. Melissa was systematically searing the skin from the man's back. Larkin swallowed hard, forcing down the bile rising in his throat, and edged his way along the stack, making sure he couldn't be seen from the ground. He stopped when he was positioned directly above the trolley carrying the gas cylinders and risked a look down.

He knew he had only one chance to get this right, so he braced himself against the warehouse wall, arms against the bin in front of him, and pushed as hard as he could.

The bin toppled over but the rest of the

stack, thankfully, held. It came crashing down on its intended target, knocking the cylinders over, wrenching the torch from Melissa's hand, raining plumbing fixtures and taps all around. Keeping the element of surprise on his side, Larkin jumped down after it.

Melissa spun to face him, her mouth gaping. She was the first to work out what was happening.

'Lenny! Get him!'

Lenny ran towards Larkin, trying to pull his gun free as he came. Larkin, thinking quickly, grabbed a length of copper pipe from the bin he had just upset and swung it at Lenny. It connected with the man's forearm, knocking the gun from his fist.

Lenny flinched in pain, grabbed his arm and still kept coming. Larkin ran to the side, dodging out of the way.

Unfortunately, his boot rolled on another length of piping, causing him to lose his footing and stumble backwards.

Lenny was on him fast, pressing his thumbs into Larkin's windpipe, his mouth twisted into a rictus of hate. Larkin tried to pull the arms from his neck but it was no good, they were locked. He tried prising the fingers back but they wouldn't budge. Lenny's arms had locked like a pit bull's jaws. They wouldn't let go until Larkin was dead.

Frantically, he groped round the floor for a weapon. He found something smooth, cold and angular. That would do. He brought the object up with as much force as he could manage, smashing it against the side of Lenny's head. The blow connected, sending Lenny's brain bouncing off the inside of his skull. He cried out in pain, his grip loosening slightly. But not enough. Larkin did it again, but Lenny kept on choking him.

Larkin managed to see what the object was in his hand: a tap. One with four long, straight handle grips. He manoeuvred it round in his hand, steadied Lenny's head by pulling his hair with the other hand, and rammed it straight up, aiming for Lenny's right eye.

He found it. Lenny screamed like a wild animal caught in a trap, and let go of Larkin completely. Larkin, who had closed his own eyes in case he got any of Lenny's in them, opened them and rolled away. Lenny staggered back blindly, stumbling against the press.

'You're gonna die for that, you cunt!' he shouted.

'I don't think so,' said Larkin and found another length of copper pipe. He picked it up, ready to defend himself from another attack.

But Lenny had other things on his mind. He was in pain and reeling around blindly, outstretched hands grasping uselessly. His fingers curled and uncurled, feeling their way along the side of the press. Inadvertently and oblivious to what he was doing, his hand fell onto the huge red starter button and pressed it. The machine clanked into life.

Larkin saw what was going to happen and called out, trying to warn Lenny. It was no good. Lenny was in too much pain to hear. He had his right hand pressed into the remains of his eye, gasping in agony, and stood with his left hand on the edge of the press, gripping it for support. He didn't see the huge razor-sharp blade come down and take his left hand off from below the knuckles.

Lenny screamed all the harder. He brought the stump of his hand up to his good eye and looked at it. As soon as he saw it, his screams started to subside. At first he fell silent but, as Larkin watched, he began to sob, slipping to the floor, back against the moving machine, inadvertently hitting the off switch. He curled himself up into a foetal ball, body jerking with pain.

Larkin found the spectacle pathetic. He almost felt sorry for the killer. Knowing he would be no more trouble, he turned his attention to the others.

Charlie Rook was still hanging there, but there was no sign of Melissa or Karen.

Larkin crossed to Charlie Rook, looked at

him. The man was in shock, his eyes blank, escape tunnels into another world. His back was a charred, bloody mess. The stench was awful. Larkin wanted to get out of the warehouse, and when he saw that the side door was open, he ran to it and exited. Into the rain, into the night.

Once in the yard, he looked round. The cars were still parked there, so they hadn't gone far. He checked the skips, the cranes. Nothing. No movement, no sound. He looked at the ground and saw lines through the dirt and gravel, being rapidly eroded by the rain. Drag marks leading to the jetty. Larkin followed.

As he approached, he began to discern two figures making their way towards the end of the jetty, one pushing the other, silhouetted against the lights on the far side of the river.

He moved cautiously closer, eyes acclimatising to the dark, wind and rain lending a sharpened coldness to his body. He saw Karen, still handcuffed, huddled, shivering and tearful. Beside her stood Melissa, a deranged gleam in her eye, a vicious-looking knife in her hand. The knife was held against Karen's throat.

Larkin stepped on to the jetty.

'Stay where you are,' snapped Melissa, 'or I'll kill her.'

Larkin stopped moving. 'Give it up, Melissa,' he said. 'Let her go.'

'Fuck off!' she shouted. 'You've ruined everything!' She sounded like a petulant child.

'Just let Karen go,' said Larkin, 'and we'll walk out of here and leave you alone forever. You've got the CD, you've got Charlie Rook's business, now let her go.'

'No! No! Leave me alone!' She pressed the knife against Karen's neck. Karen whimpered and tried to pull away, but it was no use. Melissa held her too tightly.

Fuck, thought Larkin. This isn't going to end prettily.

Just then, Karen spoke.

'Is this the spot?' she asked quietly. 'The spot where you killed Hayley?'

'It is,' said Melissa, almost proudly. 'It's the place where Lenny and Ringo killed her and dumped her. Want to join her?'

Karen gave a slow nod. 'Yes. Then I'll be free of you.'

Melissa gave a cold smile. 'That can be arranged.' She moved the knife closer.

'Do that, Melissa, and you're dead,' Larkin shouted. 'I've just got rid of Lenny. I won't stop till I've got you.' Larkin began to edge forward.

'I said stay where you are!' shouted Melissa.

Larkin looked from one to the other. Stalemate.

At that point, he noticed Melissa's eyes begin to fix on some point behind him. She was looking curiously, apprehensively at something.

Larkin turned, trying to follow her gaze. He could make out a figure striding through the yard with imposing bearing and coat tails flapping, seemingly impervious to the wind and the rain, expression one of focus and concentration. Moir.

'Wondered when you'd turn up,' Larkin said to him with relief. 'You can arrest her now.'

Moir ignored him, kept his attention rooted to Melissa. Larkin noticed the man was carrying his revolver down at his side.

'Let her go.' Moir spoke the words as a flat, uninflected command.

Melissa tightened her grip.

'You've got one more chance,' said Moir. 'Let her go. Now.'

Melissa opened her mouth to speak. 'I don't know who you are, but–'

Moir raised the gun – his father's revolver – and emptied the full six rounds into her. He would have used more: his finger was still clicking on empty chambers.

Melissa's body jerked in a different direction with each shot. Eventually she landed in a crumpled heap, head lolling over the end of the jetty.

Larkin turned to him, shock and surprise

all over his face.

Moir ignored him. He dropped the revolver, walked forward like a man with tunnel vision and gathered up his weeping daughter into his arms.

Home

Larkin took a mouthful of Chilean Cabernet, savoured the richness on his tongue and swallowed it, willing himself to relax. The dinner was, after all, in his honour, since he was going home in the morning. Or at any rate, leaving London.

He looked round the dinner table, which was laden with huge bowls of pasta, salad and sauce, bottles of wine and soft drink, crockery, cutlery and glass. Andy was on his left, Mickey on the right. Opposite sat Henry, flanked on either side by a happy Faye and a nervous but relieved-looking Karen.

The dining room of Faye's house was lit only by candles. The six of them sat there, bathed in the warmth of the glow, trying not to let the shadows touch them.

A whole week had passed since that night at Dagenham and they were still trying to come to terms with what had happened.

Like soldiers who are relieved that the war is over, they were, nevertheless, finding peace, no matter how worthwhile, difficult to fight for.

Larkin took another mouthful of wine and let his thoughts travel back. One week.

With Moir holding a sobbing, wet, shivering and blood-spattered Karen so tight, he feared she might disappear if he let her go, they had made their way back to Candleland, stopping at a callbox to leave an anonymous tip-off.

As the two cars crawled inconspicuously onto the London-bound lane of the A13, the police and ambulances were noisily announcing themselves from the other direction, breaking laws and records as they sped towards the industrial estate, tyres skidding and screeching in the pouring rain.

In their telephone conversation the previous day, Moir had insisted Larkin told him about Karen. Despite protestations, Moir managed to get him to explain about the disc and the handover, telling him it was going to take place in a pub owned by one of Mickey's old acquaintances, patrolled by some of the old gang members. Moir had insisted on being there and they had argued, eventually reaching a compromise whereby he would wait in the car he had borrowed from Faye, out of the action, but on hand to see Karen afterwards. Moir had seen Lenny drag Karen out but had been powerless to intervene since he didn't want to get caught in the crossfire. Once Larkin and Mickey set off, though, he had followed.

Back at Candleland that night, despite the fact they were overwhelmed by relief and exhaustion, Karen and Henry had gone down to the basement to talk, once her handcuffs had been cut off by Mickey, closing the door firmly behind them. Mickey and Larkin had gone into the office, uncapped the brandy and flopped into the chairs. For a few minutes they couldn't speak.

'So what happened, then?' asked Mickey, eventually.

Larkin told him everything, even down to picking up Moir's discarded revolver and wiping down any surfaces he could remember touching. By the time he was leaving, the rain was washing away any footprints.

'Who killed the guy in the office?' asked Mickey.

'Melissa or Lenny,' replied Larkin. 'My guess is Lenny. This guy was obviously in with Charlie Rook and they wanted him out of the way. They'd all agreed to meet up there after the handover, but with everything going belly up, Melissa saw this as her now-or-never moment.'

'And it turned out to be never.'

Larkin nodded. He could still see the woman's bloodied body lying lifeless on the jetty. In death she had seemed so ineffectual and harmless; the bullet holes could have marked her as an innocent victim.

He had then checked out the other two in the warehouse. Lenny had had enough presence of mind to find a strip of rigid plastic packaging and fashion it into a tourniquet. He sat, fingers twisting the plastic, face covered in blood and the remains of his right eye, hunched in pain, waiting for an end.

Charlie Rook was still hanging, still breathing. Larkin decided not to move him. Let the paramedics do that. If his eyes looked like tunnels before, the way back had now been sealed up completely.

Larkin regarded the two men; brutalised, tortured and, perhaps, dying. He thought of their victims, their miserable, wasted, un-wanted lives, the degradation and suffering that had been inflicted upon them, the un-imaginable agony of their deaths at the hands of Charlie Rook's clients. He would reserve his sympathy for those who deserved it.

He found Lenny's laptop, removed the CD, wiped it down and left it in a prominent position. Then he left, following the other two over the gate and back to the cars, phon-ing for ambulances and police on the way.

'Have you heard anything from the pub?'

asked Larkin.

'Only that two of the boys died,' replied Mickey. He sighed. 'They signed on as volunteers, both of them knew the risks. But they still had people at home waiting for them. Same as the guys on the other side.'

'Doesn't that make your situation dangerous? Won't someone want to blame you for their deaths?'

Mickey shook his head. 'Nah. They'll claim on insurance for the pub and they'll have had enough stashed away to sort their other halves out.' He looked straight at Larkin. 'Don't get the wrong idea. They weren't there because they wanted to be on our side, or believed in what we were doin'. No. They were there for the aggro, pure an' simple.'

'Don't you feel any responsibility towards them?'

''Course I do. If I hadn't asked them to help they might still be alive. But it was their choice. An' that's what I keep tellin' myself.' Mickey's forehead was creased and his eyes held a dark dolour. 'Bastards like Charlie Rook have to be stopped. Simple as that.'

'By any means necessary?'

'Any.'

'Remember what Nietzsche said,' said Larkin. "Whoever hunts monsters must in turn guard against becoming a monster himself."'

Mickey gave a sad smile, turned his eyes heavenward. 'I trust the big fella to look after me. Anyway, it's a risk you've got to take. How do you feel?'

Larkin sighed. 'Ask me in the morning.' He took a mouthful of brandy. 'So what happens next?'

'I suppose we wait an' see,' said Mickey draining his glass. 'I doubt we'll have long to wait.'

They didn't. The papers the next day were full of it. 'Massacre at the Metals Yard,' as the tabloids dubbed it. Charlie Rook and Lenny Lothario (real name Leonard Webley) were in intensive care. There was no elaboration on the state of either. The dead man in the office, Graham Agnew, was a well-known associate of Charlie Rook's. The police had long suspected his involvement in criminal activities but never had enough proof until now. They were writing the whole thing off as a falling out among thieves. At least that was the official story. There was also mention made of an unidentified young woman. Nothing was known about her, but they were working on the angle that she might have been an innocent victim. There was no mention of the CD.

Larkin wasn't surprised by the last bit of news. He had expected as much.

'We've got to do something,' said Mickey.

'We can't just let it disappear.'

'I agree,' replied Larkin, 'but we need an honest copper for that.' He was struck by a sudden thought. 'And I think I know just the one...'

Larkin imagined the scene the next morning. Detective Inspector Christy Kennedy of Camden CID coming into his office in North Bridge House to find a large package on his desk. He could see him opening it and finding a CD, two folders' worth of papers and an envelope. He would slit open the envelope and read the note inside:

'The files aren't complete and I realise it's not on your manor, but there's enough to be going on with. Put the CD in your PC, get ready to step on some toes and prepare to get angry.

'Your Friends From The North.'

He could imagine Kennedy watching the CD, reading through the papers and going to make some arrests before word got round, lawyers were called and documents shredded. And yes, Larkin thought, he would be very, very angry.

Lenny Lothario came round, but was still very weak.

Charlie Rook came off the critical list and lay there in a coma, threatening to come round, but never quite making it.

The threat was enough for Lenny, though, he wouldn't talk. So, in the absence of any alternative, he was charged with murder.

No one came to question Larkin, Mickey or Moir.

'I don't think I've ever talked so much in my whole life,' said Henry, a couple of days later.

He and Larkin were sitting in a branch of Starbucks just off Leicester Square. It had been Henry's choice, and even though Larkin knew the man wasn't drinking, he was surprised, to say the least. But then Moir had surprised him a lot recently. He had even insisted on paying for the coffees.

They were perched on high stools at the front of the shop, absently gazing through the window. The street was grey outside. Pedestrians, huddled in their clothes, cocooned from contact with others, rushed past, all seemingly annoyed by something, probably that winter was taking so long to leave. Larkin and Moir, on the other hand, were warm inside the coffee shop. Moir was so warm he was shedding layers as he talked, leaving them lying on the next stool like discarded repressions.

Larkin sipped a large latte. 'Well, you had

a lot to talk about,' he said.

Moir was telling him about his night spent talking with Karen. Neither he nor Karen had gone into specifics when talking to the others about it, but Larkin had managed to pick up quite a lot from listening between the lines, reading the silences.

Father and daughter had had a lot of ground to cover, a lot of anger to release, along with the guilt, rage and pain of a shared history. By morning they were exhausted, but at least they now possessed a clearer understanding of each other: they had actually communicated for the first time in years, perhaps ever.

'Yeah,' said Moir.

Larkin had never seen the big man so relaxed. He was cleaner, slimmer, even better dressed. And he had insisted on meeting in a chain coffee shop. The old Moir wouldn't have set foot in the place. The new one even smiled occasionally.

'I mean it's not perfect,' Moir continued. 'We both know that. We've still got a long way to go, Karen and me...' He stopped talking. There were tears in his eyes. 'But we're tryin'. That's the main thing.'

Larkin smiled. 'Glad to hear it.'

Moir kept his head down. Larkin could see the man was struggling to express emotions formerly untapped. 'Look,' he mumbled, face reddening, 'I owe you for this.' He paused, trying to find the right words. 'You did...' Moir trailed off. He steepled his hands and pressed them against his forehead, palms covering his eyes, hiding his face. He struggled to control himself.

'It's OK, Henry,' said Larkin quietly. 'Just leave it at that.'

Moir nodded and looked up. His eyes were red-rimmed. He smiled, gave a little laugh. 'I've given up the booze, or I'm tryin' to, I've got a woman in my life for the first time in years, and I've found my daughter.' He shook his head as if he couldn't quite believe it. 'Stephen, I'm so fuckin' happy.'

Larkin nodded, his smile a mask. 'Good.'

Moir gave a snort. 'I'd best get an umbrella,' he said. 'It won't last. There'll be ten tons of horseshit fallin' on my head sooner or later.'

They drank their coffee in silence.

'So,' said Larkin eventually, 'you had any thoughts on what to do next?'

'I don't know,' said Moir. 'I can't go back, can I?'

'To Newcastle?'

'To the force. To anything. I've crossed the line, haven't I?'

'Not just you, Henry. I was there too, don't forget. And Karen, she saw what happened.'

Moir sighed as a shadow crossed his face. 'Yeah, but it was me that did it.' His voice dropped. He looked round quickly, checked no one was listening. 'I pulled the trigger.'

'You did what you had to do,' said Larkin. 'It was the only way to save Karen. Any of us would have done it.'

'But it was me that did it. I was the one crossed the line. The other day I was a copper. Now ... I don't know what I am. But I know I can't go back.'

Larkin wasn't surprised by the news. He had thought something like this might happen. 'They'll miss you back in Newcastle,' he said. 'Hank Moir, scourge of evil-doers everywhere.'

'Piss off,' said Moir, managing to laugh.

'So what will you do instead?' Larkin asked.

'Workwise? I don't know. I've got a bit of money put by so I can live on that for a while. Who knows? I might move into the private sector, do something like Jackie Fairley used to, God rest her.' He took a mouthful of coffee. 'Anyway, as long as I'm near Karen for the time being, I'll be OK.'

And near Faye, thought Larkin. 'Good luck,' he said.

'Thanks,' said Moir, smiling.

They both lapsed into silence. Outside, people moved past hurriedly, blinkered, purposeful. Larkin and Moir sat and watched them.

'Do you have nightmares?' asked Larkin eventually. 'About what happened that night? About Melissa?'

Moir thought for a moment. 'Not yet,' he said quietly, then louder: 'And I don't think I will. But you never know what's around the corner, do you?' His voice dropped again. 'What about you?'

'The same,' Larkin said quickly.

Moir nodded and returned his gaze to the street outside. Larkin did likewise.

When it came time for Moir to leave, he asked Larkin to go back to Clapham with him. Larkin, who hadn't yet spoken to Faye, or for that matter, Andy, declined.

'They want to see you,' said Moir. 'They're worried about you, you haven't contacted them since–' He looked for the right phrase. '–the other night. Andy's taking it as a personal insult.'

Larkin smiled. 'Tell him not to. There's some things I have to sort out first. And I'm better doing them on my own.'

Moir understood. He relayed a message from Faye, that Larkin was invited round for dinner in a couple of days' time, then left him alone.

Larkin left the coffee shop and went walking.

As he went down Shaftesbury Avenue his eyes were drawn towards the shop doorways. Even in broad daylight, figures lay slumped and curled inside filthy blankets, old sleeping bags and pieces of cardboard. Some asleep, some, for all anyone knew, dead. Sleeping bags turned to body bags. The cocooned pedestrians hurried past them, stepped over them, treated them as if they were part of the pavement.

It made Larkin angry. Karen had been found, reunited with her father, they were working it out. Good for them. Karen was fortunate. Larkin looked at those less fortunate as he walked past. A lot of them were under thirty, most under twenty. They looked broken, defeated. No one was looking for them, no one cared whether they lived or died. They were adrift in the wasteland. No candles would be burning for them.

Larkin headed for The Spice of Life, the pub he had visited when he had first started looking for Karen. He sat with his pint, thinking. Seeing so many wasted lives on the street had left him feeling impotent. He wanted to do something. After his second pint, he began to feel that decisive action was needed. Even to satisfy his own needs if nothing else: he couldn't move on until amends had been made, some kind of truce had been reached. But he didn't know how. It wasn't until he was on his third pint that an idea came to him. As soon as it had, he downed his drink and, feeling light-headed, lurched out of the door before he changed his mind.

That was how he found himself, later that afternoon, walking down Priory End Lane. He came to number thirty-seven. It was still a place without hope. He walked up the cracked path and knocked timidly on the door. Almost as if he didn't want to be heard.

He stood there, waiting. The first inklings of alcoholic remorse were kicking in and he was starting to convince himself the visit was a bad idea. He willed himself to walk away, but didn't. Something stopped him; something stronger than just the drink. Eventually he heard footsteps coming down the hall.

The door was opened by a dead-eyed girl: limp dark hair, ineptly applied make-up, cheap, tarty clothes that exposed rather than showed off her dumpy, breastless body. She looked about thirteen. As soon as she saw Larkin, she fitted a false smile in place.

'You lookin' for fun, you come to the right place.' Call centre staff had greeted him with more enthusiasm than this girl and her broad Midlands accent.

'I'm looking for Tina,' Larkin began, hesitantly. 'Is she here?'

The girl looked momentarily confused at this deviation from the script, but recovered quickly. 'No she's not. But I can be Tina if you want me to.'

'Look, I'm not a punter,' sighed Larkin. 'I'm here to see her. Is she in?'

The girl, smelling the booze on his breath, became scared then. This was a big excursion from the script. She couldn't cope with this.

'Look,' the girl said, fear in her voice, 'you'd better go. I don't know where Tina is, I've never heard of her. Les'll kill me if she knows I've been talkin' to social workers.'

'I'm not a social worker,' slurred Larkin. 'I'm not the police, I'm not a religious nut, I'm not anything. I just want to help her.'

'Well she ain't 'ere.'

The girl began to close the door. Larkin stopped her.

'Please,' he said, digging into his pocket and bringing out a card. 'Take this. I brought it for Tina but you take it.'

The girl looked at the card. It had the word 'Candleland' on it and the phone number of a minicab company who would provide transport free of charge.

'It's a safe house,' explained Larkin. 'If it all gets too much, give them a ring. They can help.'

'Look, just piss off!' the girl shouted, and slammed the door.

Larkin stood there, staring at it. Well, he thought, I suppose I asked for that.

He turned and walked down the road, collar up, shoulders hunched against more than the cold.

He sighed. Faye's for dinner, he thought, then that's it. I'm off.

Larkin took another mouthful of wine and looked round the table. He had been so wrapped up in his memories that the conversation had started without him. Karen was telling the others of her new job.

'I start next Monday at Candleland, yes,' she said. 'Regular money and a bit of stability. It'll help, you know, when I need it.'

She looked at Larkin and smiled. A lot of the earlier fear was absent from her eyes. But not all. She still looked haunted. She always would. Larkin nodded. He understood.

Henry then announced, to no one's surprise, that Faye had asked him to move in with her. The air filled with congratulations. Faye and Larkin caught each other's eyes, then quickly looked away. Andy, Larkin noticed, was staring at him with a very brittle smile on his face.

Mickey raised his glass. 'To new beginnings and second chances,' he said.

They all drank.

After dinner, Larkin found himself alone in the kitchen with Faye. She busied herself with a cafetière. She wouldn't make eye contact.

'Congratulations,' said Larkin.

'Thanks,' she mumbled.

'I mean it.'

She stopped what she was doing, looked at him. 'Look Stephen, I know this is difficult for you.'

Larkin didn't argue.

'I'm sorry it didn't work out between us. Honestly. I just feel... I've got a future with Henry. We need each other.'

'Don't I need you?'

She stared at him, examining him with a frankness he hadn't before seen in her eyes. 'No,' she said, at great length. 'No, I don't think you do. I think you looked at me and you saw comfort. But that's not what you need. You need purpose.'

Larkin couldn't reply. The words just dammed up in his throat.

'I'll go and see who wants coffee,' she said and walked past him.

He made no attempt to stop her.

Larkin stood alone in the kitchen for a few minutes, gathering his thoughts. Faye was right, he reluctantly admitted. He did need purpose. But he wouldn't find it in London.

He turned to go back to the dining room and saw Andy standing in the doorway.

'Fuck,' said Larkin, 'you gave me a fright. What you standing there for?'

'I was lookin' for you.'

'What for?'

'Newcastle,' said Andy. 'I'm not goin' back.'

'What, ever?'

'Not tomorrow. Not with you.'

Larkin crossed to him. 'What's up, Andy? Is there something you want to tell me?'

Andy gave him a confrontational look. 'Is there somethin' you want to tell me?'

Larkin looked him straight in the eye. 'All right, then. Faye and I slept together, OK? Only once. I wanted more than that, she didn't. At least not with me. That what you wanted to know?'

Andy said nothing.

'Look, Andy,' said Larkin, 'you said so yourself. Faye might have given birth to you but she's never been a mother to you. She's a woman who needs the same things as everyone else. And you have to live with that. Unfortunately, she doesn't want them from me. And I have to live with that.'

Andy stood silently for a few seconds then turned and walked to the door. 'I'll be back up sometime,' he said. 'After all, I've got friends up there, ain't I?'

He went back to the dining room.

Larkin waited a couple of minutes then followed him.

The next morning, Larkin was up well before everyone else. He crept quietly downstairs, bag in hand, trying to make his way to the car before anyone else appeared. The last thing he wanted was a protracted and difficult goodbye session.

He crossed the hall floor, placed his hand on the front door.

'Off already?' asked a voice from behind.

Larkin turned. There stood Mickey Falco, up and dressed. Mickey had stayed the night. He had taken Moir's old room, since Moir had slept with Faye.

'Yeah,' said Larkin. 'Got a long drive, thought I'd make an early start.'

Mickey nodded, not in the slightest bit convinced. 'I was wonderin',' he said. 'D'you mind givin' me a lift back to Candleland? I know it's out of your way, but I'd like to have a chat.'

'You're not going to try and convert me, are you?'

Mickey laughed.

They got in the Saab and drove away. Larkin looked back once, hoping to see a twitch from the upstairs curtains, but there wasn't one.

'So it's back to the land of Newkie Brown for you, then?' asked Mickey.

'You know what?' said Larkin. 'It's only Southerners that call it that. No one in Newcastle does. Well, only students.'

'So what should I call the stuff, then?'

'Its proper name,' said Larkin. 'Dog.'

Mickey laughed and shook his head. 'I'm not even gonna ask.' When the smile faded, his face settled along more serious lines. 'D'you know why you're goin' back?'

Larkin thought. 'Because I don't belong here? Because I've got a job up there?' He shrugged.

'When I checked you out, I read your stuff. I liked it, it's good. Powerful. Angry. Necessary. You're doin' a good job, Stephen. An' if you need remindin', just remember the Gospel of St Matthew, the Sermon on the Mount: Blessed are the truthtellers. And John 8: The truth shall set you free.'

'You making that up?'

Mickey smiled. 'No. But it depends which translation you use.'

'So what did you want to see me about?'

'When we reach Candleland.'

They reached Candleland. It was still, the day had yet to get started.

'Down the end of the hall on the left,' said Mickey, standing outside the front door, 'is a door. It'll be closed but not locked. Ralph's in that room. Ralph Sickert.'

'So?'

Mickey shrugged. 'Thought it might be a good idea for you to talk to him. He's at peace with his past. He's found his redemption. Might help you to do the same.'

Before Larkin could answer, Mickey opened the front door, walked to his office and shut himself inside.

Larkin stepped over the threshold and stood in the hall. He saw the door at the end and walked towards it. He reached it, raised up his hand to knock, but something stopped him before fist touched wood.

What am I doing? he asked himself. The answer came: making peace with my past. Confronting the killer of my wife and child so I can put it behind me. Move my life on.

And will that change what happened? No. So he's found God, convinced himself he's over what he did. Thinks his sins have been redeemed. Well, good for him. I hope he sleeps well at night. But talking to him won't help. It won't change what he did to me.

No, Sickert is the past. My past is behind that door. I can open it and step inside or I can just acknowledge it's there, leave it and walk away.

I know where I have to go, what I have to do. It's what I was doing before I came to London. I was right, I was just scared to admit it.

It won't be easy, I know there are ghosts. But they've been with me a long time and I don't think they're ever going to leave. They've made their beds beside me. They're sleeping with me. So I've got to get used to them. Concentrate on the thumbs instead of the fingers.

Because it's better than the alternative. It's better than opening this door.

Larkin's hand dropped to his side. He turned and walked purposefully through the front door, closing it firmly behind him.

Outside in the street, the day was just starting. The air felt warmer, the sun brighter. Spring seemed to be on the way. Larkin took his fleece off and threw it on the passenger seat.

I hope I don't regret doing that, he thought, rubbing his arms. I've been fooled by a false spring before.

He climbed into the car and headed north.

Headed for home.

This Large Print Book, for people
who cannot read normal print,
is published under the auspices of

THE ULVERSCROFT FOUNDATION